IN
LINCOLN'S
SHADOW

IN
LINCOLN'S
SHADOW

ROHN FEDERBUSH

authorHOUSE®

AuthorHouse™
1663 Liberty Drive
Bloomington, IN 47403
www.authorhouse.com
Phone: 1 (800) 839-8640

Published by AuthorHouse   08/27/2015

ISBN: 978-1-5049-3357-5 (sc)
ISBN: 978-1-5049-3356-8 (e)

Social worker Bernie Johnston's frustration with how difficult it is to claim justice for innocent children is her main motivation to change professions. Her best friend, Juno Blaine, introduces Bernie to her brother, homicide detective Steffen Blaine. Why not seek out a mentor for her career transition, a step up in the search for justice? Within the first hour of their meeting Steffen is assigned to investigate the suspicious death an elderly woman who turns out to be the grandmother of a child who was a former case of Bernie's. The daughter-in-law of the murdered woman is suicidal. Steffen's traumatic first marriage has left him damaged—his wife died from an overdose. When faced with heightened emotions, he quotes Lincoln to alleviate his pain. Bernie witnesses Steffen's coping mechanism and isn't too sure his grieving heart will open for her. Envious of her grandmother's wealth, a nine-year-old appears to be the culprit. Her family has six children all living in a double-wide trailer, and the mother is expecting a seventh child. When the murder is reexamined at the parole hearing ten years later, Bernie and Steffen are asked to participate. They find the dying son of the murdered woman instigated his own daughter's poisonous act. Bernie and Steffen postpone marriage, and the story continues with the exonerated nineteen-year-old turning into a serial killer of senior citizens.

CHAPTER 1

St. Joseph's Hospital

"I'm getting an ulcer from this job," said Bernie Johnston. She pulled the lettuce out of her bacon and tomato sandwich, wishing she could yank herself out of her negative mood. "I can't digest raw vegetables anymore."

The din in the hospital cafeteria penetrated her mental replay of the court's bad decision in her latest child-abuse case. The judge sent the six-year-old home with his triumphant, drunken father. Bernie blinked through her tears giving her a blurred view of her friend, Juno Blaine, sitting across from her.

A registered nurse, Juno had provided the expert testimony for the Child Protection Agency. Juno folded her hands in her lap. "Let's bless this meal."

"I didn't pray very much before meals at home," Bernie said. "I know one. 'Give us this day our daily bread and forgive us our ... ' No that's wrong. 'Bless us, oh Lord, and these Thy gifts which we are about to receive. Amen.' How's that?"

"That will do," Juno said. "I noticed the father smirked when his back was turned to the judge."

Bernie gingerly placed her pink sweater over the back of the cafeteria's plastic chair and rubbed her aching shoulder. "So, Juno, did I prove I'm good enough for your saintly detective brother?"

Juno glanced around the noisy lunchroom. "If you can put up with Steffen for one evening, you'll be the one headed for sainthood. He's a dour man and way too old."

"Too old for what?"

"Children. He's five years older than me." Juno used her paper napkin to rip the lid off a nonfat yogurt.

"If I'd wanted children, I should have married by now." Bernie wished all the mothers of abused children had waited. Waited for what? Should women investigate the childhood of prospective bridegrooms to see if they might repeat their own abuse? "I can't erase the memory of that little boy's look of horror. I need to change professions before I lose the little faith I have."

Juno said, "I asked a priest once about a phrase in the 'Our Father': 'forgive us our sins *as* we forgive those who sin against us.' Father Joe said when Jesus was on the cross and in so much pain, He said, 'Father, forgive them for they know not what they do.'" Juno tapped the table as if to punctuate the message. "So, I ask the Lord to forgive others when I can't summon enough understanding to forgive them myself."

Bernie knew her tenderhearted friend was fighting back angry tears. "Does your brother know if the police department needs more investigators for murder cases? At least murderers are prosecuted to the full extent of the law."

Juno answered Bernie's earlier question about dating her brother. "Steffen's six-foot-six. He's got long legs, so when you sit with him at a table, you're still eye-to-eye. He only trusts women barbers to cut his hair, which is blond, not red like mine. You can smell his Old Spice aftershave as soon as he enters a room. He wears plaid shirts, a black bow tie, and a brown suede jacket with jeans. Of course I think he's handsome, but his nose might be too long, and his eyebrows are too thick. He doesn't smile often. He's not finished grieving for his late wife."

Bernie slipped a plastic spoon into her chocolate pudding. "How do you judge when a person is finished grieving?"

"Benjamin Franklin said fame was all very well, but pudding is better." Juno gave her empty spoon to Bernie, who filled it with pudding.

"Mother gave Steffen a twelve-volume set of Lincoln's sayings after Pauline took her own life. He quotes entire passages when he's upset."

"You think when he shuts the book on his Lincoln fixation, he'll be finished with the grieving process?" Bernie suspended her last spoon of chocolate pudding.

Juno swallowed. "I'm hoping you can fill the hole in his bucket."

"Forget that," Bernie laughed. "We all have burdens to bear, gifts to share, and jobs to do. And I want to change jobs." Bernie concentrated on the pleasant subject of meeting Juno's brother. Fifty years old? Maybe she would take up memorizing Lincoln's sayings too.

"Steffen will give you pointers on how to join his ranks," Juno said. "Valentine's Day should be an auspicious day to meet someone. I already described you as a five-foot-two, blue-eyed blonde with a peachy complexion."

"I'm not going to meet him without you along." Bernie shook her finger at Juno. "You can take that to the bank." Silently, Bernie prayed that the Lord would protect her and guide her in this new endeavor.

* * *

Sunday, February 14
Dead End Street, Jackson, Michigan

In his library, Steffen Blaine flipped through the pages of yet another book on forensics. The table of contents promised little of interest, but the chapter titled "Evidence: the Heart and Soul of Forensics" caught his attention, and he turned to the appropriate page. Where was his heart? He surveyed the room's rows of books on Abraham Lincoln, the law, Blackstone's Commentaries, investigative sciences, poisons, archeology, and world religions. His shattered dreams of a happy marriage could not be remedied, caught, or bound up in books.

Pauline's suicide was a crime. Steffen blamed himself for not being at the scene in time to save her life. Steffen's alibi of being at work held no weight in light of his wife's obvious mental deterioration.

What clues had he missed? When would he be freed of his continuing self-flagellation?

His oldest son, Sam, knocked on the doorframe of the study. "Nik wants to know if you care what he fixes for dinner."

Steffen laid his book facedown on his writing table. "Forgot to tell you: Juno has asked me to meet a friend of hers in Ann Arbor. The young woman wants to leave her social work job to become a detective."

"Aunt Juno's arranged a blind date? It's Valentine's Day," said Sam, shaking his head.

"I'm not sure it's even a date." Steffen unfolded himself from his chair. "Juno said I need to describe the subjects covered on the detective licensing exam."

"There should be an exam on how to court a woman," said Sam, walking away.

Steffen's gift of faith took a direct hit when his wife died. Nevertheless, he offered up a heartfelt prayer, *Please, Lord, send me someone sane this time.* His sister's friend, Bernie Johnston, sounded intelligent, but he'd seen disasters in marriages where partners and stepchildren collided. He'd concentrate on pointing her in the right direction to obtaining a detective's license.

Steffen drove toward Ann Arbor, but before he reached the first exit to the city, his phone rang. He pushed a button on the dashboard to answer.

Sheriff Beth Ann Zhang greeted him. "Hey, Steffen. One of the older ladies from my church, Marie Lee, has been found dead. I'd like you to visit the scene. 1830 Washtenaw. Something doesn't feel right."

He'd worked too long with Beth Ann not to trust her instincts. "Lee," he said as he slowed down for city traffic. Hadn't his sister and the social worker been involved with young girl named Mary Alice Lee? She could be a granddaughter. "I'm bringing along my sister and a neophyte, Bernie Johnston. She's a former social worker connected to Marie's family, and she wants to become a detective."

"Well, you might as well break her in right," Beth Ann said.

Crimes never happened at convenient times. Their Valentine's blind-date dinner would need to be postponed.

* * *

Zingerman's Road House

Steffen spied his redheaded, lanky sister as he paused at the hostess station. "There they are," he explained to the beautiful girl, who didn't look old enough to get a work permit.

Juno waved a skinny arm at him, then sat back down next to a kewpie doll, whose blue eyes widened when she looked his way.

Steffen smiled, hoping to make a possible impression—at least the woman looked older than fifteen. Her blonde hair was bobbed short. Many scruffy blondes never achieved elegance, but this woman's regal manner and the lift of her chin telegraphed untouchable polish. Delicious smells of the restaurant's food eased him into the booth across from the women.

A waitress interrupted their introductions, which relieved Steffen's initial feeling of awkwardness. He asked, "How would you two like to postpone dinner? Sheriff Zhang needs me at the scene of a crime. You both know the granddaughter, Mary Alice?"

Bernie Johnston stood and reached for her coat. "Is the child all right?"

"Her grandmother is dead," Steffen said. He helped Bernie with her coat.

Juno said, "Promise me we'll eat later."

"Hey, I'm not that much of a monster." Steffen laughed.

They walked to the parking lot. Bernie climbed into his car and looked up at Steffen as he was about to close the passenger door on his Honda. "When did you become a murder investigator?" she asked.

"Homicide detective." He gulped, looking at her enchanting and powerful blue eyes. "I changed careers after my wife died. I updated my army paramedic courses to work for a local ambulance company." Steffen folded his body under the steering wheel and continued. "I found police knew more about the instigators of mayhem. Worked as a patrol officer for five years, but I wasn't allowed time to solve crimes. So I studied for my inspector license. I thought early retirement would give me more freedom to search out truths. Once in a while legal teams hire me for their cases. Sheriff Beth Ann Zhang, my former supervisor, asked me to head up this inquiry."

"My job is killing me," Bernie said. "Not all my cases are referred from the hospital. The Mitchell Grade School called me about Mary Alice. She's seven and hid in the school when it was time to go home."

"Were you able to help?" Juno asked.

Bernie nodded. "She told me she needed a haircut."

At the long traffic light on Huron, Steffen glanced at the sway of Bernie's hair above her coat collar. "That was why she was hiding?" He faked interest in the story, fascinated with the way Bernie's mouth moved and how her nose twitched when something displeased her. Her eyes drew him in, but he turned his attention back to the traffic.

"She'd been left with her grandmother for a few days. When her mother came to pick her up, she brought along one of the younger brothers. Mary Alice was cutting out paper dolls. Her brother wanted the scissors, but she wouldn't give them up. Her mother grabbed the back of her hair and pulled it until Mary Alice shared the scissors."

Steffen was impressed with Bernie's compassion for the child. He reached for her delicate hand, lightly stroked it. "I taught a self-defense class years ago. We told women if someone grabbed them by their hair, they had little chance of escaping."

Bernie nodded and then stared at him. "Now every time the child's hair is cut, she faints."

"How did you help her?" Juno asked.

"I could see there was more going on." Bernie stared at the dashboard. "Mary Alice acted as if she was drowning in shame."

Then she turned and smiled at him.

And Steffen knew.

Her smile filled him with confidence. Wherever their adventure of getting to know each other might take them, all would be well.

"The child finally told me: when her parents leave the house, she slips into the marital bed to be cuddled in the warm sheets. She said it was the closest she ever came to being hugged by either parent."

From the backseat Juno asked, "Is she okay now?"

"I hope so." Bernie's eyes were brimming with tears. "I taught her a jingle to help: 'A-B-C-D-E-F-G, I'm singing me back to me.' I wanted her to learn to take responsibility for her own feelings."

Steffen wanted to put his arms around Bernie's shoulders. Instead, he concentrated on not running down pedestrians on Ann Arbor's busy streets.

* * *

He liked her. Bernie knew the signs. Even with his eyes on the road, his smile and the warmth in his voice telegraphed she'd made a conquest. So, she asked nonchalantly, "Tell us where we're going, Steffen."

"Beth Ann says the grandmother's death looks suspicious." Steffen cocked his head.

Bernie shifted her purse from her lap to the floor.

The slight shift in her posture must have drawn Steffen's attention. "Is there something you're not telling me?" he asked.

"No," Bernie said. "I wish I hadn't been so open about Mary Alice's case with you. I probably violated every ethic in the book."

"Mum's the word," Steffen said.

"What else do you know about the family?" Juno asked.

Bernie struggled with her seat belt to turn toward Juno. "The family has six children with another on the way. They live in the trailer park at Packard and Eisenhower. Mary Alice is the third girl with three younger brothers. Is that where the grandmother died?"

Steffen shook his head. "Beth Ann said the address was 1830 Washtenaw Avenue."

"I know that house; it's big." Juno said. "Did you remember the address correctly?"

Steffen glared into the rearview mirror.

Bernie caught Juno sticking out her tongue at her older brother.

Steffen's cell phone rang. Before he pushed the dashboard button, he said, "You answer. I'm busy."

"Blaine's automobile, Bernie Johnston speaking." Quite a length of silence ensued.

"I secured the scene," Sheriff Zhang said. "Marie's body is on the way to the morgue for an autopsy. Visit the son's trailer; they reported the death."

"Don't we need a warrant?" Juno asked.

"We can visit because of Bernie's involvement," Steffen said. Beth Ann hung up.

"Don't forget." Juno smacked the back of Steffen's head. "We still need to eat."

"I've lost my appetite." Bernie pulled her coat collar up.

Steffen coughed. "I hope we'll see more of each other in the coming months."

Juno reached over the seat and patted Bernie's shoulder.

Steffen said in a gruff voice, "Did you unfasten your seatbelt back there?"

"Bully," Juno answered.

* * *

Trailer Park at Packard and Eisenhower

Steffen opened the passenger door for Bernie. "I hate these scenes of murders' mayhem. I wish I could send you inside and wait out here for the report, but I'll learn more firsthand."

"So I'm in training as an investigator?" Bernie's smile made Steffen's knees a little weak.

"I guess that's right," Steffen managed as he opened the Honda's back door for Juno. "I don't know how we're all going to fit inside the trailer."

Bernie knocked on the aluminum door, which was opened immediately. "You must be one of Mary Alice's older sisters."

"I'm Etta," a long-limbed girl said. "Dad's out in the tool shed. I'll go get him."

Steffen blocked the doorway and bent his head to avoid the ceiling. "We'll talk to him once we visit with you for a minute." He smiled his mirror-rehearsed, one-hundred-dollar smile, and the towhead took pity on him, motioning him to a recliner. "Is your mother at home?"

Etta turned her head to stare at him as if he were daft. "She's bedridden most of the time."

She motioned down a narrow hall.

"We're here about your grandmother's unexpected death," Juno said.

"I know," Etta said.

A younger, nearly identical girl took Etta's hand. "Dad told us detectives would be coming." Then she reached out and tugged at Bernie's jacket sleeve. "Etta saw Grandma's body."

"So did Dad and Jean," Etta said as if to spread the shock around.

"Mary Alice." Bernie drew the child to her side. "You remember Juno. This is her older brother, Steffen."

"Did you find Grandma's prayer book?" Mary Alice asked. "She said I could have it."

Bernie knelt down to answer the child. "I'm sure your dad will find it for you. Does anyone else in the family want the book?"

Mary Alice shook her head. "I don't think so, but I know how to share."

"I know you do." Bernie got up to maneuver Juno and the child into the kitchen.

"Etta," Steffen said. "Let Bernie and Mary Alice chat, while you tell me what you saw." He motioned to a matching recliner. "You found your grandmother."

Etta stayed where she was by the front door. "The boys are asleep, so we shouldn't talk too loud." Etta pulled at the strings on her grey hoodie.

"I'll keep my voice low, thank you. This won't take long, come and sit down."

"That's Dad's chair."

"He's not here now. Does he get angry if you sit in his chair?"

"Oh, no." Etta plopped down in the chair. Her feet didn't touch the floor. "Only he'll want to talk to you first."

Steffen nodded but asked, "Can you describe what you saw when you went into your grandmother's house?"

"It's big." She spread her arms wide to indicate the size of their trailer. "Not like this."

Steffen didn't reply. He smiled as if acknowledging her comparison, hoping his silence would encourage her to talk before they were interrupted.

"Jean had trouble with her seat belt. Dad was helping her, so I went in the house first." Etta knotted the ties on her jacket. "I saw the soles of Grandma's Sunday shoes. She was lying next to the dining room table. That's where she fills her pill cases. When we visit, we eat at the kitchen counter next to the sink, unless Dad comes with us." Etta glanced in Steffen's direction for a second. "You know those plastic pillboxes, ones for a whole month? I remember Mary Alice saying she used the table for her pills on Saturday. Was she already sick? She did forget things. Grandma's chair had tipped over with her. I felt her cheek but it was cold."

Etta stood up and walked to the door then back to the chair. "Was there something I should have done? I don't think breathing into her mouth or pounding on her chest would have helped. Dad didn't either."

"My boss says your grandmother died around noon on Sunday."

"So why was she redoing her pills?" Etta sat back down.

"Did you notice anything else before your father and sister joined you?"

"There was still powder on the table and empty pills. You know those plastic parts they put together for a pill? Some of those were on the table, but Jean cleaned them up."

Steffen stayed very still. "How did she clean up the table?"

"With a kitchen towel. I told Dad I didn't think we should touch anything before we called the doctor, but Jean was already straightening everything up."

Steffen stood and remembered to bend over before he knocked his head on the ceiling. "Why don't you join your sister while I talk to your mother?"

"Okay," Etta said. She pulled on Steffen's sleeve. "Jean's in there, too."

Steffen sat back down. "Would you ask Jean to come out here for me?"

"I will," Etta said with approval.

A minute later the middle daughter of the household appeared. Unlike her sisters' drab attire, she wore a bright raspberry-red sweater. "I'm Jean."

"I'm glad to meet you, Jean." Steffen didn't smile at the pert child. "My name is Inspector Blaine."

"Etta says you want to know what I saw when Grandma died." Without being asked, she curled her feet under her on the gray recliner. "Dad said I wasn't supposed to dust the table. But Grandma wouldn't want anyone to think she kept a messy house. She has two cleaning girls who come in once a month to vacuum, wash the bathroom fixtures, and mop the kitchen floor."

Steffen tipped his head to show he was expecting more details.

Jean lowered her eyebrows. "Grandma Lee was on the floor in the dining room. The chair was on the floor too. You know, as if she knocked it over when she fell. I ran upstairs and checked her jewelry box, but everything was still there. We're moving in next Saturday. I have to help Mother pack now."

Steffen raised a hand for her to stay seated. "What was your grandmother wearing?"

"Did Etta say she was in her bath robe?" Jean raised her voice and added loudly, "Well she wasn't. She had on nylons and shoes and her pearl necklace and earrings." Her volume increased with her agitation. "They go with the black velvet dress she was wearing for church. It has a white satin collar, which really makes the pearls stand out."

A baby somewhere nearby started whimpering.

"That's Ben," Etta said rushing in from the kitchen.

Jean jumped down from the recliner.

Mary Alice called to her. "Jean, come meet my friend Bernie."

Hunched over, Steffen followed Etta down the hall. She opened a door to a room where a bunk bed covered the entire wall facing one small window. The oldest boy, about four, was folding clothes and putting them into a cardboard box in the middle of the room.

"Hello," he said. "I'm Bob."

Etta gathered up the big baby from the bottom bunk and jammed a pacifier into his mouth. "I'll rock him if you want to go down there to talk to Mother." She motioned toward another child on the same bed. "That's Dick; he's two."

There didn't seem to be enough air in the place for all of them to share. Steffen stepped outside to take in a few deep breaths before returning to the task of interviewing the bedridden mother of this sizable brood.

When he re-entered the trailer, Bernie put her hand on his arm. "Mary Alice says her mother, Ricky, doesn't speak anymore."

Steffen nodded his head. The cold air outside had cleared his sinuses. "Are all tall people claustrophobic?"

"A hard job is a hard job." Bernie stood on her tiptoes to kiss his cheek. "You're the good guy, even if they treat you like an intruder."

Steffen regained his ability to smile. "I like you, Bernie Johnston."

"I'm glad," she whispered.

* * *

In what might be called the master bedroom of the trailer, a woman with haunted eyes and a slight stomach bulge was pulling threads out of the bed's tan comforter. The walls were unfortunately paneled in dark wood, adding to the snug feel of the room.

"Inspector Blaine, Ma'am." Steffen sat down hard on what years ago might have been called a hope chest. "We're investigating the death of your mother-in-law. Were you close?"

Ricky shook her head.

"Could you tell me anything that might shed light on what happened?" A feminine smell he recognized but couldn't place filled the small room.

Again the woman shook her head. Her hands shook too.

Without explanation, Steffen went to fetch his sister. He gestured for her to step outside with him. "Can malnutrition cause shaking? I'd like you to look at Ricky for me. I think she needs a doctor."

Juno stomped down the hall, causing the baby to scream and the two-year-old to jump out into the hall just as she was passing. He collided with her legs and sent up a terrified howl. As if in response to Dick's shout, they could hear a man outside yelling as he approached the trailer. Juno hadn't bothered with the toddler, who was comforted by his big sister Etta.

Just as Jimmy Lee banged the trailer door open, the baby's scream pierced their ears, and Juno swept back into the living room.

"Call an ambulance!" Juno glared at the shorter man. "Your wife is miscarrying."

CHAPTER 2

Bernie's Condo

Not bad for a first date. Bernie lowered herself into her white Neon. Juno had offered to drive her to meet Steffen at Zingerman's, but Bernie explained blind dates required the safety of a quick retreat in her own car. The three of them forgot Steffen's promise for dinner. She patted the steering wheel to steady her hands after the drama at the Lee trailer.

Steffen was lean, even good-looking if you disregarded his gigantic Adam's apple, his weird wardrobe, and his big ears. Any bigger and the two of them could probably fly around town like Superman and Lois. Bernie squirmed in the convertible's seat, relishing a new sensation. Was it relief because someone found her attractive or was it a first inkling of happiness? Steffen had listened to her reasons for wanting a different profession and promised to call when he learned more about the Lee case. He didn't mind her brain power or her breadth of compassion. Not true of the men she'd tried to get close to in the past.

At her condominium, she checked the time. Was ten o'clock too late to call Mom in Florida? Buttons, her white Siamese cat, leaned into her ankle. "Hungry, aren't you?"

After she'd opened a tin of Button's favorite tuna, Bernie punched the line of numbers on her phone. "Mom, guess what? I think I found one."

"One what?" Mom asked.

"Someone for me to date." Bernie surprised herself with her openness.

"Good. Tell me all about him. We won't come home until May. Send me a picture. How old is he? Has he been married before? Any children? Sorry. I'm not letting you talk. I'm that happy for you."

"Juno introduced me to her brother, Steffen." Bernie spoke slowly, enjoying the taste of the words. "He's a detective, a murder investigator. Homicide. He's going to help me change jobs. He's fifty with two teenage boys."

"Handsome?"

Chilled after shedding her coat, Bernie turned the thermostat up from 68 to 74. "Does that matter?"

"No, but ..." Her mother coughed. "Does he dance?"

"I don't know yet, Mom." Bernie laughed. "How long has it been since I even dated?"

"Too long." Bernie could almost hear her digesting the changes in her daughter's life. Then her mom said softly, "You take very good care of yourself, won't you?"

"What do you think of my wanting to change professions?"

"This Steffen can help?"

"He has all the right contacts and knows how to train me for the job." Bernie hit the speaker button on her headset and set it on the kitchen counter. "Tonight he included me in the investigation of an elderly woman's murder. One of her grandchildren, a seven-year-old, was one of my cases." Bernie pirouetted and Buttons scurried away from her crazy owner. "I'm going to send an email to my supervisor tonight. I'm quitting my job as a social worker, Mom." Sliding down the dividing wall to the front room, she held out her palm for Buttons, who ignored her empty peace offering. "I don't want to go over the details, but today's judge abandoned another child to his abusive father."

"You do whatever it takes to lead a happy life, Bernie." In a quieter tone, almost as if she didn't want to be overheard by Bernie's stepfather, she added, "With your dad's inheritance, you needn't worry about finances while you're establishing yourself in your new field. You know I'm with you 200 percent."

Bernie's head spun with all the work she wanted to finish before giving up for the night. "Love you, Mom. Say hello to Jack."

"I will. Guess this means you won't be visiting us down here this winter?"

Bernie felt a pang of guilt. "We'll see," she said.

Her mom said a warm goodbye, but Bernie delayed getting up to shut off the phone. "Tomorrow looks promising," she told Buttons, who moved closer for an ear rub.

After remembering to ask the Lord to bless a cup of microwaved cream-of-tomato soup, Bernie sat quietly on a stool at her kitchen counter, engaging in a longer conversation with her Maker. Although conceivably a one-sided chat, she believed if she knocked long enough the Lord would let her know His answer—somehow. *Am I using Steffen, Lord, or is he attractive to me? Is it Your will for me to seek justice for innocents by becoming an investigator? Is this the man You want in my life, or am I supposed to lean on You more as a lonely person?*

A surge of energy flowed to her toes, and she scurried upstairs carefully avoiding Button's accompaniment.

The resignation email to her boss was short but final. She'd given her two weeks notice. She had shut off the computer screen before remembering to delete an entire trove of messages she wouldn't need in the future. As she swung around in her chair, she was reminded of scenes from the reality show, "Hoarders." The tables and bookshelves—even the floor—in her workroom were stacked with reference materials she no longer needed.

"I've got boxes left over from my last move," she told Buttons.

Buttons followed her up and down the basement steps as Bernie filled fifteen boxes of books for Purple Heart. Six large garbage bags were stuffed with old magazines and trade papers. She donned her coat and dragged the bags down the snowy side door steps out into the garbage room that was attached to the string of condo garages.

"Tomorrow will be here sooner than you think," she told Buttons as she shut off the lights, locked the doors, and headed for a hot shower.

Mom was right. She had waited too long for happiness. *Please, Lord,* Bernie prayed, *Let this man of integrity stay in my life.*

* * *

Jackson

That same night Steffen pulled up the covers, exposing his feet to the chilly room. He wanted to court Bernie Johnston correctly. They could learn to have fun together and base their long-term relationship on a thorough knowledge of each other. Sure of Nik and Sam's love, he wasn't willing to live without their affection, even if he needed to remain single until they were out of college and employed with families of their own. He'd seen disasters in marriages where stepchildren collided with stepparents.

Steffen spent a restless night. When he married Pauline he'd made a commitment to make her happy for the rest of her life. He'd failed miserably.

What made him think he knew how to ever live with a woman again? And he was way too old for Bernie. She needed a life of her own with children of her own making, didn't she?

Why had she come into his life now? And why was she so cute? Fetchingly so. Those eyes. Why hadn't she found someone to love her already? Did Juno know her history with previous men? Too much of a gentleman to ask his sister, he hoped she'd never been married, never fallen in love. That was ridiculous—the woman was not that young. Surely men found her attractive. He didn't have a chance, did he?

* * *

Monday, February 15
Trailer Park

Etta did not hear Benjamin crying when she arrived home from school. Out of habit, she checked the trailer's back bedroom. Of course, her mother wasn't in the bed. What did the word miscarriage mean, the specifics of it? In her twelve years Etta Lee had seen her mother pregnant six times, including this last child. The baby wouldn't be coming home. Had Mother named the child? Probably not, unless they let her hold him or her.

17

Etta didn't want to think any more about the baby, who probably would have been another towhead since all the Lee children sprouted Ricky's blonde hair. Before opening the door to the boys' room, Etta hushed her sisters, Jean and Mary Alice, as they took off their coats.

The three boys were napping together in the bottom bunk. Bob opened his eyes, but Etta motioned for the four-year-old to stay where he was. The baby, Benjamin, would be shrieking in pain when he woke. He was teething and being weaned at the same time. Dick had fallen asleep with his thumb in Ben's mouth.

The doctor agreed their mother was too rundown to continue nursing. Etta could testify that when Ricky wasn't sleeping she dragged herself around acting tired, not combing her hair and even smelling bad from not showering. Etta's dad, Jimmy Edward Lee, set down a new rule. Mother needed to be dressed at least by the time he came home for dinner.

Her dad entered the trailer, stomping the snow off his boots, making the whole trailer shake. Sure enough, the baby started fusing. He tapped Etta on the head as she stirred the beans on the stove and went in to change Ben's diaper and talk to his sons.

After they ate the hot dogs, burnt beans, and potato chips, Etta heard an odd racket outside.

Mary Alice was tipping Benjamin over in continuous somersaults so he would forget to scream. Dick, just two, helped make sure Ben didn't knock into anything harmful by rearranging the red couch pillows on the floor. All three were giggling.

Jean was drying dishes, still pouting about not receiving any valentines from her schoolmates. On Thursday night the three girls had stayed up, whispering in their room way past bedtime, to complete the last of the homemade hearts for Friday's party at school. Etta tried to assure Jean it didn't matter that they didn't have envelopes. Jean didn't think writing each person's name on the back would solve the problem, but that was all they could do.

Mary Alice said she didn't need any. Two years earlier Etta had figured out people stopped being friendly if you couldn't invite them home for sleepovers.

Her sister, Jean, once asked Grandma Lee if she could invite girls to the big house, but Grandma said she wouldn't be able to sleep. Dad said that was the end of it, which of course meant never bringing up the possibility again.

Bob placed each dish and glass along with the cutlery directly back onto the table for tomorrow's breakfast. Bob's method of setting the table saved him from climbing on a chair to put the dishes in the cupboards and then getting a chair to take them down again for each meal.

The continuing noise was not in the house. Etta slipped on her gray hoodie to search out the cause.

Probably one of the neighbors decided to get even for all the baby screams they had to put up with. Jean said Mrs. Staples next door gossiped to Mrs. Spradlin on the other side of the trailer that Mother was the old woman in the shoe who had so many children she didn't know what to do. Dad said they were just jealous. Etta wasn't sure she would be jealous of a woman with six kids with another one on the way. In fact, she didn't think she would ever marry.

Outside the clamoring sound was louder and seemed to come from behind the shed where Dad actually lived a good part of the time. He usually played old music too loud for Mother to sleep. Of course Ben was too loud too.

Dad had explained, "I use my time out here to pray so all our prayers can be answered."

Without calling out, Etta walked around the small tin hut to find the source of the odd clanking. With his face a deep beet red, Dad concentrated on pounding the burnt bean saucepan onto a boulder. The pan was dented already, so Etta slipped away.

The house rules included never hitting anyone.

"Only cavemen hit people," according to Etta's mother.

Of course cavemen didn't have pots to pound. Etta smiled. She didn't think she would tell on Dad. He probably needed to get mad in order not to cry about Grandma dying and mother miscarrying the baby.

Dad called their home a doublewide. He worked hard to keep them all fed. He tried to be a good parent, folding clothes while they watched TV and helping with homework if he didn't dose off before their bedtime. He used a funny voice for silly stories to make them laugh. Mother had not read stories aloud since Ben was born, and she hadn't laughed for ages.

The last time Etta could remember her mother laughing was when her brother Bob was born. He was almost ready for kindergarten, so that meant Etta had been eight, in third grade. Next year she would enter middle school. Dad had said she would need to take time from school to help Mother with the new baby.

They were all praying for a bigger house, which might be evil or even materialistic. The twenty-third psalm promised the Lord was their shepherd and they would not want. Etta thought the word 'want' was a peaceful word. It didn't mean a bigger house or more food or clothes, surely. She hoped the Lord meant to guarantee they needn't worry about their futures. School and a warm place to live would be provided, just maybe not by Dad.

Etta had heard that people who stop drinking said a prayer called 'Serenity.' The verses steadied her too. *Grant me the serenity to accept the things I cannot change* (which was Etta's whole life), *the courage to change the things I can* (Etta tried to keep the kids quiet and clean, even attempted new recipes, like bean soup, once and a while), *and the wisdom to know the difference* (that was the hard one).

Mother had stopped speaking altogether when she found out another baby was coming. Etta guessed Mother didn't know how to get mad at the Lord, so she just cried inside. Her eyes looked like that: empty-of-tears, yellowish, and dry, nearly dead with just a slim flickering of light. It was useless to try to cheer her. Would Mother get even sadder now that the baby was gone?

Jean was the only one who kept Mother company in the back bedroom, talking nonstop without a word in return. Etta wasn't sure that had been good for Jean, but Dad said to leave them alone.

Now Grandma's death, even more than the baby's death, had changed everything.

Her father finally returned to the trailer. His face wasn't nearly as red. "Girls," he called as he sat down in his recliner. "I'm going to see Mother in the hospital. I'll be bringing more boxes home for you to help me pack. We'll bring Mother home to Grandma's house."

Mary Alice and Jean stood on either side of his recliner. Jean smiled from ear to ear. Mary Alice's frown showed she hadn't understood.

"When will we move, Dad?" Etta asked, hoping to answer Mary Alice's unspoken question.

"Mother will be coming home tomorrow." Her father reached for Jean's head. "Pack your mother's things so she can stay at Grandma's. We'll move out completely on Saturday." He seemed to notice Mary Alice was still frowning. "We won't change schools this year."

Etta nearly laughed as the faces of her sisters changed dramatically. Mary Alice smiled and Jean frowned.

* * *

But Etta couldn't sleep. In her head, she went over the recipe Grandma had given Jean for Sunday night again and again. Sunday was when the detective said her grandmother died. She was forgetting something but not from the list of ingredients. Some truth slipped away from her. She was glad the giant of a detective wondered what had happened to Grandma. Etta wondered too. She remembered the stew hadn't looked right.

She'd even called down the hall to Jean, who was ensconced on the bed in the back bedroom, talking away to their mute mother. "Did you write everything down?"

Jean had skipped down the hall toward her. "Why don't you call her?" Jean had taken the recipe from her. "Do you think something is missing?"

Then Mary Alice had taken the slip of paper over to their father. "Dad, is anything wrong?"

"Darling, I wouldn't know if the words made a cake or a stew." He laughed but not loudly enough to wake Ben, who lay face down on his bouncing knees.

"Should I call Grandma?" Etta had asked. "The stew smells funny."

Their mother came into the kitchen.

Etta stepped aside, relieved to turn the cooking over to her. "Should I put in a jar of spaghetti sauce?"

Mother had nodded. Then she went into the family room and sat down in her recliner.

Jean had already dialed the phone. "Did Grandma say to add sauce? There's no answer, Dad." She held the mobile phone to his ear so he could hear it ringing.

"Mother, take the baby," he said, as he placed a sleeping Ben on what was left of Mother's boney knees. "I'll drive over. Who wants to go with?"

"Me." Jean already had her coat on.

"Etta," he said, "you come too. Grandma will let us bring home a bunch of chocolate chip cookies from her freezer."

Etta put a heavier coat over her hoodie. When she pulled the hood over her hair, she noticed Mary Alice's brow was puckered. "Did you want to come with?"

Mary Alice shook her head. "I better help Mother with the stew."

"Okay, we're off," Dad had said.

Etta knew he used any excuse to visit his mother. His eagerness would hurt her feelings if he were her husband. Mother probably gave up trying to change anything years ago. Etta remembered a Bible verse saying a son should leave his mother and father and cleave to his wife. Of course, all that cleaving probably just made more babies. Not marrying was definitely a great idea.

Jean climbed into the front seat of their secondhand Blazer— Grandma had given it to them when she bought her new Chrysler. Etta sat in the back listening to their dark-headed dad chat on and on about a dream. Etta didn't remember her dreams. Her alarm interrupted them, and then she was too rushed to dwell on the details.

"I had a dream last night that pretty much describes my life, the life of Jimmy Edward Lee and Ricky Elaine Walker Lee." He had turned around to make sure Etta was listening. "I was swimming and giving advice to my family while I towed an empty row boat. Ricky and all you kids—all six of you—were in a motorboat next to me."

The ride to Grandma's wasn't long, so Etta tried to relax into the scenes of snowy tree-lined streets. Some people must have been out of town or lazy, because their Christmas lights were still blinking away.

"Etta, are you listening?"

"Yes, Dad." Etta leaned forward to feign interest.

He continued his self-absorbed tale. "You thought the water skiers should stay farther away. Mary Alice came up with the idea that someone should lower the river. I just kept talking as the water got higher and higher."

A life-like dream. Etta knew enough about her dad's easily pricked pride *not* to share her insight.

"I saw my life is okay," he said. "We live in a doublewide with the family room the size of a normal house. My boys have bunk beds in their room, as do the girls. Our seventh child would have stayed in our room until we could afford a bigger place."

Etta could not keep quiet any longer. "But Dad the budget is stretched about as far as it can go."

"Just put more water in the soup. That's what Grandma says. I know my salary is not keeping up with our growing brood. Grandma helps all she can. She lives on her social security. The big house is paid for. Since I'm the only child, I love having all you kids around. Eventually, I'll inherit the house, which has more than enough bedrooms for all of us."

Etta tuned back into the discussion. Jean had been silent. That was a change. Was she angry at someone, or was she pretending to be Mother sitting next to Dad? Jean had it right. The only time Etta remembered Mother talking to Dad was to give directions or continue her critique of his driving skills.

And then they found Grandma.

Now, Mary Alice was having trouble sleeping too. Etta replayed exactly when Mary Alice had frowned and when she'd stopped. Her stomach hurt when she thought of moving into Grandma's house. If she remembered anything, she promised herself, she would immediately tell the giant detective. Etta was sure he was a good guy.

CHAPTER 3

Mary Alice couldn't sleep Monday night either. She wiggled out from under the covers she shared with Jean. The[1] floor was cold. She pulled clean socks from her drawer and crept into the silent family room. Etta's hoodie hung on a peg near the door. It was way too big for her, but its warmth helped. "A-B-C-D-E-F-G, I'm singing me back to me." Mary Alice was glad for the new prayer. Maybe it wasn't a prayer at all. Bernie was nice too.

She snuggled down into her father's chair. The plastic would get warm soon to help her keep from freezing. Her teeth chattered in the cold room. The night prayer Grandma made them say made Mary Alice's eyes fly open. In fact every time she heard it, she thought she would never want to sleep or dream again. "Now I lay me down to sleep. I pray the Lord my soul to take if I should die before I wake!" Some monster who hated children must have made that one up.

It wasn't Grandma who made up the prayer. Now Jesus had taken Grandma to heaven. Bernie came to see if she was all right. Maybe. But why did the skinny, tall man need to visit? Mr. Blaine—Steffen—talked to Etta and Jean about finding Grandma. He questioned them. Why would he do that if he thought Jesus decided Grandma needed to come home?

The prayer held special terror now that their new baby had died, and Grandma was gone too. Mary Alice was glad she hadn't seen

---

1

her grandma's dead body. Half dozing, Mary Alice replayed the last weekend.

* * *

Big House on Washtenaw

Grandma Lee had elbowed Mary Alice away from the butcher's block in the middle of the huge kitchen on Saturday. "Let Jean knead the bread in peace," Grandma said in her dry raspy voice.

Mary Alice had backed up to the sink. She'd turned to look out the window at the snow-covered evergreens against the back fence. No one cared if they hurt her feelings. She breathed in the lovely smell of raisin and cinnamon rolls already baking in the oven. Grandma always chose Jean over her, just like Dad did. Mary Alice refused to get down about it. Bernie told her it was her choice to feel happy or sad. "Could I go upstairs?"

"Oh, wait for me," Jean demanded. "Don't go up without me."

"Now, Jean," Grandma said, "Mary Alice is a big girl. Here, take up these clean towels for your bathrooms."

Mary Alice had skipped off. She spun around in the spacious dining room, hugging the warm towels just out of the dryer to her chest. With Mother so sick because of another baby on the way, Grandma had invited them to stay for the whole weekend: Friday night, all day Saturday and Saturday night, then home after church on Sunday. Bob liked Grandma Lee's church, so he was invited too.

Bob had played with Dad's old train set in the basement. You couldn't even hear the whistle on the toy train. The house was that big!

On the second floor, Mary Alice hung a fresh dark blue towel in the bathroom Bob would use. Grandma had her own pink bathroom in her bedroom. On the third floor the bathroom only had a shower, but that was great for washing hair with no one hurrying you.

Mary Alice understood why Mother was ill about having another baby. She was tired of loud babies too. Grandma Lee said they ought not complain. That was easy for her to say because they all went home to the trailer and the screams, and Grandma stayed in the big quiet house by herself every night.

They loved to stay over because Grandma cooked something wonderful every night. Mary Alice knew she usually said something wrong about how much space some people have to themselves while others barely have room to sneeze. Dad spent most of the time in his toolshed. He even bought an air conditioner for summer and a heater for winter.

Mary Alice had heard the neighbors making fun of them. Grandma Lee said they were filled with envy because the Lord had blessed her son with a full quiver. Mary Alice didn't know what that was, but if he could empty it somewhere else they might have enough to ask for second helpings every night.

Jean had told her once Grandma's closets were emptied, they would have room to hang up every T-shirt. Mary Alice liked Grandma's walk-in pantry best, with its shelves full of canned hams, vegetable soups, glass jars of red sauces, and different kinds of crackers and cookies and even canned fruits and pie fillings. Pies were even better than birthday cakes. Grandma was always good about making them cakes. Mother said the oven in the trailer was tilted, or lopsided, or something making her cakes uneven.

Mary Alice remembered following Jean a year earlier, when they were at Grandma's for Dick's third birthday. Mother hadn't come with them. Jean showed her Grandma's perfumed clothes, the filled medicine cabinet, and jewelry boxes. Jean said Grandma didn't want for anything.

It might be true. Except Grandma probably wished she didn't have to take so many pills. Jean didn't know it, but Mary Alice had seen Jean put a handful of pills from Grandma's big brown plastic bottle into her sweater pocket. Maybe Jean was brave enough to try them herself. Grandma wouldn't miss a few because she fixed a month's supply in those long plastic boxes. Mary Alice didn't ask for any pills because she was afraid she might turn immediately old, like Grandma. *Alice in Wonderland* told the story of dire things happening to girls who swallowed pills or drank medicines.

The Friday night before the real Valentine's Day, Jean stood in the doorway of the third floor bedroom with the fireplace and said, "Mother needs the peace and quiet Grandma's big house affords."

Mary Alice told her, "I wish Grandma or Jesus would figure that out."

Jean answered really quietly, "God helps those who help themselves."

* * *

Coming home after church on Sunday with Grandma, Mary Alice had repeated Bernie's silly ditty to herself: "A-B-C-D-E-F-G, I'm singing me back to me." She wished Bernie had given her a phone number to call in an emergency. Mary Alice's hands were sweating, and she could feel even her hair was wet under her grey knit cap.

Grandma had stopped her new Chrysler in front of the trailer and unfastened Jean's seatbelt. "Mary Alice, help Bob with his seat belt. Tell your mother my blessings are on all your heads."

Then Grandma's shiny, black Chrysler inched its way past all the trucks and old cars on the narrow street. On Sundays everyone was home so the street was crowded. Mary Alice remembered wanting to run screaming after her grandmother, not understanding why. Of course she could hear Ben's unhappiness and didn't want to enter the trailer, but something worse had tugged at the corner of her mind. Had she known she wouldn't see Grandma again?

Jean had held the door open for Mary Alice but spoke to Etta, "Grandma gave me a recipe for stew. She said you could make it with one hand tied behind you."

Mary Alice had tried to read the recipe as she stood looking over Etta's shoulder. Jean was acting different, not such a sourpuss. Etta sat in her mother's recliner. She waved the slip of paper around trying to keep Ben from grabbing it to shove in his mouth. Nonetheless, Mary Alice read every word and nothing seemed harmful, but something was not right. "Should I give Ben a ride in the stroller?" she had asked. "The streets are dry."

Etta seemed relieved to get the noisy infant out of the house. She had helped Mary Alice carry the stroller down the steps, with the bundled, screaming baby strapped in. "Thanks, Mary Alice. Now I can concentrate on what Dad needs to buy for the stew."

"Call Grandma if you get stuck," Mary Alice had said. "She did say it was complicated."

Etta gave her a hug. Actually, Etta was the only member of the family who remembered seven-year-olds still needed hugs. "A-B-C-D-E-F-G, I'm singing me back to me." She hadn't cared if the neighbors thought she was crazy and decided to sing loudly to drown out Ben's cries. Grandma's church ended with everyone singing, "Come Holy Ghost, Creator blest, and in our hearts take up Thy rest. Come with the grace and heavenly aid to fill the hearts which Thou hast made—to fill the hearts which Thou hast made."

Ben had been silenced. Mary Alice stopped the stroller so Mrs. Staples's small collie could lick the baby's face. Ben giggled. Mary Alice hadn't pushed the dog away; instead she buried her face in his soft long hair. "Nice Pepper," she crooned to him. He smelled like shampoo. Pepper was a funny name, but the black-and-white dog seemed to like hearing it. He had great dark eyes, which looked right into your soul and almost wept for you.

However Mrs. Staples must have thought something was wrong; she called Pepper back into her trailer.

Surprisingly, Ben remained silent. Mary Alice had continued her trip around the park. The trailer lot wasn't much of a park: never any flowers and hardly any trees. Most of the trailers were junky. Trash bags, spare tires, wire fences, and all kinds of useless stuff—metal, boards, plastic—seemed to collect around the homes.

One yard had a sofa and chair covered in snow sitting in it next to a table with a lampshade on it, holding its own share of heavy snow. The trailer directly behind their own was occupied by an old man with a dirty, white beard and nobody else. His house was the worst.

Mary Alice peeked once at Ben and found he was asleep. After three turns around the cold streets, Mary Alice headed for home. At least at their house, Dad insisted all the garbage be taken back behind the toolshed until the day the giant green garbage truck came by.

* * *

Waking up in her father's chair, Mary Alice hadn't found anything specific to tell the tall detective even after going over her memories of the days surrounding Grandma's death. It was no longer dark outside when she crept back into the lower bunk with Jean. She wondered if Mr. Blaine would ever ask *her* about Grandma. No one asked seven-year-olds anything important, did they?

Grandma was in heaven where people didn't eat at all. The pills must have tasted bad too because Grandma always frowned while she tried to get them down. Sometimes they stuck in Grandma's throat, and she acted like she was dying, vomiting green flecks and turning kind of blue-white. It was scary. So Grandma must have prayed for a lot of things. At least Grandma wouldn't have to take the pills anymore. Too bad she couldn't have let up about never having enough grandchildren. Grandma only had the one boy, Dad. Couldn't she understand Mother had had about enough? Sleep finally blessed Mary Alice.

* * *

In Route to Jackson
Monday, February 15

Steffen's hands tapped the steering wheel on his Honda hybrid. He couldn't name Bernie's perfume and couldn't ask her in front of his sister. "The boys better find you to their liking or I'll disown them."

"Bit drastic," their Aunt Juno said from the back seat. "Did you at least tell them we were coming?"

Steffen wiped perspiration from his upper lip. "Of course. They're cooking New England boiled dinner for us. I told them I hadn't delivered on the meal I promised you both on Sunday night."

"Do you even like corned beef, Bernie?" Juno asked.

Bernie nodded. "When you called, Steffen, I thought you had news from the sheriff. And Juno could have driven me to Jackson."

Juno laughed. "My big brother stayed with me last night to get up the courage to call you. The boys take care of themselves fairly well."

Bernie admitted, "I am more accustomed to dealing with grade-school children than teenagers."

"I wouldn't put you in harm's way," Juno said. "I keep telling Steffen to buy a home in Ann Arbor. Jackson society is dominated by a prison-guard mentality."

"What about the poets at the community college?" Steffen asked.

"A weak lot," Juno said. "Not a good ACLU member in the bunch."

"Oh, good," Bernie said. "I just love it when families split up about politics. I thought the Civil War got rid of the worst of you."

"Hey, beauty, you're on my side," Steffen said. "And I'm on Juno's. She's right about the staid politics of the community. Democrats run out of gas this side of Chelsea."

"Amen," Juno said.

"Juno, did you see today's rape victim?" Bernie turned to engage Steffen's sister in a different conversation.

"No, too busy in Emergency."

"Well, this twelve year old poured brandy ..."

"Wait a minute, the guy with the severed ..."

"Yep. He'd used the last of his vodka on her when he'd finished, then fell asleep."

"Wait," Steffen said. "What are you two talking about?"

"Guess," Bernie teased.

"I refuse." Steffen said. "Please let's not discuss it any further." He wiped his brow. "Especially not in front of the boys."

"Well," Bernie crossed her arms. "At least I don't have to worry about the judge sending a child home to a fiend."

"Will she be housed in juvenile detention?" Juno asked.

"She'll be safe until she's eighteen." Bernie seemed pleased.

Steffen shook his head. "A horrible loss of childhood."

"Not as bad as her home," Bernie said. "The subject is closed and in two weeks I'll be free of these horrors."

* * *

Dead End Street in Jackson

Steffen laid his fork on his emptied plate. "Nik, the meat smells great. Did you want to say grace?"

"Let's hold hands," Nik said before praying. "Lord, we come together to share Your bounty. Bless this food with Your living Spirit. And help us discern Your will for our lives. Amen."

"Heavy," Sam said. "We don't usually pray before meals."

"The truth will set us free," Steffen said, hoping Bernie didn't think the impression he'd tried to give was hypocritical.

Juno and Bernie sat across from him, while Sam and Nik commanded the head and foot of the table. Juno wore a dark green sweater over her nurse's uniform. Bernie's blue sweater revealed a bit of modest cleavage.

While they ate, Bernie stared past Steffen to the orchard outside the dining room windows. "What kind of fruit trees do you have? I don't recognize any apple trees."

Steffen lifted his chest. "One is a pear tree; the others are cherry trees. Usually the birds get the cherries before we realize they're out there."

"The view must be spectacular come spring," Bernie said.

The house phone rang. Sam got up and answered the kitchen extension, "Blaine residence. Hello, Sheriff Zhang. Beth Ann. Yes, we're just finishing up. New England boiled dinner. Thank you." Sam brought the handset to Steffen.

"Yes, Ma'am," Steffen said. There was a long pause, in which Bernie made faces at his teenage boys. Sam started picking petals off the yellow roses in the centerpiece and throwing them in Nik's direction. He did the same in return. Steffen's ornery sister encouraged Bernie to join in.

Steffen raised his hand to stop their laughter.

"I'll bring Bernie … Johnston … along and Juno." Steffen stood up, barely ducking in time to miss hitting the light hanging over the table.

Juno waved her hand, but Steffen had already pushed the disconnect button. "I should check on Ricky Lee," she said. "I promised her."

"Boys, sorry. Bernie won't be eating your chocolate cake. I need to go back to Jackson to review some new evidence."

Bernie stayed seated. "Could we plead for doggie bags?"

The boys hustled about while Bernie and Juno seemed to put their boots and coats on in slow motion. Finally, Nik handed each of the women large plastic containers. The entire cake must have been divided between the two women.

Bernie kissed the cheeks of both boys, who shuffled their socks on the slate entranceway.

"I might stay at Juno's, if she'll put up with me for another night," Steffen said, holding the door open for the women.

Juno hugged Sam and then Nik before leaving. "Aren't they jewels?" she asked Bernie outside.

"A credit to their father," Bernie said as Steffen nearly pushed her into the Honda's passenger seat.

* * *

In the passenger seat of Steffen's hybrid, the threshold of a new world opened for Bernie. She crossed her arms, hugging the new happiness she'd found. Nik and Sam were grown gentlemen as far as Bernie was concerned. The oldest child Bernie had ever counseled was an eleven-year-old girl who hadn't wanted to stay with her paternal grandmother. The case was resolved when the maternal grandmother stepped in to provide a needed home. Most of Bernie's patients were under ten years old. These strapping young men were both charming added pillars in Steffen's life.

Sam was blond—sandy-haired like his dad. Steffen's hair needed styling. Bernie remembered Juno saying he only let women cut his thick hair. But not lately, as far as Bernie could tell. Nik was shorter, maybe still growing. His hair was nearly black, and his features resembled his father's more than Sam's did. Nik's nose held the same prominence with the same deep set of dark eyes. Sam was more cheerfully handsome, while Nik and Steffen's looks were more romantic and brooding.

Bernie congratulated herself. Here she was, investigating her first case with Juno and her brother again. They needed her, and she was ready to learn. Shutting the door on counseling hadn't been difficult because she looked forward to a sound profession in the investigative field. Life was good. The Lord was meeting all her needs.

She smiled, then turned again to share her happiness with Juno. "Thank you," she said to her friend.

Juno shook her head.

Bernie wondered if Juno doubted their future. Maybe Juno saw pitfalls Bernie couldn't fathom. Nevertheless, she was committed for the long haul, whatever happened. She hoped she was fulfilling the Lord's will in her life.

CHAPTER 4

Washtenaw County Court House

In Sheriff Beth Ann Zhang's second-floor office, Steffen routinely sat down before uttering a word. The woman did not like to be intimidated by size, gender, or intelligence. Her polished chrome desk and the imitation Van Gough irises painted on giant mirrors represented the tastes of her modern, Chinese-American culture.

Steffen's long legs were not a problem. Once he was seated his old boss, Beth Ann, could converse at eye level. He introduced Bernie and waited for her to choose one of the purple chairs facing Beth Ann before he sat down.

"Tell me what you two thought of Marie Lee's family." Beth Ann swiped at her black bangs. "I'm having herbal tea. Do you want any?"

"Their living arrangements are the opposite of the Grandmother's." Steffen hadn't meant to imply a motive.

"Do you have Earl Grey?" Bernie asked. "The oldest granddaughter seemed the most distressed. Had you met them previously?"

Beth Ann's tea ceremony was perfunctory; tea bags were left in unmatched cups of hot water, and there was no sugar and no cream.

"I knew Marie from church. Her son's family rarely attended." Beth Ann tilted her head. "No, that's wrong. I remember christenings—quite a few if I'm correct. Why did you ask me if I knew them?"

"The wife." Steffen stalled, checking his notes as if he couldn't be sure of a name. He felt he was on shaky ground. Was he assigned to the case because the condition of the daughter-in-law resembled the start of his wife's illness?

Bernie cleared her throat. "Ricky Elaine Walker Lee didn't respond to Steffen's questions."

"Why not?"

"Besides living in a cramped trailer with six kids—one of whom could easily pierce your eardrums with his cries—and an additional baby she was literally miscarrying as I spoke to her …" Steffen swept his hand into empty space.

Bernie finished his thought: "I'd say the woman was about as depressed as a woman can be without doing herself in."

Beth Ann stood and stomped around the room. "I did not send you out there knowing that!"

Bernie stood up too and blocked Beth Ann's march. "You have known Steffen for how long?"

Beth Ann pulled at the back of her hair as if wanting to make it grow. "Do you think I'm a lunkhead, or cruel?"

Bernie placed her hands on her hips. "How *do* you explain yourself?"

Beth Ann went off like a firecracker. She picked up a paperweight and threw it at one of her mirrored paintings. "Who do you think you are?" she screamed at Bernie.

Steffen leapt to his feet, placing himself between the two women. "Wait a minute." Below his left shoulder Beth Ann's black, shiny hair gave off a pungent, unknown scent. "What's going on?" Looking down to his right, Bernie's blue eyes glistened. He drew in a deep breath of her rose perfume.

Bernie pushed past him. "I've only known Steffen for a few days; but I'm enough of a friend not to place him in such an emotionally charged situation, when he's still grieving."

Beth Ann collected herself. She sat back down and looked at the havoc she'd wreaked. "Get out of my office." Her tone was quiet but distinct.

"I will not." Bernie sat down too. "Apologize!"

Steffen resumed his seat. Beth Ann appeared embarrassed at her lack of control. Why had the two women sparked each other's tempers?

The truth dawned on him. Beth Ann never overstepped her boundaries as his superior, but now her personal involvement was evident.

"Hey, forget about it. You didn't know." Steffen wished he could erase every detail of his wife's death. After years and years of self-torture, he was beginning to control his thoughts and his emotions.

He put his hand on Bernie's arm, struggling to change the subject. "Is it possible Ricky Lee was grieving so intensely that she lost the child?"

"Do they inherit her house on Washtenaw?" Beth Ann rifled through a stack of files.

"Only son," Bernie said.

"Right. They were close." Beth Ann had a vertical crease in her forehead, starting right between her eyes. Worry or concentration turned the slight indentation into a red, angry scar. "They sat together at Christmas. Could any of them have harmed Marie?"

"What their process of reasoning was, I can only judge from what none of them told me. But I believe they all could have said, 'We are not to do evil that good may come.'[2]" Steffen sat back and lifted his chin.

"I know that look." Beth Ann shook her finger at him. "Is Lincoln talking again or is that what *you* surmise?"

"Both." Steffen grinned, pleased he had restored calm.

Bernie sipped her tea.

"Somebody killed the woman." Beth Ann downed the rest of hers. "She had rat poison in her blood."

Steffen sat up straight. "Did you check her pills? The twelve-year-old said there were opened pills and powder on the dining room table." He flipped through his notes. "Etta came into the house first, before her father or the other sister, Jean."

"Was she seriously ill?" Bernie asked. "Why was she taking so many pills?"

---

[2] Abraham Lincoln to Williamson Durley, Springfield, October 3, 1845, p. 10; Volumes 1 to 8; The Life of Lincoln, 1858-1865, P.F. Collier & Son, New York, 1906.

Steffen answered, "Old people commit suicide rather than suffer long illnesses, don't they?"

"I was there, remember?" Beth Ann's scalp must have been itching, but she refused to scratch; instead she pulled on her bangs and then the back of her hair. "There were pills but no loose ingredients, no powder."

"That's because the child called Jean cleaned up the mess," Steffen said, "according to Etta."

"Why would their father let her do that?" Bernie asked.

"Does her insurance policy cover suicide?" Beth Ann stood.

"We'll need to see them again, won't we?" Steffen decided he was not fond of the Lee crew. "Some members of the family give me the creeps."

"Do you know Marie's family lawyer?" Bernie asked.

Steffen's cell phone rang. "Excuse me," he said, checking the number. "It's Juno."

Juno sounded excited. "Ricky came through the miscarriage. They gave her strong antidepression drugs. She's on some sort of high and wants to finish your interview."

Steffen's backbone tensed. He didn't know if he was up to facing a roller-coaster ride again. His wife, Pauline, would intersperse talking jags with weeks of silence. "Could you stay there with us, Juno?"

Juno's tone telegraphed she understood Steffen would be reliving his painful past with Pauline. "You know I will."

Steffen explained the situation to Bernie and Beth Ann. "Ricky, the mother, wants to finish our interview."

Beth Ann walked them to her office door, avoiding the shards of mirror on the floor. "I'm glad Juno is there. I'll check on the lawyer. Take Bernie with you when you return to the trailer tonight. Here, I already arranged for the warrants. Search everything they own—cars, everything. Talk to the neighbors. Marie's house is included."

Steffen couldn't help smiling. "Thanks."

"Sure," Beth Ann said. "What are friends for?"

Down the hall out of earshot of the sheriff, Steffen asked Bernie, "What just happened?"

"Changing of the guard." Bernie smiled up at him. "The lady was in love with you, Steffen, but she knows I'm here now."

Steffen gave her a quick hug.

* * *

On the ride to the hospital, Bernie questioned herself. Was she ready to receive this tall man's affection with all the responsibilities included? Would she need to move to Jackson? She hoped not. Steffen's house was presentable, but wasn't that where the boys had found their mother? Could she ask the entire family to uproot themselves? Nik was still a sophomore, and Sam would graduate in the spring. One step at a time.

She liked the man—might learn to love him—but could Steffen put away his sorrow, let go of his first wife's trauma long enough to let Bernie move into his thoughts, his heart? Steffen's chiseled face showed his reluctance to encounter Ricky, whose suffering surely reminded him of his failure in the face of his dead wife's suffering.

Bernie wished she could wave a magic wand over his head to disperse all of Steffen's fears, erase his painful memories. *Please, Lord, lift his painful burdens.*

* * *

St. Joseph Hospital

Ricky was pacing her hospital room when Steffen and Bernie arrived. "They can't discharge me. My doctor needs to sign the papers."

Juno didn't need to reintroduce Steffen. "This won't take long."

"Will you drive me home, after we talk?" Ricky's eyes were too bright. "My husband wants to move into his mother's house by Saturday. I only have two days to pack, and today is half over."

"I'm sorry to hear of your loss." Bernie kept her voice steady.

Steffen waited for Ricky's reaction. His facial muscles strained to form a smile. If he could have gracefully jumped out the window, he would have. The clean, rank smell of bleach nauseated him. He attempted to clear his mind of ancient fears to listen closely.

Ricky shook her head. "A blessing. I didn't mind pregnancy with Dick, but Ben was a surprise. This one knocked me for a loop. I couldn't even pray for the Lord's will to be done. I could hear everything going on around me, but my mind felt like a trapped rat. I couldn't quiet it down enough to speak. Did you know the park has rats? Jimmy told me. I'm glad to get out of there." She paced the small room, knocking into Juno's shoulder.

Steffen stood in the doorway, afraid the woman might escape before the doctor saw how manic she'd become after her depressed state.

Bernie sat down in the only chair. "Ricky, you'll wear yourself out. Don't you want to rest until the doctor comes in?"

"No." Ricky rubbed her back. "I have bedsores. I never want to lie down again."

Juno motioned for Bernie to get up. "Here, take this chair."

"No." Ricky walked up to Steffen. "How tall are you?"

"Six-foot-six," he said. "What did you want to tell me, Ricky?"

"Jimmy." Ricky put both her hands into her long blonde hair. "He had no reason to want his mother dead. I know you came out to the trailer because you suspected us."

Steffen paced his words slowly, hoping despite her drug induced state that Ricky could quiet down. "Even though your family knew of the tragedy, we wanted to answer any questions you might have about our involvement."

"I heard your voice in the trailer." Ricky turned to Bernie. "Jean told me you helped Mary Alice decide to stop hiding after school. Why did she?"

"Who?" Juno got lost in the woman's rapid change of subjects.

"Mary Alice," Ricky said. Then she quickly moved on to another topic. "We'll have to sell the house. Jimmy's salary as a custodian at the university will barely pay for the heat. He thinks a miracle will happen, and he'll be able to live at his old home again." She stopped to peer between the hospital's vertical blinds. "He wouldn't be happy anyway. He's accustomed to wandering those halls all by himself. Six noisy children are going to make the place ring with activity. Besides the taxes—there's no way we can stay there for long."

Bernie gently guided the distraught woman to the chair and nearly pushed her into it. "The doctor is not going to let you go home if you can't relax."

Ricky was all attention. She folded her hands after straightening her sweater's buttons. "I need to go home."

"Did the children visit their grandmother often?" Steffen closed the door to the hall and sat down on the bed.

"Jean loved to," Ricky said. "Etta was usually too busy picking up my slack. Bob liked his father's train set. It's still in the basement. What will we do with that? Storage? That's probably too expensive. We'll sell all the antique furniture. I'm going to get a job at night. Jimmy can watch the kids."

Ricky got up and started pacing again. She headed for the door, but Juno placed herself in front of it.

"If I can find a high enough hourly wage, we could make it for a while." Ricky's spastic hands caught in her hair again. "Sell the china, the silver, those chandeliers. Still there won't be anything left for schooling. They don't have enough clothes now, besides shoes. At least we'll eat right for a while. Her freezer and pantry will last until we start selling things. See Jimmy had no reason to want his mother out of the picture. The children will need to change schools? And then we'll have to move them again, because we can't afford to stay in that big house. You can see it doesn't make sense."

The doctor knocked on the door. Juno let her in. Steffen, Bernie, and Juno stepped outside.

* * *

"She would be crazy to let that woman go home." Steffen rubbed his neck.

Juno stared at the room's closed door. "I'll tell the doctor to lower her medications."

"Will you take her home, if she's released?" Steffen asked. "Beth Ann wants me to interview the neighbors. I'm taking Bernie with me. The autopsy showed her mother-in-law was poisoned."

"I'll drive her home if she's released." Juno wrapped her arms around herself. "Someone murdered the grandmother?"

"What did you think of Ricky's testimony?" Bernie asked.

"Protecting Jimmy seems like a smoke screen," Steffen said. "Did you notice she didn't mention Mary Alice?"

"She did," Juno said. "Remember? In connection with Bernie?"

"That's right, she did." Steffen couldn't wait to leave the hospital.

In the sterile hall outside Ricky's room, Bernie and Juno took their time rehashing the situation. Steffen stomped his cold feet to get their attention.

Ricky did not resemble Pauline in the least. Pauline was graceful in her injured state, almost operatic, or like a driven ballerina. Ricky's movements were jerky. Her ravaged face and sunken eyes made Steffen want to weep. Pauline had maintained a poetic dignity, an abject state of royal tragedy, a Grecian idol—cold and aloof.

Steffen tugged at his thick hair, trying to clear his thoughts. He'd seen casts of Lincoln's hands, one holding a broken broomstick. What good were his hands to right the world? Lincoln ruled in a turbulent time. Steffen felt his world was spinning out of control again. What made him think he had anything to offer another woman, a delicate spirit like Bernie Johnston?

When the women finished their discussion, Bernie took Steffen's arm. "Okay, Sherlock, let's roll."

* * *

Juno had agreed with Bernie, Steffen's painful memories held sway. "I wish I'd known Steffen was going to get involved with this case," Juno said. "You're not seeing him at his best."

"Your brother hasn't finished grieving," Bernie had told her.

Sitting next to Steffen as they drove back to the Lee's trailer, with Steffen tapping on the steering wheel, Bernie realized she would be front and center as the poor man came to terms with his memories. "Steffen," she asked as gently as she could. "Have you and the boys gone through grief counseling?"

"Mother," Steffen said. "Their grandmother insisted the boys go. I did too, for all the good it did. Memorizing Lincoln helped occupy my mind." He looked in her direction for a minute, then turned his attention back to the road. "I haven't been able to shed Lincoln's words. I guess that's bad, right?"

"You're continuing to grieve for your wife." Bernie's heart sunk. Had she come into his life too early?

"Ricky is triggering a lot of old tapes." Steffen smiled. "Sorry."

"You never need to be apologetic for truthfulness," Bernie said, but she cried out in the depth of her soul at the unfairness of life. When would she be given a chance to safely love a man, a good man like Steffen Blaine?

CHAPTER 5

Trailer Park

Steffen drove Bernie around the entire place. Snow was falling in that fantastical sort of way, reminding him of an upturned Christmas globe. Since Valentine's Day his world had been turned upside down. A barbed murder case promised to reopen wounds he'd tried to stitch shut and cover with Lincoln's balm. The excruciating case was entangled with the universe's gift of another beautiful woman to stand at his side. He wanted to explain to Bernie how Ricky's manic state threatened to overwhelm him, drive his thoughts down to the dark caverns of grief. Instead, he counted the twenty-five trailers. "Where do these children go to school?"

"Mary Mitchell on Lorraine Street," Bernie said. "Kind of junky, isn't it."

"I don't see any rats, do you?"

Bernie screamed. "Oh no. I should be looking for rodents?"

Steffen laughed. Her reality was going to save him. Was it unfair to count on her happy nature to drag him out of his quagmire of grief? He did welcome the reprieve. "Let's go interview the neighbors."

Mrs. Spradlin was sweeping new snow off her porch as they drove by for the second time. They parked in front of the Lee trailer. Their neighbor was nearly as wide as her front stoop. "Good afternoon," she called. "How is Mrs. Lee?"

"Fine," Bernie answered, walking carefully toward her on the snow-packed walk. "This is Inspector Blaine. You and I talked on the phone about Mary Alice."

"I remember," Mrs. Spradlin said. "I don't have much more to tell you. How do they keep all those children in that trailer?"

"Bunk beds," Steffen answered. "You haven't heard any violence in the home?"

The portly woman tucked her broom inside the front door of her trailer. "That baby, Benjamin, makes enough noise without that going on."

"Do you visit with Mrs. Lee often?" Bernie asked.

Mrs. Spradlin crossed her arms. "I don't take kindly to people invading my privacy."

"So you didn't have coffee clutches, like Mother did when I was young?" Steffen knew his mother would have a fit if she knew how many times he used her name in vain. His widowed mother went to book clubs and bridge games, never anything as tame as a coffee clutch.

Mrs. Spradlin smiled down at him from her perch on the porch. "When I was younger and my husband and I owned our first home in South Elgin. The boys were toddlers then—I had coffee klatches. We would talk until lunchtime. I'm a widow now, just getting by. No time for all that nonsense."

"Does Mr. Lee help when you ask for his assistance?" Bernie asked.

"Jimmy Lee? He wouldn't put a fledgling back in its nest. I don't know what possessed the man to father so many children."

"He's an only child," Steffen explained.

"No excuse," Mrs. Spradlin decreed, slamming the door as she re-entered her impregnable castle.

Bernie came down the one step she had mounted to the porch. "Jimmy Lee seems not to be the ideal neighbor."

"Six children could be an excuse," Steffen said. He felt like laughing but he didn't want Mrs. Spradlin to think he was ridiculing her. He was just happy. There was this beauty standing next to him, which lightened his mood considerably.

Bernie walked past the Lee trailer to the one next door. The sidewalk had recently been shoveled and salted. Steffen followed, enjoying the view. She must have sensed his interest. "Steffen, concentrate."

"Right." He laughed as quietly as he could. "Mrs. Staples, right?"

Bernie knocked on the trailer's door. Mrs. Staples, as slim as Mrs. Spradlin was thick, invited them in. Her dog barked not at all. Steffen hoped he'd be asked to sit down, because his neck was beginning to ache from his crouched position in the low room.

"What did Mrs. Spradlin have to say about the Lees?" Then Mrs. Staples noticed Steffen's dilemma. "Sit, sit. I have coffee."

"Were not at liberty to reveal the details," Steffen said, thankful for the couch and coffee. He checked his watch: nearly nine o'clock at night. "What is your opinion of your neighbors, the Lees?"

"Loud," Mrs. Staples said. "Noise is about the worst of it. I turn the television up as high as it will go, and I can still hear that squalling baby. Is he sick?"

"No," Bernie said. "He's teething and being weaned at the same time."

"Mercy," Mrs. Staples said. She handed them chocolate cookies along with the coffee. The cookies were more like small cupcakes or dime-sized pancakes.

"Have you known the family long?" Steffen asked.

"Since they first moved in. Old Mrs. Buchmann died in there about ten years ago. Her lover—sorry, her friend, Mr. Prettenhoffer, still lives in the trailer behind the Lee's. Her married daughter emptied out the trailer and let the Lee's rent it. They only had two babies then. I guess Etta and Jean." Mrs. Staples refilled Steffen's cup. "Etta's the worker in the house. Always has been. I remember her when she wasn't as tall as the broom she was sweeping the porch with."

"You have a close relationship with the children?" Bernie asked.

"No. Nothing like that." Mrs. Staples nearly lifted her skirt, as if the very thought of children in her house contaminated the floor. Realizing her reaction was out of place she added, "The children are generally well-kept and behaved. My dog, Pepper, loves them all, even the screamer. Last Sunday, Pepper licked the baby's face into silence, but I called him in. I thought the parents might be afraid of germs. Mary Alice might have had her feelings hurt, but I couldn't very well explain."

"Thank you," Steffen said, afraid to overstay his welcome. "Let us know if you remember anything that might shed light on their grandmother's murder."

"Oh, no! They murdered her?" Mrs. Staples clutched her throat. "I suppose they'll be moving away, into her house?"

"I'm not sure." Bernie seemed to take pleasure in tormenting the old woman. "They probably can't afford to keep up the big house for long."

When they had returned to the privacy of Steffen's car, he called her on it. "That was a little cruel ... to suggest the murderous family would remain her neighbor."

"The uptight dame deserved it. The children are such angels."

"Someone in that family," Steffen pointed out, "probably killed their elder relative."

* * *

Etta opened the door for the detective and his partner. Mr. Blaine showed her a folded piece of paper. "Is your father home?"

"I'm in charge," Etta said, wishing she was at least as tall as Miss Johnston, the social worker Mary Alice knew from school.

Mary Alice ran down the hall toward them. "Bernie, you *did* come back."

Bernie hugged Etta's little sister. "Is anything wrong?"

Jean appeared at the doorway of the back bedroom.

Mary Alice peeked around Bernie's stooped position and instantly let go of her friend. "No, I'm just glad you're visiting us again."

Etta became more formal under Jean's tattletale eye. "My father is visiting Mother. The doctors won't let her come home yet. Bob and Dick wanted to see Mother, so he took them along. Ben is sleeping."

Jean approached, finally standing in the middle of the room. "Why are you here?"

Bernie answered, "We have a search warrant to examine the trailer, your father's shed, his car, and your grandmother's house."

Etta stepped back into the kitchen. "Why would a judge ask you to search our things?"

Steffen was stuck in his bowed position because of the ceiling. He smiled as if to reassure her. "Your father is coming home soon?"

"I don't know," Etta said.

Bernie directed the affair. "Steffen, sit down in the kitchen before your neck stays frozen in that hideous position."

Mary Alice laughed, and then held her hand over her mouth when Jean yelled at her.

Steffen sat down before extending his hand and pleading with Etta. "I could use a cup of coffee, or tea?"

Mary Alice was quick to respond. "Dad brought home Grandma's cookies. They're good." She set Etta to work by turning on the stove under the teakettle.

"Careful." Etta said, shooing the seven-year-old away from the stove. "I'll do it."

Jean hadn't moved. "Is something wrong about my grandmother?"

"Very," Bernie said. "Let's start in your mother's room. Steffen, do you want to come along and supervise the search?"

"Go ahead," Steffen said. "Mary Alice, could I taste one of those cookies while the tea is brewing?"

"Sure. Dad took clothes over to Grandma's for Mother to stay the night, but doctors know best." Her welcoming smile turned serious in the midst of the sentence, as she craned her neck to watch Bernie and Jean.

Steffen helped her out. "Go ahead. Etta can help me with that tea."

Etta knew Mary Alice did not go gladly down the hall toward Bernie and Jean.

When she was out of earshot, Steffen asked Etta, "Does Jean often yell at Mary Alice?"

Etta shook her head. "Jean's so mean she usually doesn't have to raise her voice."

"Should I tell you what we're looking for?" His voice was lower than her dad's.

She liked him, trusted him—maybe more than her own father. Etta brought him a cup of tea. "Tell me," she said, breathing in his nice manly smell.

"We need to find more of the powder that Jean swept off the dining room table in your grandmother's house."

Mary Alice had crept into the kitchen without their noticing. Her dark eyes seemed frightened. "Bernie wants a cookie too," she said. Grabbing three, she ran back to the bedroom.

Etta decided to keep busy, in case her dad came home while the detectives were still in the house. "Dad wants everything packed up by Saturday. Not the dishes," she remembered.

She opened the cupboard holding the cereal boxes and stacked pans.

"Do you need help?" Steffen asked.

"Could you tape up the bottom of some of those boxes?" Etta thought about filling the carton she had prepared. "Dad said he would have helpers from work to move." She opened the bottom of the gas stove, pulling out the cast iron skillet. "Could the powder have been laundry soap?" Etta leaned over to place the frying pan on the bottom of the box. "These are going to be too heavy to lift."

"Put kitchen towels and cereal on top," Mr. Blaine suggested. "The powder was white? Was there lots of it?"

Etta shook her head. "Not very much. Yes, white. Why would Grandma open her pills?"

"We're trying to find out," Steffen said. "I think Mary Alice overheard me ask about the powder. Did she seem frightened to you?"

Etta had taken Steffen's advice and only added two pans and the cereal boxes to the first carton before emptying out the hot pad and dishtowel drawers on top of them. Four empty boxes now stood in front of the refrigerator. "Don't make anymore!" She almost laughed. "The trailer will explode."

"I know how to pack dishes." Steffen said. "Do you have any old newspapers?"

Etta opened the door under the sink. "We don't get a newspaper, but I hoard advertisement fliers."

Mr. Blaine turned his chair in her direction. "Are there any cleansers under there?"

"Yes," Etta said, "but that's a green powder."

Steffen's long arm pointed toward the cleanser. "What else is under there?"

Etta noticed the box of rat poison. She shoved it behind the garbage pail. She handed Steffen the box of lye. "I think this is a soap. Dad put it under the trailer when the pipe froze in January. It's white."

Steffen used a dishtowel she hadn't packed to wrap around the box. He put the box under his folded coat on another chair.

Then Etta hauled out a sizable stack of papers and placed them on the table. "Dad said to leave out dishes to eat on until the day we move. Oh, dear. I've packed all the cereal."

"Maybe you could have pancakes?"

Etta pulled out a chair and sat down. "I packed the frying pan." She started to cry. "Oh, no," she stuttered in sobs. "I won't … be … able to stop."

"Never mind, Etta," Steffen said. "Sometimes it's good to cry, even if you think you won't stop."

Etta looked at Steffen for the first time through her tears. Was she crying for the frying pan, or because Mary Alice *was* frightened, or because Grandmother was murdered by somebody in her family?

Steffen's black tie bobbed as he swallowed. His eyes were nearly as dark as the tie.

Mary Alice came back into the kitchen. She put her arms around Etta and glared at Steffen. "Don't frighten my sister."

"Are you frightened?" Steffen asked the two of them as they clung to each other.

* * *

Mary Alice started to look back at the bedroom to check if Jean was with Bernie emptying out her mother's dresser drawers. Then she changed her mind. She might not have another chance to talk to the detective. "Did you see the movie about Cleopatra?"

Steffen nodded.

"Remember when the servant girl tasted the wine for her and then wiped the cup?" Mary Alice hoped this giant knew how to follow her hints.

Steffen nodded again.

Etta got rather still, as if any movement might cause something awful to happen.

Mary Alice let go of her sister. "Another servant noticed and asked her about it."

"Bernie said you were a very intelligent young woman." Steffen didn't smile, but Mary Alice knew he caught on.

"What happened then?" Etta asked. "I don't remember."

Jean entered the kitchen area.

Mary Alice knew she'd been listening, but she didn't care. Sure it was scary, but that's what they said courage was: action in the face of fear.

Jean answered for her. "Cleopatra made the servant drink the poisoned wine, and she died."

Mary Alice refused to show her fear. "I'll just go help Bernie. Steffen has some questions for you too."

Safe with Bernie in the back bedroom, Mary Alice couldn't stop talking. "Did you empty out the hope chest? That would be a good hiding place for things, wouldn't it?" She tried to look under the bed before she remembered it was boxed down to the floor. "Would anything be hidden between the mattresses, or under the springs?"

"You're a very good detective," Bernie said. She held out her arms to Mary Alice.

Mary Alice didn't want to cry, but Bernie didn't seem to mind until Jean came back.

"Bernie," Jean's voice was cold. "Your partner wants you to help him search my father's work shed."

Mary Alice took one more deep breath of Bernie's rose perfume before she joined Etta in the kitchen. Dad would be home soon.

* * *

Steffen tapped Mary Alice's head as she came back into the kitchen. "Thank you, both of you." Then in case that cagey Jean was listening he added, "The cookies were great."

Bernie touched his shoulder, causing him to jump inside his skin. "Are you going to wait for their dad to come home to tackle his tool shed?"

Steffen ushered her outside. "I think we'll get better results by not questioning him right now. Although I hate to leave those children alone."

"I'm surprised someone hasn't reported him for leaving an eleven-year-old as a babysitter." Bernie said.

Steffen didn't want to comment. He didn't want to think about living in the same house—a small trailer—with a murderer. Instead, he placed the box of lye on his car's backseat, where he found Nik's packages of chocolate cake. "Did you want to take this cake back in for the girls? You could ask if one of their neighbors is supposed to be keeping an eye on them."

He waited in the cold until Bernie returned.

She was shaking her head. "Jean took the cake. You don't suppose she'll keep it for herself, do you?"

"Three sisters couldn't be more different," he said. "But my boys are opposites too. Let's go question old Mr. Prettinhoffer."

Mr. Prettenhoffer's trailer was rank. Steffen refused to allow Bernie to step inside. He invited the old man to join them on the snow-trampled porch. "We don't want to inconvenience you."

Mr. Prettenhoffer pulled his tattered sweater around him. "I'm all right. Seen you two going door to door. What are you after?"

"The Grandmother of the family living behind you was murdered last Sunday," Bernie said. "Had you ever met her?"

"Probably the dame in the black Chrysler, right?" Prettenhoffer scratched himself, where men don't usually scratch in public.

Steffen turned Bernie away from the sight.

As they withdrew, Prettenhoffer called after them. "The Lee family's all right."

Steffen turned back to watch him close the door.

The old man was talking more to himself than to them. "Haven't seen the inside of that trailer since Millie Buchmann died."

Bernie shrieked. "A rat!"

She jumped up to the step below Steffen just as he placed his bad foot down. He grabbed her or they both would have fallen into the snow bank. Steffen kept his arms around her: not to steady her any longer but because he couldn't let go.

Bernie looked up and smiled. "I think you saved me."

Steffen wanted to release her—that was the sane thing to do—but her closeness, her perfume, the way the snow lit piece by piece on her soft blonde hair, mesmerized him.

Bernie drew his head down and kissed him. "I can see this is the start of something big."

Steffen didn't release her as he jumped down the final step. He twirled her around as if he were a teenager on his first date. "How old am I?" he asked, as he placed her carefully down.

"Old enough to know better," Mr. Prettenhoffer yelled at them from his dirty window.

* * *

Bernie's heart had lifted off the ground with her feet. Steffen was capable of loving her in the midst of this terrible case. His affections reached out for her.

"Old enough to dream," she whispered into his ear before he sat her down.

Steffen regained his composure and seriousness as they drove back to her condominium.

Songs of love rang through Bernie's head: *'Someday he'll come along, the man I love and he'll be big and strong ... a home from which I'll never roam. Who would, would you?'* Ella Fitzgerald knew how to croon love.

Time might be required for their relationship. But what else was time for, if not for loving?

For learning a new profession, a little voice in her head warned her.

Bernie never wanted to see another child's bewilderment when justice was denied. Never. Was Steffen teaching her anything about his craft, his profession, or had she let herself fall into a gentler category in his mind—a plaything instead of a comrade or colleague?

Thirty years had taught her hard lessons. She knew how to take care of herself and her emotions. Danger flags were flying high. Steffen might not be the man she wanted. He might not be able to provide her with the love she deserved. The end of St. Francis' prayer presented itself: *Grant that I might seek to comfort, rather than to be comforted; to understand rather than to be understood, to love rather than to be loved.*

She smiled in his direction, but he was busy minding traffic.

* * *

When Bernie invited him into her condo, Steffen's curiosity overcame any trepidation. He suspected their first kiss meant more to him than to her. Ten years was a long time not to be kissed. He wondered how long it had been since she'd been close to a man.

"Buttons," she said, stooping to pet an imperial white Siamese cat. "Meet my friend, Steffen Blaine. He's my instructor." Bernie looked up at him.

His hands itched to touch her. Instead he fumbled to help her with her coat. He knocked his foot into Buttons, who complained loudly. "I didn't step on her, did I?"

"She's objecting to not being fed. Come into the kitchen while I start the coffee and open a can of tuna for her."

Before he joined her, Steffen took stock of her front room's fireplace and comfortable-looking couch and matching chairs. "No television."

"Reader," Bernie said. "I have a brain-eater in my study, but I relax better with a good book. My job as a social worker demanded escape into fiction."

Steffen leaned against the counter. "When people mention famous authors, they always refer to fiction writers who have changed their lives."

"I think fiction allows us to share what makes us human."

Steffen accepted a blue mug of black coffee, dismissing an offer of sugar or cream. "I've learned how to name my emotions from fiction."

"What's the first word that comes to mind when you think of the two of us?" Her eyes were bright with anticipation.

"Potential." Steffen sat his cup down carefully on the counter and spread his arms for a hug. She moved to him, but the top of her head only reached the middle of his chest. He bent down and tipped her head up, saying, "What word comes to your mind?"

"Possible." She moved away too quickly.

After they said their goodbyes, Steffen sat in his Honda outside pondering what he might have done better. Why hadn't he kissed her again for Pete's sake? "I'm new at this." He started the engine. "There's a lot of room for improvement."

He hoped Juno wouldn't mind him staying over another night. Steffen wanted to see Bernie Johnston in the morning light—maybe every morning from now on.

CHAPTER 6

Tuesday, February 16

Steffen hoped Bernie didn't mind eating with his boys again. He couldn't take visiting the Lee's new home on an empty stomach. So he picked Bernie up at her condo off of Pauline Avenue at four o'clock. He tried not to give any significance to the name of her street, but maybe his deceased wife, Pauline, free of earthly cares, was directing him toward a woman fit to know his sons.

Because of their upcoming visit to the Lee's, Bernie had dressed casually. Her petite figure made her slacks mimic a long, gray skirt. Her thighs were sleek and her waist smaller than athletic younger women. Her matching gray sweater's softness tempted him. He did touch her shoulder as he helped her on with her coat. "I told Beth Ann I liked working with you," Steffen coughed. "On the Lee case."

"Thank you." Bernie smiled up at him. "How much training do you think I'll need to be certified as an investigator?"

"There are courses and tests online." Steffen appreciated this beautiful creature who wanted to be around him. "You have honed most of the intuitive skills required with your experience in child counseling."

"Would you include me in any further cases?" Bernie's blue eyes pulled at his heart's muscle. "Even if I've not been certified?"

Steffen coughed again to break her spell. "What do you think of Sam and Nik?"

Bernie ducked her head as she seated herself in the Honda. "I don't know them very well yet. They're still working through grief stages. I know they feel well-loved by their father."

"Thanks," Steffen appreciated the compliment. "Hey, I wanted to explain why I almost knocked you off the Prettenhoffer's porch. I'm originally from Illinois, where they grow them tall, like Lincoln. I played college basketball for Western Michigan until I collided with a teammate, tipping in a rebound. I shattered my knee cap when I landed. The season ended and I graduated before my knee replacement allowed me to walk without crutches."

Bernie touched his arm. "You might as well mention Pauline; Juno already gave me the harsh details."

Steffen thought he might be blushing. "Do you have a pushy sister?"

"Only child." Bernie was still looking straight at him.

He wanted to stop the car, but the boys were expecting them. "Pauline was my nurse in rehab. The bluest eyes in the universe, except for yours. Hers didn't hold any hints of trouble. Truth be told, she was a little high-strung, with a temper, but never mean or unkind. After I returned from the army in Germany where I served as a paramedic, I asked her to marry me."

Steffen surveyed the prospect next to him. Probably too young to consider him as a mate. He relaxed and continued, "Then I traveled a lot for a sports equipment manufacturer. I thought Sam's birth and then Nik's, two years later, would ... what keep my wife busy while I was away? I don't know."

Was Bernie using her professional skills as a counselor? Nevertheless, he was compelled to delve into his past as honestly as he could. "I thought she was fine. When I came home about one weekend a month, I mopped floors, washed the johns and showers, even moved laundry from the washing machine to the dryer. I never realized Pauline was in trouble until my mother took me aside. She'd found Pauline naked in the house with both boys screaming and hungry in their locked bedroom. Pauline's doctor prescribed strong antidepressants."

Bernie didn't speak.

Should he shut up or continue his tale? "I quit traveling. Became sales manager for the company and tried to keep my family together. Pauline started a roller-coaster ride of emotions the pills couldn't keep up with."

Bernie nodded her head, as if she'd witnessed similar horrors.

So he continued. "My mother moved in temporarily to help. Sam was in second grade and Nik had started kindergarten before Mother moved back to her house. Pauline was initially diagnosed with postpartum depression, but she never fully recovered. I think the pills were addictive."

"Absolutely."

Steffen struggled to trudge through the entire tragedy. "I was married to a stranger, who wouldn't let me touch her and seemed to hate the sound of my voice. My boys couldn't reach her either. Psychiatrists suggested I commit her for treatment. I was sure our love would break through her defensive walls. I was wrong."

Bernie patted his arm on the steering wheel. "Juno told me the boys had nightmares for years, because they found her asleep when they came home from school."

Steffen coughed but chose not to be a coward. "She never woke up from the overdose she must have started as soon as the boys caught their bus."

The ride from Ann Arbor to Jackson seemed too short for the first time in his life. "Do you like to travel?" He didn't care one way or the other. He liked the sound of her voice. It cheered him to his core.

Bernie looked steadily at him for a full minute before she answered. "We're going to travel together for a long time, Steffen; no matter where we go."

The Honda swerved slightly as Steffen digested her words. "I think so too." He smiled at the straight road before him, relaxing his hands on the wheel. The car seemed to know where they were going. The green recharging light of the hybrid even flickered. All was well with the world—for the time being.

* * *

Nik hung Bernie's small, black coat with a white lamb's wool collar in the front closet. He wondered how tall his mother had been, but now was *not* a good time to ask anyone. "My friends think it's so cool that Dad is a detective. I tell them cancer took my Mom. It's easier for them instead of thinking she was so unhappy with us she took her own life. Besides, you know, they say suicide is catching."

Bernie looked up at him, "Kids have enough problems with bullies and girls and trying to be perfect."

"Like my big brother, Sam," Nik said.

Bernie grinned. "Is he a saint like your aunt's brother?"

Nik took a second too long to catch on, then he laughed. "Like Lincoln says, 'People are about as happy as they decide to be.'"

Bernie scowled at him. "Your Aunt Juno explained the reasons for your dad's Lincoln obsession."

"Yeah, he's got me doing it. I hate it when Sam and Dad talk to each other in Lincoln quotes. Grandmother started it after Mom died. They just don't know how to let go of Mom."

"So they use that tortured man's words to comfort themselves."

"I don't want to be a party to it. Sooner or later they both need to let go and seek the Lord's comfort. I'm not afraid to pray for what I need, which is the Lord's guaranteed love." He thought Bernie might be losing interest as she stepped into the living room.

He touched her shoulder to keep her attention. "No matter what mistakes I make, no matter who loves me or hates me, I depend every day on trusting the Lord to guide me to do His will. Dad and Sam think they can function on their own. I don't know if they pray, but they try to work out their own personal problems. The Lord is so willing to hear from us. I pray He keeps them as happy as they want to be."

"Well said." Bernie sat down on the blue love seat facing the fireplace. "Can I help with dinner?"

Sam joined them. "Has Nik been hammering on about God's comfort?"

Bernie smiled at them both, "He has."

"It works for him." Sam sat down next to their guest.

Nik didn't appreciate the extra two inches his brother had on him. "He's the oldest."

"So how come I'm not in charge of dinner?" Sam got up and rested his elbow on Nik's shoulder.

"You can set the table." Nik shrugged off his brother's arm. "Aunt Juno is coming, isn't she?"

Bernie got up to help Sam. "She said she might stay with the Lee children until their mother comes home from the hospital."

Nik returned to the kitchen, but he could hear Sam talking to Bernie as they set the table.

Sam's voice took on a mocking tone when he mentioned their mother. "I was embarrassed by Mother in grade school. Dad says he never figured out why she hated clothes. But you can understand. A kid doesn't want his buddies surprised by a lot of flesh when he was hoping for a cookie or hot chocolate."

Nik stirred butter and salt into the microwaved mashed potatoes. He guessed they needed a sweet-smelling woman around the house. It wasn't about the fact that Bernie looked like Marilyn Monroe. Her chest didn't measure up, for one thing. But being a blonde certainly helped taciturn men like him, his brother, and his father to open up.

Sam couldn't seem to stop talking. "Even now after ten years, I hate to come in my front door. I always step back and let Nik or Dad in first. It's not quite sane, but it's the best I can do. I'm not a loner. The girls kind of fight over me. I'm not too stupid, I'm athletic like Dad, and I get invited to help them with their homework a lot. I just don't invite them home."

Their father brought in more groceries. "Hey, I thought when I dropped Bernie off you guys would come out to help me."

"Are there more bags outside?" Nik apologized. "We can't stop gabbing with her, Dad."

Dad smiled and cuffed him on the back. "Me either."

Sam was still chatting with his back to the kitchen. Nik wondered if he was deaf. Surely, he'd heard his dad come in.

"Dad lets us in on his casework," Sam said. "We're under strict rules of confidentiality, no talking outside the home about anything."

Steffen caught Bernie's eye but didn't interrupt Sam. Nik figured Sam needed to get something important off his chest. They stood stock-still, as if waiting for someone to yell, "Action" on a movie set.

Sam raised his hands to ruffle his curls, as if he knew they were listening but didn't want to be stopped. "Dad loves to quote Lincoln ever since Mom offed herself. It helps him take a step away from his emotions. I humor him and memorize as much as I can too. Dad enjoys arguing with Lincoln's words. Nik's not into it and usually leaves the room. I asked him why he doesn't get with the game, but he says it's too heart-wrenching to watch us not grieve for Mom."

Steffen could stand still no longer. He stepped past Nik and wound his long arms around Sam. Then he hugged him hard. "We're almost done with all that, aren't we?"

Sam turned around and Nik was horrified to see he'd been crying. Nik sat down on the kitchen stool, put his head on his arms on the counter and wept too.

"What a reception," Bernie said. "I didn't know I had so much power to move men to tears."

Nik turned toward her, angry at her ridicule, until he saw that she was weeping too. "Sorry, so sorry." Nik rushed at the short woman, nearly knocking her over in his hurry to embrace her. "You're just too good for our sorry lot."

* * *

Bernie knew if Juno had come with her, the boys would not have broken down. She was somewhat taken aback that her presence had triggered the cathartic release. A new woman in their father's life was surely intimidating. The funny thing was all three—man and boys—towered over her. Perhaps her size helped them show their vulnerability in front of a nonthreatening person.

"Well, let's eat," she said.

The storm had passed. The boys cheerfully carried in the food, while Steffen smiled from ear to gigantic ear.

"Bless this meal and our new friend" Nik prayed before they dug into the food.

Bernie made a toast with her water glass, "To our arrival on this high plateau after pushing our grief and loneliness uphill for ten years."

"Amen," Steffen said. His eyes glowed with affection.

* * *

"Nik," Steffen said. "Have you thought about becoming a world-renowned chef? Your meatloaf was great."

Bernie smiled at Nik too. "Do I smell a cherry pie?"

Nik could feel his face growing warm from all the praise. "I don't want to work in a restaurant. I want to be able to help my future wife cook, when she's busy with the babies."

Sam teased, "Do you have a girl picked out yet?"

"Of course not." Nik passed the sautéed spinach to Bernie. "I need college under my belt before I start all that nonsense."

"Nonsense?" Bernie laughed. "Now I'm just a bit of nonsense."

"Never," Steffen said.

Nik noticed Sam took a minute to absorb the new fact too.

Bennie broke the silence. "Did your dad tell you what we're working on?"

Nik recovered more quickly than Sam. "He's examining what first was deemed a suicide. Later they found out the deceased woman's capsules were spiked with poison. Since she owned a big house and her only son lives in a trailer with six kids and had a pregnant wife, I am convinced the son did it."

"Dad, I agree." Sam put his fork down, as if to concentrate. "I'll bet twenty dollars the son did it. He's the only one benefiting from her will."

"If inheritances were motives for murder—" Steffen stopped to swallow a particularly dry piece of bread. "The jails would have to add three floors to each facility."

Nik helped himself to more mashed potatoes. "I miss Mrs. Mac's homemade bread."

"Really, Dad." Sam frowned at his brother. "If he can not or will not confess, if on any pretense or no pretense he shall refuse or omit it, then you should be fully convinced of what I more than suspect already—that he is deeply conscious of being in the wrong and that he feels the blood of his mother like the blood of Abel, crying to heaven against him.[3]"

Frustrated by another night of Lincoln quotations, Nik pounded the table. "I've had about all I can take!"

Bernie shook her head. "Nik, grief never occurs the same way in any two people. The Lord made us such unique persons. Your answers can't be Sam's or your Dad's."

"Sorry." Nik acknowledged his rudeness. "When you trouble poor Lincoln's grave, I remember Mom's the more."

Steffen stood up. "How about if I play waiter and bring in that pie?"

"Ice cream on mine," Sam said. "Sorry, Nik. I'll try to stop."

Steffen divided the cherry pie into fourths. "We shall have no split or trouble about the matter; all will be harmony[4]."

"You know, Dad," Sam said, placing his slice of pie onto his plate. "Lincoln never tasted Nik's cherry pie, and he was the only president to start a civil war."

"Yeah." Nik swallowed quickly to speak without his mouth full. "Can't we eat in peace without Lincoln joining us at every meal?"

* * *

Bernie helped Sam with the dishes, while Steffen agreed to untie a knotted calculus problem for Nik. Sam loaded the dishwasher as Bernie brought in the remains of the meal from the dining room. "One of the things I like about this family—" She almost laughed because Sam turned toward her with a rinsed-out pan at half-mast. "I appreciate how

---

[3] IBID

[4] Abraham Lincoln, to Joshua P. Speed, Springfield, May 18, 1843, page 3, "The Writings of Abraham Lincoln," Volume Two, 1843-1858, P.F. Collier & Son, Publisher, New York, 1906.

you allow each other to try to understand the Lord without imposing your own views."

"Well," Sam said. "Nik gives it a go once in a while."

"Do you and your dad agree?"

"We do," Sam said, as if surprised by his statement. "I don't believe in Lincoln as much as Dad does." Among the clatter and bang and the noise of rinsing dishes and pans, Sam continued his philosophy. "I know the Creator started the whole shebang, gave us free will and all, but I'm not sure of his constant involvement. The end results might interest Him."

"So, you don't pray?" Bernie wondered if her numerous pleas set her right with the Lord.

"When I'm in the foxhole."

"Me too." Bernie knew what he meant and worried the Lord might find them both wanting. "I'm thankful too."

Sam shut off the water and studied her. "I have more questions than prayers."

Bernie nodded her head. "I guess Nik would say that's where trust comes in."

* * *

1830 Washtenaw Avenue

All the lights were on inside the stately home in Ann Arbor. Steffen and Bernie walked up to the entrance between the three-car garage and the house. Steffen had barely knocked when Etta opened the door.

"I saw you drive in," she said. "I'm glad you're both here."

"Why is that?" Steffen asked.

But before she could answer, her dad appeared.

"Come into the den," Jimmy Lee said, as if he'd lived there all his life. He had grown up in the house, Steffen remembered. "We won't disturb the kids' program."

Etta joined the other children lounging in front of the fireplace. Above the unlit grate and marble mantel, a huge screen pulsated with cartoon characters.

Bernie asked, "Sir, is it all right if I stay with the children? *Square Pants* is one of my favorites."

Mary Alice tugged on her father's sleeve. "Please, Dad, Bernie helped me at school when I didn't want to come home to the trailer."

Jimmy visibly searched his mind for any alternative but gave in. "I suppose that will be okay. Etta, ask our guest if she wants any coffee."

Steffen realized the second oldest, Jean, watched him longer than was natural. Did the little imp think she could bully him with those foul looks?

Steffen stood in the den's doorway, so Jimmy couldn't slide the door shut. He wanted the little scamp, Jean, to hear his mission statement. "I felt, that for (us) now to meet face to face and converse together was the best way to efface any remnant of unpleasant feeling, if any such existed.[5]" Steffen sat down on the couch facing the den's fireplace, declining to inform his host that Lincoln's words were flowing.

Jimmy made the interview awkward by sitting at a small writing desk perpendicular to the arm of the couch.

Steffen faced him by scooting back to the opposite arm and casually crossing his long legs, dangling his feet off the couch in Jimmy's direction.

Jimmy stood, as if remembering his manners. "Would you like something to drink, coffee or something stronger?"

Steffen sucked his teeth, tasting the remnants of the cherry pie from home. "Coffee with a little sugar would hit the spot."

Jimmy moved to the doorway, so Steffen stood. "Etta, could you wheel in the coffee cart?"

A picture of Marie Lee was prominently hung above the den's fireplace. "Your mother loved nice things, didn't she?"

"Don't we all." Jimmy smiled broadly, showing his pride.

---

[5] Abraham Lincoln, to James Berdan, Springfield, April 26, 1846, page 14, IBID.

Steffen waited until the coffee was served, taking his time to survey the room and its nervous occupant. Finally he replaced his empty cup on the carved rosewood cart. "I would like to see the house. When was it built?"

Jimmy flung open the sliding door as if escape was at hand. "I'll show you the place. Mother said the house was built in 1886. There are gas lines still in the walls for lighting."

Steffen noticed Jean had inserted herself into their tour.

The dining room, sun porch, pantry, and enormous kitchen—which contained an entire wall of refrigeration units—were remarkably clean. He could still smell the recently-made popcorn without finding any traces of the task.

The trailer hadn't been ill-kept, but these spacious rooms allowed any clutter from the brood of children to go virtually unnoticed. In the trailer he had needed to step over children and toys.

Jean blocked the stairway to the upstairs. "Mother's resting."

Jimmy pushed past her. "Mother won't mind me showing off the house."

Steffen followed and smiled at the fourth-grader, who only glared at him and monitored their trip upstairs.

The second floor consisted of two bathrooms, a master bedroom—where Ricky slept undisturbed—a dormitory for the boys, and a smaller bedroom where Jimmy's single bed was wedged between shelves of books.

Long white cabinets with locked doors lined the second-floor hall. At the end of the hall, one of the second-floor rooms was used as a toy room and the other—as far away from the sleeping mother as possible—was a nursery with two empty baby beds. Presumably the house had employed a bevy of maids when it was built, because a stairway led from the third floor down to the kitchen.

Jean preceded them up to the third floor. "My room is up here," she explained, as if to warrant her presence.

"Mother—" Jimmy's voice lapsed into a moment of grief, "—decorated the rooms for the girls' visits."

"Who occupies the one with the fireplace?" Steffen asked, knowing full well this aggressive nine-year-old child was the owner.

"Mine." Jean actually smiled for the first time. "Etta says there's a draft from the flue and Mary Alice didn't care."

Steffen didn't accept either excuse. "You're very lucky." He tried to pat her on the head, but Jean pushed his hand away, nearly growling in protest.

"Jean," her father remonstrated. "Mr. Blaine is our guest."

"No he's not." The little snot stamped her foot.

"Go to your room," Jimmy directed. "Stay there until you can remember your manners."

Steffen failed to follow Jimmy down to the next landing immediately. He intended for Jean to hear every word of Lincoln's: "If (I) have been out of order in what I said, I take it all back so far as I can. I have no desire, I assure you all, ever to be out of order—though I never could keep long in order.⁶" Then just to make sure Jean appreciated his efforts at her education, he admitted, "That's a quote from a book on Lincoln."

"What?" Jimmy asked. "Oh, interesting."

Steffen invited Bernie to join them in the den, then he asked Jimmy, "Is there an exit to the house through the den? I don't want to disturb the children."

"Yes," Jimmy said. "It was called the tradesmen's door when the house was built."

Steffen stopped with his hand on the doorknob, keeping Jimmy's face in full view. He remarked as if the news was of no importance, "Your mother's death was not an accident, or a suicide."

Jimmy turned a lighter shade of pale. "What then, a heart attack?"

"Yes." Steffen chose to sit down at the writing desk and motioned for Jimmy and Bernie to occupy the couch. Steffen thought '... *besides this open attempt to prove by telling the truth what he could not prove by telling the whole truth. So that I cannot be silent if I would.*⁷'

---

⁶ Abraham Lincoln, House Remarks, January 5, 1948, page 23, IBID.

⁷ Abraham Lincoln, Speech to the House, January 23, 1848, page 28, IBID.

Bernie informed Jimmy, "Arsenic poisoning does present initially as a heart attack. The blood test found enough traces to kill your mother."

"But how?" Jimmy pulled at his forelock of dark curls. "You've got to be wrong."

Steffen quoted Lincoln, "There's no dispute as to the facts. The dispute is confined altogether to the inferences to be drawn from these facts. It is a difference not about the facts, but about the conclusions.[8]"

"Everyone loved Mother." Jimmy would be bald by the end of the week if he didn't stop pulling out his hair.

Steffen couldn't count the times he'd heard a similar statement. "Someone did not."

Jimmy stood somewhat shakily. "Tell me when you find out who murdered my mother."

Steffen inwardly repeated, *'He knows not where he is. He is bewildered, confounded and miserably perplexed.[9]'* Then Steffen assured Jimmy. "Of course."

After Steffen and Bernie descended the narrow brick stairs of the tradesmen's exit, they walked past the front of the house to the driveway. Steffen couldn't help but note the idyllic scene of four children in pajamas splayed out on various couches and rugs, watching their favorite cartoon movie. Four? Jean was upstairs. Steffen looked closer to find out who was missing.

Steffen waited until he was safely in his car with the doors locked, before he asked Bernie, "What did you glean from that visit?"

"Lincoln held sway," Bernie said.

Steffen laughed. "Murder is not a happy subject to investigate. Whenever blackness overcomes me, the words of Lincoln reach out a lifeline."

Bernie nodded. "I suppose that's how Biblical scholars or ministers find words to help others."

Steffen decided to place his King James next to his bed. In his edition, the words of Jesus were printed in red for easy reference.

---

[8] Abraham Lincoln, page 24, IBID.

[9] Abraham Lincoln, page 42. IBID.

"Maybe I'll find peace someday about Pauline. Why couldn't she find the courage to live another day for the boys?"

"Do the moods of the mother of the Lee children resemble your own wife's angst?" Bernie slipped her hand onto his arm.

Steffen was surprised to find his face wet. "How many tears do I need to shed before I feel relief?"

"Oceans," Bernie said. "Oceans won't be enough."

CHAPTER 7

Washtenaw County Court House
Wednesday, February 17

Bernie was already seated in Beth Ann's county office before Steffen arrived. Bernie handed him a paper cup of coffee.

Steffen sat down before he said, "When I got back home last night, I found these pills in my coat pocket."

"Did one of the Lee children put them there?" Bernie asked.

"When we left only four children were in the front room watching television," Steffen said. "And Jean was still upstairs."

Beth Ann reached for the phone. "You expect they're laced with poison?"

Bernie stood up. "The children need to be taken from the home and separated, now. Or at least until the case is solved ... before one of them is killed by a sibling."

"You think one of the grandchildren killed their own grandmother?" Beth Ann's tone reflected Steffen's disbelief at the possibility.

"What do we need to do?" Bernie asked.

"I'll call Judge Wilson to get the necessary paperwork ready," Beth Ann said. "How many children are there?"

"Six," Steffen said. "But we only need the three girls."

"Why not the boys?" Beth Ann asked.

"They're below four years of age," Bernie said.

"Let's ask to see Bob too," Steffen said. "He's very articulate."

"Their poor mother," Beth Ann said.

"She needs help too." Steffen stopped. Lincoln's words ran around in his head, *'(He) would have gone farther with his poof if it had not been for the small matter that the truth would not permit him. A further deception was that it would let in evidence which a true issue would exclude.*[10]*'* "I think their mother is close to suicide."

Bernie was silent. Both women were no doubt thinking of his wife's death. Beth Ann said, "I'll talk to the judge. Is the mother under a doctor's care now?"

"Can't they institutionalize her until she's better?" Steffen wanted to hammer his cell phone to dust. Where was the anger coming from, the fear? He remembered hearing a minister ask, "Where does all this fear come from?" Steffen knew the answer: Fear never came from God. "She was hospitalized for a miscarriage on Monday."

Back in the car, Bernie leaned over the gearshift and hugged Steffen. "Do you know that I'm quite fond of you?"

"I know that," Steffen said, trying to make light of her statement even though he felt like a cad not to be able to say equal words in return. "Hang in there for me."

"You got it," she said, but he could hear her disappointment.

* * *

Margaret Mitchell Grade School
Thursday, February 18

Etta's teacher, Mr. Wilkinson, shouted her name. "Etta Lee!"

Etta turned away from the shocked expressions of the kids playing volleyball in the gym. A small Asian woman and a fat policeman were standing one on either side of old Mr. Wilkinson, who pointed straight at her.

She stumbled in their direction. What had happened now? Did Mother die? Was someone in the family in trouble with the police?

---

[10] Abraham Lincoln, page 29, IBID.

"Should I change my clothes?" she asked, afraid to learn why they wanted to talk to her.

"This is Sheriff Beth Ann Zhang, Etta." Mr. Wilkinson said before he escorted the uniformed policeman out of the gym.

"Hello," the woman said. "Call me Beth Ann. We have plenty of time for you to change. Is it all right if I come with you?"

Etta felt like crying. Instead, she looked straight into the short woman's eyes. "I'm in the habit now of showering and washing my hair." Her courage started to slip when she admitted, "When we all lived in the trailer there was usually not enough hot water for all of us."

"Plenty of time," Beth Ann said. "Your sister Jean doesn't attend the same school as you and Mary Alice?"

"Not since ..." Etta could hear her dad's words: *No one needs to know all our business.* "She attends St. Francis' school."

"I'll send Patrolman Schultz over there," Beth Ann said. "I think I can handle you and Mary Alice."

Under the shower, Etta wanted to stall before going with the sheriff. She needed time to think. Etta surveyed herself in the mirror. Did her eyes give away the fact that she was lying? Did anyone see her hide the rat poison, or had the detectives found it after the family moved out of the trailer?

When Etta finished drying her hair, Mary Alice came into the steamy shower room. "I don't like Beth Ann as much as Bernie," Mary Alice said.

"Do you know why the detectives want to see us?"

"Here's your coat. Mrs. Forbes said we're not going home." Mary Alice smiled, then she patted her jacket's pocket. "She gave me a hug and peanut butter cookies for both of us."

Etta wanted to caution her sister, but couldn't think of what to say except, "We'll just tell the truth." She hugged Mary Alice again, more to receive comfort than to give any.

Beth Ann opened the door to the smelly changing room. "Your father has been informed that we picked you up from school. He's arranging a lawyer, so it might take some time before he joins us."

"Where are we going?" Mary Alice said, with her dark eyes as wide as they would go.

"Just to my office," Beth Ann said. "We'll wait for your dad there."

"I want to stay with Etta," Mary Alice said.

"Of course, child," Beth Ann said, looking at Etta for approval.

"Mary Alice likes to have milk and cookies after school." Etta had to pull on the back of her sister's hair to keep her from saying anything different.

"Are you going to question me, like Steffen did Jean and Etta?" Mary Alice happily jumped in the back seat of the policewoman's car.

"You should wait until Dad comes." Etta buckled herself in next to Mary Alice.

"I only want to talk to Steffen." Mary Alice said. "Not when anyone else is around. Well maybe you, Etta."

* * *

1830 Washtenaw Avenue

Steffen wondered if they would need to break into the Lee residence, after ringing the doorbell for at least five minutes.

Bernie asked for the fifteenth time, "What can a four-year-old possibly tell you?"

Finally Ricky—wearing only a bathrobe—opened the door and quickly stepped behind it. "Bit nippy out there. Come in before the furnace turns on."

Steffen leaned against the shut door. He hated coming to the house. Ricky's eyes darted about. Still high on the medication. The popcorn smell of the house revolted him. What was it that put his senses on high alert? He felt sweat trickling down his back. *'How like the half-insane mumbling of a fever dream ...* [11]*'* Lincoln's words reached for him, gave him comfort.

---

[11] p. 39, IBID

Bernie noticed his disconnect. "We'd like to speak to your son, Bob. Is he here?"

"He's playing with Jimmy's trains." Ricky clutched the throat of her robe. "In the basement. How can he help you?"

"That's what I've been asking this monster." Bernie pointed in Steffen's direction.

"What?" Steffen asked. Was she playing good cop, and he was the bad cop? "What's the problem?"

"He's only four," the two women said in unison and then smiled at each other.

Steffen stayed where he was as the women bonded, leaving him behind as they walked into the living room. He watched them go through the dining room and into the kitchen. Ricky was a head taller than Bernie. Bernie was wearing ridiculous, but sexy, high-heeled boots. He couldn't remember how tall Pauline would have been in comparison. Steffen was shocked that he'd lost that particular detail.

Maybe it was time to court a woman like Bernie. If he couldn't remember Pauline's size, surely his heart needed the love of another woman. Steffen wondered if he knew how to act as a lover. The ten years—fifteen years if you counted how long it had been since he was intimate with Pauline—conspired against him.

He tried to collect his wits. Was the access to the basement off the kitchen? How was he going to explain to Ricky that they needed to take Bob away with them?

Lincoln's words presented themselves, '*His mind, taxed beyond its power, is running hither and thither, like some tortured creature on a burning surface, finding no position on which it can settle down and be at ease.*'[12]

Steffen wondered if he had repeated the words aloud or only heard them ringing in his ears. He pushed himself away from the door and followed the women's path into the kitchen.

Bob was just emerging from the basement.

Bernie held his hand. "Where is your coat, little man?"

---

[12] p. 41 IBID

His mother fetched the little one's winter coat off a peg near the back door. "Bobby, these people think you and your sisters might help them find out who hurt Grandma."

Steffen felt a strong urge to hug the woman. She certainly retained enough of her right mind not to frighten her child … not like Pauline who had terrified his sons routinely. "Thank you," he said.

Bernie marched past him with Bob in tow. "Ricky, I'll call you as soon as I can bring Bobby back."

As Steffen shut the rear door to the backseat of his Honda, where Bernie was buckling Bob in, he noticed Ricky wasn't as calm as he'd thought. She stood in the open doorway, braving the cold and the expensive furnace's reaction to wave goodbye to her oldest son, as they drove him down the circular drive out onto Washtenaw Avenue. Steffen wondered how long Ricky would wait at the open door.

* * *

"Is my mother going to be all right?" Bob asked.

Bernie answered for Steffen, "We'll make sure your mother is taken care of."

"Good," Bob said. "I worry too much. That's what Grandma used to say. She said I was born with an old soul. What does that mean?"

"Your grandmother knew you try to take care of too much because the adults around you aren't doing their job." Bernie glared at Steffen as he looked her way in the rear-view mirror.

She reviewed her own romantic motives for complying with Steffen's directives. Why did they need a four-year-old's testimony? In her experience as a social worker, judges rarely wanted to hear from children.

Ricky was certainly teetering on some emotional brink. Perhaps the spaciousness of the bigger house unmoored her flimsy stability. Confines sometimes acted like swaddling to a soul. *Please, Lord, keep the children and Ricky safe until I can return her son.*

* * *

Washtenaw County Court House

The county's sophisticated, computerized visual taping system allowed Steffen to review the questioning of all those involved in the Lee murder. He hoped raising his sons qualified him to speak alone to Bob, the four-year-old.

Bernie half-heartedly challenged his parenting experience. "I know you would never harm the psyche of a child." Bernie reached up to pat his shoulder before she opened the door to the room where Jean waited.

Steffen breathed in deeply, feeling he was the one being tested.

Bob was dressed in a blue sweatshirt that Steffen suspected was a hand-me-down from one of his sisters. For some reason Steffen thought he smelled baby powder. He arranged himself on the same side of the table as Bob. "I have two sons."

"Dad has three," Bob said, sitting as tall as he could. "I'm the oldest."

"When I visited the trailer, I noticed you were helping your dad pack." Steffen tilted his head to encourage more information. "I bet you're a big help to your sisters."

"I even change Ben's diapers." Bob blushed. "When the girls or Dad are too busy."

"See," Steffen laid his big hand on the table, palm up. "I knew it."

Bob smiled, then his little face got serious. "You want to know everything about my family, because somebody hurt my grandmother."

"Do you think your grandmother might have been sad enough to take the bad medicine herself?"

Bob shook his head. "Not Grandma. She told me she was going to live forever. I think she knew we wanted her big house."

Steffen was inclined to agree but decided silence might be more rewarding. He smiled in accord. "Do you want a Coke or something to eat?"

"I'd rather just go home." Bob smiled slightly. "Grandma's freezer is full of cookies. She was a good Grandma. She sent a dozen home with us for the trailer whenever we visited."

Steffen settled back to listen.

Bob opened up. "We were awful crowded in the trailer. I liked to keep everything in its place, which Mother used to smile at. She had stopped watching me straighten the forks in the drawer, or the scatter rugs, or the couch pillows. Her eyes were open but they didn't see nice things anymore."

"We asked a doctor to examine your mother," Steffen said. "Now that she's getting better. Did anyone tell you that you won't be adding a new baby to the family?"

"Etta told me." Bob shook his head. "It's sad, because now we have room for him or her."

"You have every reason to be sad," Steffen said. "Tell me more about your mother."

"When we were still in the trailer, when the baby was still coming, she cried when Dad needed to spread rat poison under the trailer. Cried for a long time. I guess rats meant we were poor people. Not like Grandma. I guess we're not poor now? I don't even think Grandma even knew about the rats. Jean said not to bring it up when we visited because it was not polite, like not tucking in your shirt, or having on different colored socks, when Dad mixes up the laundry. I hate that. So Etta said she didn't mind if I helped with the socks, which I can do better than Dad, 'cause he's watching television instead of being as careful as you need to be."

Steffen maintained his silence.

"Dad's okay." Bob sounded unconvinced. "Grandma says any other man would be driven to drink. I don't know why she says that except she said Grandpa was a drunk. In the trailer, Dad slept in Mother's bed after Ben went to sleep. Now he has his own room?"

Steffen nodded, realizing the child was asking for more information about married life, which didn't need to be addressed immediately.

Bob seemed to accept the fact his implied questions were not going to be answered. "Jean was the only one who talked to Mother. I haven't heard Mother answer her. I know Mother loves us. Sometimes when we still lived in the trailer, I'd sneak in to her back bedroom and put her hand on my head. It used to make her laugh. Back then, she let water come out of her eyes, but she didn't make any crying sounds."

"Would you like to join your sisters?" Steffen asked. Bob seemed undecided, then raised his head when Steffen added, "Etta and Mary Alice are in the next room."

"Good." Bob hopped down from his chair and headed for the door. "We need to go home." He smiled at Steffen. "Mother's up and about, Dad says."

* * *

Etta and Mary Alice had been ushered into Beth Ann's office with a promise of hot chocolate and instructions to wait for their dad. Bernie had taken Jean into another interrogation room. After returning Bob to two of his sisters, Steffen retired to the video taping room to review both of the women's sessions.

On the first tape, Beth Ann sat quietly while Etta and Mary Alice walked around her office. Finally to open the conversation Beth Ann said, "Your sister's red sweater is beautiful."

"She stole it," Mary Alice said.

"You're not supposed to tell on people here," Etta said.

"Yes you are," Mary Alice defended herself. "This is a police station, isn't it?"

Beth Ann started to explain they were not in a police station. "Well, really ..."

The quarrelling girls ignored her. "She did not steal it, Mary Alice," Etta insisted. "Jean said Betsey gave it to her."

"Did you ask Betsey?" Mary Alice's arms were on her hips. Steffen thought he saw the makings of a natural if miniature detective in the child. "Did she ever wear the red sweater to our school?" Mary Alice asked.

Etta thought for a minute or two, then answered somewhat undecidedly, "No. But why would Jean lie?"

"She always lies, to everybody, even when she doesn't need to." Mary Alice walked to Beth Ann's side of the shiny desk. "I think some people are born that way."

"What else does she lie about?" Beth Ann asked.

"Ask Etta why Jean cleaned off Grandma's table." Mary Alice glared at Etta.

Etta threw up her arms. "Mary Alice! I do not know why she did that. She said the police would think Grandma kept a dirty house."

"And you believed her, again." Mary Alice nodded her head to Beth Ann as if she had proven her point.

"Do you know why she cleaned off the table, Mary Alice?" Beth Ann asked.

"Etta says I shouldn't tell on people." Mary Alice returned to her seat next to Etta. "I might tell Steffen."

Try as she might, Beth Ann was not able to get another word out of either of them. Steffen watched until Bob joined them.

* * *

On the second tape, Steffen observed that Jean found it difficult to stay in her chair. She paced around the table, glaring at Bernie.

"Where's Dad?" she asked.

"He's bringing over your family's lawyer," Bernie said. "As soon as he can get him out of bed."

"I should be home!" Jean whacked the chair with her fist.

"Why do you think Mr. Blaine asked you to come?" Bernie opened her notebook.

"How am I supposed to know?" Jean shouted. She tried rubbing her eyes as if she was crying, but when Bernie failed to notice she gave up the pretense. "I'm only nine."

"I'm thirty," Bernie offered.

Steffen was shocked. He'd hoped she was closer to his sister's age. Juno was at least forty-five. Bernie was twenty years younger than him? Would she want more children? Steffen tried to concentrate on Jean's body language. Their conversation had come to an end.

Steffen decided to join them. He turned the machine to the record position.

As he opened the door to the room, Jean's head snapped to attention. "Jean, let's get a few questions answered, so you can go home."

"What kind of questions?" Jean sat down with her hands in her lap.

"Why did Mary Alice give me some of your grandmother's pills?" Steffen folded himself into one of the chairs on Bernie's side of the table, then tipped his head waiting for an answer.

Jean's eyes flicked once. "Did she kill my grandmother?"

"No," Bernie said mildly. "We don't think so. How could a second-grader think of substituting arsenic for the medicine inside?"

"Etta is in seventh grade," Jean said. "Dad says she's the smartest." Jean smoothed down her hair. "I'm the peacemaker."

Bernie smiled. "My sister was our family's peacemaker."

Steffen knew Bernie didn't have a sister. Then he realized he'd believed her as easily as Jean had.

"The boys are always fighting about something." Jean relaxed for the first time.

Steffen bore home. "I bet you're wondering, 'how any man with an honest purpose only of proving the truth, could ever have thought of introducing such a fact to prove such an issue is equally incomprehensible.[13]'"

"What?" Jean asked.

"Did you fill the capsules with rat poison?" Steffen asked.

"Why would you say such an ugly thing?" Jean's frightened tears were real.

"I have sometimes seen a good lawyer struggling for his client's neck in a desperate case, employing every artifice to work round, befog, and cover up with many words some point arising in the case which he dared not admit and yet could not deny.[14]'"

"Can't he speak more plainly?" Jean asked Bernie.

"It's a nervous tick," Bernie explained. "You know, like when you pound the chair with your fist when you're frustrated."

"I'm not frustrated." Jean said, trying to manage her temper, then resorting to loud sobbing, "I … want … to … go … home!"

---

[13] Abraham Lincoln, page 31, IBID.
[14] Abraham Lincoln, page 36, IBID.

Steffen stood and leaned over toward Jean, bending nearly in half, "Then let her answer fully, fairly, and candidly." He stood abruptly. "Let her answer with facts and not with arguments.[15]"

"Etta did it," Jean said, quiet now with the accusation. "Why, I don't know."

"Wasn't it so she could have her own room?" Bernie asked.

"With a fireplace?" Steffen added.

Jean crossed her arms.

"Did Etta get the room with a fireplace?" Bernie asked.

"No," Jean said. "Etta doesn't like drafts from the flue."

Steffen and Bernie exchanged glances.

Bernie asked a policewoman to set with Jean, before they left the room to consult with Beth Ann.

---

[15] Abraham Lincoln, page 38, IBID.

CHAPTER 8

Washtenaw County Court House

In the narrow hallway outside Beth Ann's office, Bernie pulled on Steffen's arm. "You've got to let me call Ricky."

Steffen gave her appeal serious thought. "Beth Ann might agree to let Bob go home. Should I go with you?"

"Please." Bernie crossed her arms.

Steffen searched for a Lincoln quote, but none came readily to mind. This small woman—in stature only—was determined to have her own way. Pauline had been easy to maneuver, maybe too easy. The woman facing him possessed all her faculties. She was formidable, not easily crossed. Steffen breathed in deeply. At least he could freely partake of her blessed perfume. He tugged at his hair. He wanted to touch Bernie's shoulder to ease her tension or his, but the strength of her determination brooked no advance.

He opened the door to Beth Ann's office just a crack and called, "Beth Ann, could you excuse yourself for a moment?"

Steffen could hear Beth Ann direct the children to more cookies and Bob's response, "Grandma makes *good* cookies."

Etta hushed him as Beth Ann closed the door.

When Beth Ann sized up Bernie's angry stance, she asked, "What has our mastermind detective done now?"

"Ricky Lee needs her children around her now." Bernie glared at both of them. "You need to rely on my experience. Keeping Bob away from his mother could tip the scales. The mother of these six children is on an emotional brink."

Beth Ann swiped at her bangs.

Steffen read the familiar gesture as a hostile act. Instinctively he stepped back to let the ladies quarrel.

"If she's that unstable—" Beth Ann took a step toward Bernie. "The children should be placed elsewhere."

"Not a good idea." Steffen reached out his arm to stop Beth Ann's advance on Bernie.

"Don't even think about it," Bernie said. "You are more of a threat to these children than their mother. I'm not afraid to bring charges against both of you."

"What?" Beth Ann raised her voice and then caught the harried look of the children who heard her on the other side of her office window. She shook her head. "I give up. You want to take only the boy back to her?"

"Yes," Bernie said. "For now."

* * *

1830 Washtenaw Avenue

The front door was wide open to the elements. Steffen kicked himself for not listening to Bernie earlier. Bernie rushed in, then stopped and took Bob's hand.

"Where's Mother?" he asked.

Bernie stalled. "Maybe you could wait for me in your dad's study with Steffen."

"Oh, no." Bob's face turned white. "I want to see Mother."

Steffen tried to reassure them even though he was frightened too. Would they find Ricky asleep as his children had found Pauline after her fatal dose? "We'll find her." He picked the four-year-old up, holding him close. "Together."

Bernie smiled at them. "Let's try upstairs."

Ricky's room and Jimmy's library were empty. They followed Benjamin's screams into the nursery. Ricky's back was to them. She was kneeling on the floor, holding Benjamin to her breast.

Dick, the two-year-old, was leaning against his mother's shoulder, stroking her long blonde hair. His voice was barely audible over the shouts of his frustrated brother. "Ben wants to sleep, Mother."

Bernie walked around Ricky and lifted the baby away from her. "Bob," she said quietly, helping Ricky up with the arm that wasn't holding Ben. "Come kiss your Mother."

Steffen set the boy down but kept his hand in his. "Ricky, Bob is home."

Dick crept behind Bernie's leg. "Mother's sick," he said.

When Ricky turned around, Steffen felt he might drop to his knees in pity.

Her fevered eyes didn't recognize anyone.

Bernie handed the baby to Steffen. "Take the boys downstairs." To Bob she said, "Dick is right, Bob. Your mother is running a temperature, and Steffen needs to call the doctor. Can you show him where the phone is, very quickly?"

Bob didn't move toward his mother. "Yes," he said. "Mother, go lie down until the doctor comes. Dick, let's go downstairs now."

Dick took his big brother's hand. "I was so scared."

"You're too little to worry about this," Bob said. "Everything will be all right now, because Bernie understands how sick Mother is."

* * *

Steffen paced the first floor of the Lee's quiet house. His wristwatch told him food would probably be a good idea for everyone. Something in the way Bernie acted toward him told him he shouldn't ask her about anything if he wanted to remain unscathed.

Pauline's temper was a sudden thing: plates crashing, tears, and then the silence. Bernie's righteous ill mood was based on his inhumane treatment of a woman dealing with an emotional condition similar to Pauline's depressive state.

Bob and Dick sat on the couch in their father's study quietly staring at him.

"Shall I start a fire for us?" Steffen asked.

Neither boy responded.

"Hungry?"

Both boys nodded.

Steffen reached for the phone. "I'll order pizza. What do you both want put on for extras?"

Dick looked at Bob before saying, "I like those salty, little fishes."

Bob stroked his chin. A habit he must have picked up from this father. "I like lots and lots of mushrooms."

"Done." Steffen relayed their requests over the phone. He ordered another large with extra cheese and pepperoni for the grownups. Then he telephoned Juno to help with Ricky and the boys. "Do you remember the nurse who came to your trailer?" he asked the children.

"She made Mother go to the hospital," Bob said.

"Didn't she stay with you in the trailer when your dad visited your mother?" Steffen recalled her excuse for not joining Bernie for another dinner with his sons.

"She came by the trailer," Dick recalled.

Bob nodded. "Dad said we missed Mother, and he took us with him. They wouldn't let us see Mother. She was sick then too."

"The nurse is my sister," Steffen said. "Juno is coming over to help with your mother and Benjamin after the doctor leaves."

"When is Dad coming home?" Dick asked.

Luckily the telephone rang. Steffen couldn't come up with an answer for the two-year-old.

Beth Ann wanted to know when he planned to return to the office. "A neighbor of the Lees in the trailer park, a Mrs. Staples, called. She was at the vet's. He had just given an antidote to her dog, Pepper."

Steffen looked at the boys, realizing he couldn't very well ask about the poison or the dog's condition. "Tell me more," he said.

"Okay. I understand," Beth Ann said. "You can't talk. The children's father is on his way here with Joe Wilcox. They're demanding to take the girls home."

"Don't do that," Steffen said. "I'll be there as soon as Juno can take over for Bernie."

Juno arrived with the pizza delivery boy. Juno pulled Steffen's head down for a kiss on the cheek before he introduced her again to Bob and Dick. "I'll send Bernie down," she said.

Just like Juno to read his mind. He didn't relish seeing Ricky again in her present state of mind. "Bernie and I need to get back to Beth Ann's office. Bob can show you where the dishes are kept and where all the cookies are stored."

* * *

Washtenaw County Court House

Etta saw her father through the window of Beth Ann's sheriff office before he slammed open the door. She only had time to touch Mary Alice's shoulder to stop her endless chatter to the officer.

"Come along, girls." Her father glared at the sheriff.

The little man beside him was Grandma's lawyer, old Mr. Wilcox. Mr. Wilcox was shorter even than her father, who wasn't tall like most men. But Mr. Wilcox was chunky— 'fighting fat' as Grandma used to say. To Etta he looked more like an angry teddy bear. His tweed suit and vest might feel scratchy like the white bear she had touched in the big grocery store before Christmas.

"Thank you for coming, Mr. Lee." The sheriff stood up and extended her hand.

Dad seemed a bit confused but stepped forward and reached across the desk to shake her hand.

Mr. Wilcox picked up Mary Alice and sat her on his lap when he commandeered her chair. Mary Alice fidgeted, got away, and went behind the desk. Beth Ann put her arm around Mary Alice's shoulder and then sat back down in her desk chair.

Etta wished someone would think to hug them, but Dad was not demonstrative, Grandma said. He was still dressed in his janitor clothes from the university: red suspenders with numerous keys jangling from his belt.

Mary Alice hid her face in Miss Zhang's shoulder.

Etta thought she was whispering to the sheriff.

"Mary Alice," her father scolded. "Come here this minute."

Mary Alice shook her head, not facing him at all.

"She's frightened," Etta said.

Mr. Wilcox cleared his throat. "Do you have any questions to ask my clients?"

The sheriff must have pushed a button under her desk because the fat policeman, Officer Schultz, and a grinning policewoman came into her office. "Mr. Wilcox, would you accompany Jimmy Lee to an interview room," Beth Ann said. "The girls can stay with me until Steffen Blaine finishes his interrogation.

"Are you asking questions about his mother's sudden death?" Mr. Wilcox stalled at the doorway leading to the hall.

"Her murder," Beth Ann said and then gripped Mary Alice closer to her, as if that would help her not to hear.

Etta was just as happy to stay with Mary Alice, but she wished Mr. Wilcox had cautioned her little sister to stop telling all their business to Beth Ann.

* * *

First of all, Mary Alice liked the sheriff's office. The metal desk was cold to touch, but the purple chairs and pretty mirrors with flowers on them made her think growing up to be a policewoman might be nice. The room was bigger than the double-wide's family room but not as large as Grandma's living room with the big fireplace and television mounted above it.

"Do you live in a house?" she asked the sheriff.

The sheriff answered while her eyes searched the hall outside her office window. "I'm living in a loft apartment on Liberty. You know, across the railroad tracks where the old furniture factory was."

"Etta might know where that is," Mary Alice said.

Etta was getting into a habit of shaking her head. Almost everything Mary Alice said was greeted with a mean look from her big sister. Usually they agreed about things. "Why are you always shaking your head since we got here?"

Etta did it again. "I don't think we're supposed to talk unless Mr. Wilcox is in the room."

"Why not?" Mary Alice shook her finger at Etta. "You told me we would be okay if we just told the truth."

The sheriff took notice of their argument for a second, then she rushed around the desk to open the door.

"Bernie!" Mary Alice flew at her friend.

Bernie hugged her and then went over to Etta and hugged her. Etta started to cry, hard. Bernie sat down in the other chair and kept one hand on Etta's lap. "Come here, Mary Alice. Everything is going to be all right."

Mary Alice walked over slowly. Etta didn't cry very often. "Is Dad in trouble?"

* * *

In the interrogation room, Steffen felt up to form. "'No man can be silent if he would. You are compelled to speak; and your only alternative is to tell the truth or lie. I cannot doubt which you would do.[16]'"

Joe Wilcox jumped out of his chair, knocking it backward against the wall. "You can stop that nonsense right now! I've heard about your brow-beating tactics and I'm here to tell you if you mention Lincoln or quote one more of his sentences to me, I won't be able to control my temper." Mr. Wilcox collected his chair and reseated himself, wiping his brow.

Steffen grinned. This was going to be fun. "Well, 'as his faith is, so be it unto him.'[17]"

Mr. Wilcox failed to deliver on his promise of a tirade.

Jimmy seemed disappointed too. "I can tell you I had no reason to kill my own mother." He reached for a handkerchief from his back

---

[16] p. 48 to William H. Herndon, Washington, 2-1-1848, IBID.

[17] p. 101, IBID

pocket and covered his eyes with the red-and-white rag for a minute. "Mother was living in the big house because I wanted her last days to be peaceful." He stuffed his hankie away again. "The deed and my father's resources were put in my name when I married Ricky."

Steffen realized he was an inch away from physical violence. "Then I ask, is the precept, 'Whatsoever ye would that men should do to you, do ye even so to them' obsolete? Of no force, of no application?[18]" Steffen growled, "Why didn't you have the decency to relieve your wife's worry? She still thinks you will need to sell the house even to pay the taxes."

Mr. Wilcox stood up. "We'll take the children home now."

Steffen regained his calm; he knew he was in control. "I know you'll want to find out who poisoned your mother with her own pills."

Jimmy stood too. "You'll have plenty of time to do that. My children are not leaving town anytime soon." He actually smiled.

"You can not fail in any laudable object unless you allow your mind to be improperly directed.[19]" Steffen stretched his long legs out under the table and spread his large hands over its surface. "Someone in your household murdered your mother. The children are going to remain in custody until we answer the question: Who spiked her pills with rat poison?"

Jimmy and Joe Wilcox quietly sat back down in their vacated chairs.

Beth Ann entered the room.

Steffen asked, "Did the children know the circumstances of your mother's stay in your house?"

Jimmy shook his head.

"I believe it was Shakespeare who said, 'Where the offense lies, there let the axe fall.'[20]" Steffen turned to take stock of Beth Ann's reaction.

She motioned for him to join her outside the room. Once in the hall, she cautioned Steffen. "I'm going to ask Bernie to question the girls." Beth Ann swiped at her bangs. "We can't keep all three girls here. They didn't all agree to off their own grandmother."

---

[18] p. 66, to Rev. J. M. Peck, Washington 5-21-1848, IBID.
[19] p. 90 to W. H. Herndon, Washington, 7-10-1848, IBID.
[20] p. 268, IBID.

"Jean told Bernie that Etta did it." Steffen felt a physical shift as he filed his quotations of Lincoln beyond his conscious mind.

"Go in and hassle Jean," Beth Ann said. "I'll join you in a minute."

Steffen felt he ought to check on the recording devices in the taping room instead. He poured himself a cup of horrible, burnt coffee from the pot. He knew he was postponing his questioning of Jean. Approaching the meanest child was a daunting prospect. He watched as Beth Ann briefly joined Bernie and the two sisters, then shifted his attention to Beth Ann's entrance into Jean's interrogation room. Bernie's scenario was of more interest to him, so he sat down to listen and watch.

* * *

Beth Ann's Office

After crying for a time, Etta felt relaxed.

Dad was in the building, and she was almost certain Mr. Wilcox would not leave without taking them home. She accepted another tissue from Bernie. "Thank you."

"Dad did not kill Grandma," Mary Alice said when Beth Ann joined them for a moment to talk with the social worker.

Etta thought she must have been mistaken, but for a moment she thought she heard old Mrs. Staples' dog, Pepper, mentioned.

Then Beth Ann smiled at them. Etta noticed her eyes were not warmed by the smile. She pushed her hair away from her black eyes. "We don't think he did either." She put her hand on Bernie's shoulder, and she shuddered as if from cold. "Bernie is going to ask you a few upsetting questions, and then I think you can go back to your house."

"Home," Etta corrected, then blushed at her own courage.

Bernie waited until the officer was out of the room, but Mary Alice didn't.

"One time," she started, as if trying to give a date to her story, "when Bob had his third birthday party at Grandma's, when Dick was just starting to walk and Mother still spoke but wasn't slim anymore, Jean took me into Grandma's bedroom and bathroom."

"No she didn't." Etta tried to stop her, but Bernie signaled to her not to interfere.

"Did Jean go through her jewelry box?" Bernie asked.

Mary Alice shook her head at Etta. "I'm not saying she stole Grandma's jewelry, but you should check with Betsey's mother about the red sweater. Did I tell you Betsey is a special child?"

Bernie shook her head.

So Mary Alice went into needless detail. "I bet Betsey's mother just thinks she left it somewhere, even if she told her Jean took it. People don't believe special children. Although Mrs. Forbes says it is a proven fact that special children are in … un… can't lie!"

"That is true," Bernie explained to Etta. "They are incapable of lying."

Etta said, "Betsey's mother probably just thinks Betsey got confused."

"Maybe," Mary Alice said. She turned to Bernie, "Did you find out why only Jean went to a Catholic school?"

Bernie nodded. "Jean didn't fit in with the other children at your public school."

"Because she was so mean." Mary Alice's face was red, as if she had been controlling herself not to shout the words instead of merely whispering them.

"Did the sheriff tell you about Mrs. Staples' dog?" Etta asked Bernie.

"Pepper?" Mary Alice asked. "Did someone hurt Pepper?"

Bernie held out her arms for Mary Alice, who promptly climbed on her lap and hid her face. "Pepper was at the vet's," Bernie said. "They gave him an antidote."

"For poison?" Mary Alice asked.

Etta jumped up. "I should have told Steffen. I hid the rat poison behind the garbage can under the sink in the trailer."

Bernie held out a free arm for Etta. "It is all right, Etta. Steffen saw the rat poison and understood you were embarrassed because of the rats. No one tried to hurt Pepper."

Etta understood and tried to explain to Mary Alice, "The poor thing went under our trailer and got in trouble all by himself." Etta pulled one of the purple chairs up close to Bernie, and curled herself into it out of gratitude.

Bernie turned back toward Mary Alice. "Did Jean get into anything else?"

"Oh, yes." Mary Alice nodded energetically. "Jean opened Grandma's closets and said once her clothes closet was empty we would have room to hang up every one of our T-shirts."

Bernie remained silent, stroking Mary Alice's hair and patting Etta's hand.

"And the medicine cabinet." Mary Alice was whispering again.

Etta knew then Steffen had somehow been listening to everything, because he came into the room.

No one said anything to him as he went behind Beth Ann's desk and sat down.

Steffen put his elbows on the desk and propped his chin in his hands, just watching them.

Under his scrutiny, Bernie's position in her chair shifted, making Mary Alice uncomfortable enough to get off her lap.

Etta had been shocked to hear Jean had invaded Grandma's privacy.

Mary Alice seemed to realize Steffen was especially listening to her story.

She continued as if uninterrupted by his entrance. "Jean put a handful of pills in her jacket pocket, but she didn't know I saw her." Mary Alice walked around the desk, right up to the detective. "You found pills in your pocket."

"I did." Steffen turned toward her. "I didn't know who put them there."

"Did they have poison in them?" Mary Alice's eyes always signaled when she was frightened.

Steffen placed his big hand on Mary Alice's head. "You were a great help, Mary Alice." To Etta he said, "We found rat poison in those pills."

"Mary Alice," Etta said. "Jean could have ..."

"Hurt me." Mary Alice finished Etta's sentence. "That's why I don't want to go home, if she's going to be there."

CHAPTER 9

Washtenaw County Court House

Etta watched as her father and Mr. Wilcox brought in enough unmatched chairs for every one to sit down. Beth Ann was overly polite, providing tea for everyone. She tapped the detective on his shoulder, so Steffen got up to give back her desk chair. He pulled a chair up next to Etta's purple chair. Sitting in the matching chair, Bernie asked if Mary Alice and Etta should be excused from the conversation, but their father thought they should stay.

Beth Ann began, "Mary Alice and Etta are free to go home with you, Mr. Lee. We might need to call them back for statements."

"And Jean?" Mr. Lee asked. He and Mr. Wilcox had placed their folding chairs perpendicular to the desk and Steffen's chair.

Standing at Bernie's side, Mary Alice must have felt courageous. "Bernie knows I won't be safe at home, if Jean comes home, too."

"Did Jean say she hurt your grandmother?" Mr. Wilcox asked.

"She won't." Mary Alice walked over to Etta to make her agree.

Etta looked at Dad. Why had he allowed this to happen? "Jean, Jean …" She couldn't continue.

"Jean loved her grandmother," Dad said, although his voice sounded unsure.

Mary Alice couldn't keep quiet. "No, she did not. After you told Jean not to talk to Grandma about having friends sleep over at the big house, she was mad at her."

Steffen unfolded himself from his chair next to Etta and began to stomp around the room. "Jimmy Lee, explain to your children why their mother need not have lived in fear of deprivation."

Bernie tried to get Steffen's attention by waving her arm, but the tall detective leaned over Mr. Lee. His long arms gripped the back of the metal chair Mr. Lee sat in. When Bernie clapped her hands and shook her head at the detective, Steffen snapped to attention.

Everyone craned their neck to look up at him as he said, "'I would like to know how it then comes about that when each piece of a story is true the whole story turns out false.'"[21]

Mr. Wilcox got right up and stood on his chair, waving his arms like a scary windmill. "I told you I wouldn't allow any Lincoln tactics to harass my client." He got down from the chair with a wobble, as if he felt faint being up so high. "We are *all* going home now." He pulled on the bottom of his tweed vest.

Bernie spoke very quietly. "If you take Jean home with you, some one else might be murdered before the night is out."

"Me." Mary Alice went up to her father and put one of her hands on his chair the way Steffen had. "Then you wouldn't have to feed me. You'd have Grandma's house and only five children. You could hide out in your study the way you did in the toolshed. Mother would have to worry about everything, and you could listen to your stupid music." Without waiting for an answer, Mary Alice turned her back on him. "I'm staying here, if Jean goes home."

Dad took out his ugly red handkerchief and wiped his mouth. He turned toward Mr. Wilcox. "Etta and Mary Alice need to know I lied to their mother."

Etta felt her brain was going to explode. "You what? You let Jean sit in Mother's room, tormenting her with whatever her mind could come up with. Why did you not stop her?"

"I thought Jean was good to keep her company," Dad said.

"Good?" Mary Alice yelled. "What has Jean ever done for anyone except herself? She wanted Mother all to herself. I don't know what

---

[21] p. 65, Volume Four, Lincoln Douglas Debates, II, 1858.

Mother wanted. You wouldn't let us find out. What was the lie?" Mary Alice advanced on him again.

Etta thought if she owned a weapon she would have handed it to Mary Alice. "Tell us!"

"The big house has been mine since I married your mother, as well as all my father's funds." Dad got out of his chair, standing behind it as if he realized how angry they were.

"I hope she divorces you!" Mary Alice said. "You don't know how to be a father."

Etta hoped so too. "You destroyed Mother. She loved you, and you watched her suffer, watched all of us do without, knowing you could have done better." Etta went back to her chair and turned it so she couldn't see him. "I don't want to live with you anymore."

"Make him move out." Mary Alice stormed up to Mr. Wilcox.

Bernie came around in front of Etta and leaned against Beth Ann's desk. "People make mistakes, Etta. Your father was helping his mother, just the way you're trying to help yours. Your grandmother was very old and compared to you, he thought she would suffer more."

"Have you tried to talk to Mother?" Mary Alice put her arm around Etta's shoulder.

"I know," Bernie said. "Your father has made everyone in the family sick by lying to all of you."

"Jean murdered Grandma?" Etta didn't want to believe it.

Steffen stood behind Beth Ann's desk, as if he could arrange everything to come out all right. "Etta, Jean told me you killed your grandmother."

Etta wasn't surprised; she had expected nothing less from Jean. "She'll say anything to get out of trouble."

"Mr. Wilcox, we need to fingerprint all three girls." Steffen continued to direct Beth Ann, who called in assistants and proceeded—with Mr. Wilcox's blessing—to ink and make a fingerprint on transparent paper for each of the girls' fingers.

"This isn't going to help," Mary Alice said to Steffen. "I put those pills in your pocket."

"We're matching prints to the pills your grandmother left on the table," Bernie said.

Dad coughed. His whole manner had changed. His shoulders were slumped. He wasn't crying, but the strut short people use to seem taller had left him. He looked older than their mother for the first time. "I'll make it up to your mother and both of you."

"What about Jean?" Mary Alice said. "How are you going to get the meanness out of Jean? She's already killed your mother, because you lied to us."

Mr. Lee broke down.

Bernie pulled Mary Alice aside and spoke quietly to her, trying to calm her down.

"He's sorry," Etta said. "We have to go home for Mother."

Mary Alice wouldn't have it. "Mr. Wilcox, you take him to your house. Etta can tell Mother, and then we'll see what she says." Then Mary Alice turned to Etta, seeming to realize how difficult that was going to be for Mother. "Bernie, could you and Steffen come with us?"

"Of course," Bernie said, without even looking at Steffen, who seemed very surprised.

Steffen tried to look even taller and quoted Lincoln once again: "'I know there is a God, and that He hates injustice … truth is everything. A house divided against itself cannot stand. God cares, and humanity cares, and I care.[22]'"

Mr. Wilcox put his arm through Dad's arm and walked him out of the office. Though they were not dressed any where near the same, Etta nearly giggled in hysterical relief. They looked somewhat like Tweedle Dee and Tweedle Dum, her father being the stupid one.

Beth Ann told Bernie that Jean would be kept in the juvenile detention home in Ypsilanti for the night.

Bernie shook her head sadly. "Steffen, pull yourself together. We need to return the girls to their mother."

---

[22] P. 209, Abraham Lincoln after reading Mr. Bateman's list of Springfield clergy, who would vote against Lincoln, before November 1860.

* * *

1830 Washtenaw Avenue

Juno opened the door of the Lee residence. Bernie ushered the children upstairs to see their mother. Steffen shuffled after Juno as she headed to the kitchen. "Smells familiar," he said.

Steffen was taken aback when his son, Nik, greeted him after replacing a large soup pot's lid. "Hi, Dad. Aunt Juno pleaded for mercy."

"He offered," Juno said. "I was running ragged trying to change diapers, carry trays up to Ricky, and keep the laundry going."

"You two are amazing," Steffen said. "It's good to know there are people I can count on to pick up the slack in someone else's life."

Juno nudged him with her bony elbow. "Bernie needs you upstairs."

"I know," he said. Still, he lingered in the vegetable scented room. He lifted the pot's lid, then opened the oven door to excited shouts from Nik and Juno. The crescent rolls were browning nicely without his help. He coughed, and a Lincoln quote came out of his mouth: "'I shall try to correct errors when shown errors; and I shall adopt new views so fast as they shall appear to be true views.[23]'"

Juno and Nik looked at each other, but failed to comment on his crazy affliction.

So with nothing further to keep him, Steffen mounted the two flights of steps to the second floor. Did men on their way up the gallows steps feel as doomed as he did? He knew nothing he could do would relieve the suffering of this mother of six children. When he entered the pink master bedroom, Steffen tried to concentrate on anything other than his thoughts of Ricky's condition and its resemblance to his dead wife's.

The girls were dressed in jeans and sweatshirts of a pale blue, an almost gray color. Their gym shoes were scuffed. Mary Alice had on one pink sock and one blue sock, which peeked out from under her

---

[23] Abraham Lincoln, to Hon. Horace Greeley, 8-22-1862, Vol 8, 1862-1865, G. P. Putnam's Sons, 1906

jean cuffs. She obviously had grown out of that size, but no one had bothered to give her a new or used pair. Etta's hair was pulled into a tight ponytail, while Mary Alice's feather-like hair flew around her shoulders. Her bangs were too long, and if she tipped her head down you couldn't see if she was frowning.

Bernie seemed to place all of her frustration about the case on his shoulders, as if he had instructed the nine-year-old to solve all their problems by killing her grandmother. He had read enough psychology books in his search to understand the criminal mind to realize that Bernie's displaced anger couldn't very well be directed toward Jean, so Steffen was elected her target. He felt her anger's palpable vibrations. He dared not touch her and was barely able to look directly into her unfriendly eyes.

Nevertheless she was beautiful and intelligent. Her splendor couldn't be denied. She had unbuttoned a bright blue sweater and pushed up its sleeves as if ready for a fight. Her black skirt didn't cover her knees, and her shapely legs were enhanced by those high-heeled black boots.

"Steffen," she called his attention back to the matter at hand.

All three boys were on Ricky's big bed. Dick was taking his turn pulling the baby's toes, thoroughly engrossed as if making sure the baby did indeed have ten toes.

Bob sat close to his mother. Ricky's arm was around him, not to comfort the boy but as if the child was supporting the entire weight of her body or soul.

Etta went up to the bed and took Bob's hand, not her mother's. "We need to tell you the truth."

Mary Alice kept close to Bernie on the opposite side of the bed from Etta. "Dad's been lying to you since your wedding day!"

Steffen positioned himself at the foot of the bed, watching their interactions with Ricky as if refereeing a tennis match.

"Mary Alice," Ricky scolded. "Don't talk about your father that way. He loves us all."

"I don't want a liar to love me," Mary Alice said, and then she broke down in Bernie's arms.

Bernie glared at Steffen. "Tell her."

He couldn't help himself, Lincoln's words fell unbidden from his lips. "'Neither let us be slandered from our duty by false accusations against us. Let us have faith that right makes might and that in that faith, let us, to the end, dare to do our duty as we understand it.[24]'"

"Stop it," Bernie shouted.

But seeing Ricky's distraught eyes led Steffen further into his own illness of denial. "'You say you will destroy (their marital) union; and then you say the great crime of having destroyed it will be put upon us. That is cool. A highwayman holds a pistol to my ear and mutters through his teeth, 'Stand and deliver, or I shall kill you, and then you will be the murderer.[25]'"

Bernie took his arm and led him out of Ricky's bedroom. "I understand, Steffen. Stay out here. I'll tell her."

Steffen sat down on the floor near the steps, letting his feet dangle down the stairway.   Etta, carrying the baby, made her way down the hall to the nursery. Dick and Bob followed her.

Mary Alice came out of the bedroom and sat down next to him. "Don't worry. Bernie likes you. Why do you make her mad with those old words?"

Steffen gently pushed Mary Alice's hair behind her ears. "You're very old yourself, for a child."

Mary Alice patted his arm. "Everything will be all right, won't it?"

"Of course," Steffen was surprised to hear himself say. He could clearly hear Bernie's words, thankful that he needn't watch their terrible consequences reach Ricky's soul.

Mary Alice nudged him. "You should lose that black bow tie. It just draws attention to your Adam's apple."

"Really?" Steffen remembered a young girl giving Lincoln advice about his appearance, which Lincoln took to heart, hence the beard in the later pictures. Steffen unsnapped the tie. "It's yours, for a keepsake."

---

[24] p. 188, IBID, Volume 8, Chapter XIV, After a Great Struggle Speech early in 1860 in Plymouth Church where   Henry Ward Beecher was Pastor. The audience was too big and the venue was changed to Cooper Union.

[25] P. 189, IBID, Chapter XV, Cooper Union speech.

Mary Alice handed it back. "I don't want it."

Steffen's feelings were hurt, but he placed the tie in his pocket and tried to smile.

"Oh, give it here, you big baby."

"Are you seven or are you a forty-year-old small person?" Steffen sheepishly handed her the offending tie.

"Now that Bernie's told Mother," Mary Alice told him, "You should probably go in and make small talk."

"Yes, Ma'am." Stephen slowly made his way back to the master bedroom.

* * *

Bernie had moved a chair closer to the bed. She reached for Ricky's hand.

"Tell me," Ricky said. "You know who murdered their grandmother?"

"I'd only be guessing," Bernie said. "I need to give you news that might relieve a whole world of financial fears for you, but the information might be painful to hear."

Ricky fidgeted with the edge of her cover. "Relief about money? I know my family loves me. What could be painful?"

"Your husband … " Bernie began.

Ricky stiffened and held up her hand for Bernie to stop. "Let him tell me."

"Yes," Bernie agreed. "He should be here to respond."

"To my anger?" Ricky brushed her face with both her hands. "You are telling me that financially, my worries were groundless?"

"Any plans you have for your children will be easily met." Bernie stood.

Ricky's revival at this partial view of Jimmy's deception convinced Bernie this mother of six possessed the inner resources necessary to hear the entire truth.

"I better shower and dress," Ricky said, sliding to the edge of the bed.

"The children need your calmness," Bernie said, wanting to cheer her.

"I've been praying nonstop," Ricky said, as she stepped into the adjoining bathroom.   Bernie could only nod. She wanted to shout, "He's answered."

Ricky stuck her head around the frame of the door with almost a smile on her face. "I know," she said.

Bernie met Steffen at the door. "She's going to be okay."

"Shouldn't we call the doctor?" Steffen asked. "Is she safe in there by herself?"

Bernie knocked on Steffen's chest with her balled up fist. "Pauline is not in that room, Steffen."

"I know," he said, but he didn't look relieved in the least. "Is Ricky going to divorce the children's father?"

CHAPTER 10

Bernie walked past Steffen, smiled for the boys in the nursery, then pushed past him in the hall, saying, "We need to talk downstairs."

Lincoln's words fell in a jumble in Steffen's brain. He tried to sort them out, wondering if any of the phrases in his repertoire would fit his downtrodden situation. Bernie Johnston's moods were seeping into his ken, wreaking havoc as they shoved their way through his defenses. *'Discourage litigation. Persuade your neighbor to compromise whenever you can.'*[26] Bernie didn't qualify as a neighbor but Steffen wished he could at least convince her of his good intentions. *'As a peace-maker the lawyer has a superior opportunity of being a good man.'*[27]

Steffen considered giving up investigative pursuits. Perhaps the law would be less emotionally stressful for him. He followed Bernie down the stairs and into Jimmy Lee's empty study.

Bernie slid the door closed before motioning for him to sit on the couch. She stood with her back to the unlit fireplace. "You need to seek out counseling."

Steffen shifted his gaze from her disapproving eyes to the oil portrait of the dead woman above the mantel. Neither woman looked at him with any sympathy. "I thought I could handle my emotions on my own." He twisted his hands, wondering if they resembled Lincoln's.

"How's that working out?" Bernie shook her head. "I don't want to sound cruel, but I think you could use someone else's suggestions."

---

[26] Fragment: Notes for Law Lecture, July 1, 1850, IBID

[27] IBID

"Lincoln," Steffen said, then couldn't stop his words. They seemed so appropriate. "'Intoxicated with unbroken success, we have become too self-sufficient to feel the necessity of redeeming and preserving grace, too proud to pray to the God that made us: It behooves us, then, to humble ourselves before the offended Power, to confess our (national) sins, and to pray for clemency and forgiveness on a day of humiliation, fasting, and prayer.'"[28]

Bernie's expression hadn't changed. "Are you implying I am the offending person?"

Steffen tipped his head, which generally worked when he tried to elicit information from a close-mouthed witness. Silence reigned.

Bernie's impeccable attire, her perfect hair, her delicate complexion, her set mouth, and her angry eyes brooked no nonsense, gave no inch of reprieve.

He gave in. "You think my reactions are inappropriate for the situation?"

"Don't you!"

"Of course." Steffen hung his head. He wasn't convinced Lincoln hadn't come to his rescue, but obviously Bernie hadn't appreciated even one of Lincoln's insights. "I wish ..." He dared not continue, kept his head down, and tried to think. Then it dawned on him: he would let her take over. "Can you help?"

Bernie stared straight into his eyes.

Could she detect he was trying to manipulate his way out of her bad opinion of him? He waited, feeling a chess game lay before him. If he had the patience to outwait her, not give in to a passion to explain his behavior, he might still have a chance with this intelligent, unrelentingly honest, lovely woman he had every intention of keeping next to him for the rest of his life, if she'd only see fit to speak to him.

He knew Bernie had won, and he might have lost his future with her, when Lincoln wetted his tongue. He hoped it was for the last

---

[28] Thursday, the 30th of April, 1863; Proclamation Appointing a National Fast Day, p. 271, IBID

time. "'No one is good enough to govern another without the other's consent.'"[29]

Bernie approached, placed her small hand under his chin. "I have no intention of telling you what you need to do." She turned her back on him and tried to slide the door open.

Steffen jumped up, used his long legs to reach the door before she accomplished her escape, and still Lincoln came out, "'With other men to be defeated was to be forgotten; but with him defeat was but a trifling incident, neither changing him nor the world's estimate of him.'"[30]

Bernie placed both her hands up on his chest. "Can you stop?"

Steffen wrapped his arms around her, kissed her with all his frustrated passion evident in his embrace.

She was flushed and breathing rapidly when he set her back down. Still she turned without a word, opened the door, and started to walk through the living room.

Steffen grabbed the back of her sweater just in time. "He never spoke merely to be heard."[31]

"No," Bernie said, as she straightened her sweater. "You use his words to stuff down your real feelings. A woman could live her whole life with you and not hear one original thought."

"That's not true." Steffen held her close. "I will never quote another word of Lincoln's."

Bernie lifted her wet lashes to stare at him. "We'll see," she said, then went into the kitchen to seek refuge from him.

But there was hope. All Steffen needed to do was to stomp Lincoln back into his grave, erase the comfort he'd derived throughout the last ten years, and open his heart to this new, somewhat small piece of womanhood. That, and re-enter the real world of emotional minefields.

* * *

---

[29] p. 209, Speech at Peoria, Illinois in reply to Senator Douglas, October 16, 1854, IBID

[30] p. 161, Eulogy for Henry Clay, State House at Springfield, July 16, 1852, IBID

[31] p. 163, IBID

Bernie's Condo

Bernie almost asked Steffen to come in when he brought her home. The only thing that stopped her was a need to think things through. Buttons greeted her coldly, not leaning into her ankle in her traditional mode of greeting. Instead she meowed harshly and almost stomped into the kitchen.

Bernie made her apologies, opened another tuna can, and stroked the cat's back until Buttons complained at the continuous interruption to her meal.

Bernie adjourned to her study, flipped on the Turner Classic Movies channel, and muted the sound. The black-and-white scenes soothed her. She believed Steffen about never quoting Lincoln in her presence again. Would that open his heart for her? She wasn't sure. Who was his first wife ...? Pauline. Why had her mind wanted to avoid thinking of her name?

The children were Pauline's. Well they were raised from the age of five and seven by a housekeeper and their grandmother. Steffen's brand was on both boys. They were grown. It wasn't as if they would need guidance from her. Well maybe some. They didn't yet have families of their own. What did she know about families? She was still single at thirty.

Bernie was glad the hard-jawed Crawford dame wasn't in the movie. She released the mute button to listen awhile to the accents of England, then muted the scene in order to consider her options.

She didn't have any, not really. Steffen held sway in her emotional world. But her future was her own, so far. She wanted to work, to learn more about solving crimes.

Next time they were together, she'd ask to see Steffen's library. Borrow a few books, discuss them with him, insist he become her favorite tutor. That would work.

The couple on the screen kissed, and the credits began to roll.

* * *

Livonia Juvenile Detention
Thursday, February 18

Bernie agreed to accompany Steffen. He'd driven her home the night before but didn't ask to be invited in. His drive back to Jackson with Nik seemed to take hours. Steffen felt he was in a daze. He didn't remember much of what Nik preached about on the way home or even what dinner consisted of. However, in the morning, the commute back to Bernie's condo had required only minutes.

The ceilings in the detention facility appeared deliberately lowered. Did the children feel safer with less headroom for their brains to expand? He did not. He sat down in one of the chairs in the hall as they waited for Jean to be brought from wherever she was kept.

Two feet away from him, Bernie patiently waited near the open door of the designated room. "What will you ask first?"

Steffen rubbed his wet palms on his pant legs. "Could you ask her what she talked to her bedridden mother about, all those days in the trailer?"

"Good idea," Bernie said. Then she actually smiled at him.

Before Steffen could rack his brain—now that it was devoid of Lincoln's words—for something pleasant to say, Jean Lee was escorted down the hall toward them.

As she stepped into the visitors' room, Jean said. "I hate this uniform." She wore her long, blonde hair in two pigtails, which hung down over her shoulders onto the front of her shirt.

Bernie smiled at the nine-year-old. "Grey is never a flattering color."

"You'd think they would at least *try* not to make us unhappy." Jean walked to the window.

Bernie stood beside her. "The courtyard probably has a flower garden. Is this where you walk for exercise?"

"So far I've only been allowed into the gym." Jean sat down and folded her hands on the wooden table, then looked up at Steffen.

Steffen immediately sat down across the table from them. He took out his notebook and nodded to Bernie.

"Do you mind talking with us?" Bernie asked, as she seated herself next to the child.

Jean shook her head. "I'm dying of boredom in here. Dad made sure we were kept busy, even in the trailer."

"Is that why he liked to have you talk to your mother?" Bernie asked.

"I was the only one." Jean sat up a tad straighter. "Everyone else ran out of things to say."

"Your mother was a good listener." Bernie encouraged her to keep talking.

Jean tapped the table for Steffen's benefit. "Are you writing all of this down?"

"Shall I?" Steffen asked.

"Dad might like to know," Jean said.

Steffen wrote the date and time down, checking his watch.

Jean seemed pleased and scooted her chair closer to Bernie's. "I talked to Mother about the future we would have in the big house. I described the rooms in different seasons, at different holidays, where we could put the Christmas tree—maybe even two trees."

"Where you would sleep?" Bernie asked.

"Yes." Jean was losing herself in her story. "And what color the rooms could be repainted, and the clothes we girls would wear, and how mother could have her hair done, and her fingernails and toenails painted in a shop."

Jean broke the line of her thought, pulled on each pigtail in turn. "Dad will retire from the university, eventually." She bobbed her head knowingly at Bernie. "That's why we can go to the doctor and dentist without breaking the bank."

"What else did you talk about?" Bernie spoke quietly.

"About the boys going to college and becoming doctors and dentists and lawyers, and about the big weddings Etta and Mary Alice would have, with lots of bridesmaids because they would all be our friends once we lived in the big house and could have sleepovers."

"That is important," Bernie said.

"To young people." Jean acknowledged Steffen and Bernie might be too old to appreciate the finer points of social reality.

"I understand," Bernie said.

"And Mother could have tea parties with Grandma's fancy bone china and those big silver teapots. They're just sitting there collecting dust, you know." Jean went on. "The boys could have all the toys they wanted to go with Dad's train. They could have whole towns with little people and street lamps and churches with lights in them, and then they would have friends over too." Jean rocked back and forth in satisfaction. "Dad said he used to make pizza in Grandma's big ovens; we could entertain."

"Did your mother like your plans?" Bernie asked

"She didn't say no to them," Jean said. "I think it sounded nice to her. I had a good time cheering her up."

Steffen slid his notebook over to Bernie. "We need to tell you that your father lied to you about the house."

"He did not!" Jean stood up and pushed her chair away from her. "Policemen are told to lie to make people talk."

"Has he visited you?" Bernie asked, as she wrote down Jean's response.

"He's busy." Jean said. "Don't write that down."

"Okay." Bernie laid her pencil down.

"I'm not going to talk to you anymore!" Jean lifted her chin. "Make Dad come see me. If he tells me he was lying to us, I'll tell you what happened."

"That's a good idea." Bernie walked toward the nine-year-old.

Jean stepped away. "Get out! I don't trust you—either of you—anymore." Her bravado shifted as she sobbed, "I want my dad."

The matron, who had been waiting in the hall, came into the room as Bernie and Steffen left.

"I'll call Jimmy," Bernie said. "I'm sure he can take off work."

"Go ahead," Steffen said, thinking they might have time for lunch before Jean's father arrived. "Should we eat in the cafeteria, or find a restaurant?"

Bernie shut her cell phone, saying, "Jimmy will not be here until two."

As Steffen opened his Honda's passenger door for her, he said. "I wish we had time to drive to Zingerman's."

"I'm not very hungry," Bernie said.

"You establish a rapport with children easily." Steffen wished she would work a little harder to make him feel as comfortable.

Bernie laughed. "Now that's a backhanded compliment if I've ever heard one."

"And you pick up on hints …" Steffen smiled at his attempt at wit.

"A nice vegetable soup with lots of bread sounds good, doesn't it?" Bernie patted his hand.

"I can never remember the name of that place." Steffen was glad the conversation wasn't headed toward analyzing Jean's motives. "It's not Olga's."

"Olive Garden," Bernie said, laughing good-naturedly.

"I'd like you to meet my mother, Helen," Steffen said, fully realizing the risk of rejection.

"Does she live in Jackson?"

Steffen relaxed a bit, as he spied a familiar sign for the restaurant in Livonia. "She's in Ann Arbor in Burns Park."

"A nice area."

"She's close to the Senior Center." Steffen smiled. "She's a dedicated bridge player. Do you play?"

"I don't," Bernie said. "Do you?"

"I'd rather carry on a conversation." Steffen's stomach growled. "And eat," he said.

* * *

Livonia Detention Center

Jimmy Lee seemed to have shrunk since Steffen had seen him last. All the swagger had gone out of the man. While he waited for Jean to be brought into the visiting room, Jimmy constantly shook his keys as if to ward off unwelcome fears.

Jean ran right up to him and stayed in his fatherly embrace as long as she could.

Finally Jimmy pushed her away. "The police were not lying," he said, before breaking down.

Jean slapped his face. Then sat down next to Bernie, across the table from her father. "Tell me," she said.

Jimmy tried to calm down. His voice was broken with sobs as he admitted what he had done. "Since the day I married your mother, I owned my father's house and his fortune. I thought Mother would be more comfortable living alone among her things."

"While we slept two to a bed?" Jean's little fists banged on the wooden table.

Jimmy rose to leave.

"Stay where you are!" Jean roared at him. She stood up and went around to him.

Jimmy backed away.

"You coward." Jean said. "You don't want to hear the truth, do you?"

Jimmy put his hands over his ears.

Jean pulled at his elbows. "I killed her. I killed Grandma. Did that make her more comfortable among her things? Do you remember her lying on the carpet with her expensive, upholstered dining room chair lying next to her? Did she look comfortable to you? I laced her pills with the rat poison you kept under our sink. Her guts were torn apart; her heart couldn't stop beating until it burst. Does that sound comfortable to you? And she knew I did it!"

Jean slipped down to her knees, holding on to her father's pant leg. "And now you know what you did by lying to us for... how long, twelve, fifteen years?"

Jimmy fled the room.

Jean got up from the floor. She straightened her pigtails and sat down. "So I get to rot in here for the rest of my life while Dad gets to enjoy his big house."

"I think you guaranteed," Bernie said, "that your father won't enjoy one day of the future."

CHAPTER 11

1830 Washtenaw Avenue
Thursday, March 11

Mary Alice heard her mother tell Etta mothers usually need six weeks to recover, emotionally, after a miscarriage. Both Etta and Mary Alice enjoyed having Mother up and about. She was clean and smelled like soap.

Her blonde hair glistened when the sun shone through the beveled glass panes in the sun room. They had thrown out all of Grandma's green plants with their dusty, spider-strewn leaves and crumbling clay pots. Mother started what she said was a compost pile with the green trash and the potted soil. The broken pots she threw away without even asking Dad. The moldy carpeting was harder to get rid of, but finally the trash men did throw the tattered roll into their big truck. Now the floor was just wood planks, which Mother oiled and oiled until they shone in the sun too, smelling like fresh lemons.

Mother had set up an easel and laid out all her oil paints on Grandma's old dining room chest in the sun room. She smiled often. The picture she was painting reminded Mary Alice of a Christmas tree, although this one had a lake and mountains for decorations. It was nice. More importantly, Mother liked painting. You could watch her worried forehead erase all its lines and her eyes began to focus—like she felt at home with the sun warming her shoulders, even though the snow wouldn't let up outside.

Nik came over almost every day to fix supper for them. On the days when he didn't come, he had Etta thaw out and bake a chicken or fish casserole that he had made earlier. His food was nearly as good as Grandma's had been.

Mary Alice did miss the smell of cinnamon bread baking.

Etta acted silly around Nik, making eyes and wringing her hands behind her back. Mary Alice guessed she must be falling in love with the older teenage boy. Nik was a good guy, and the detective would probably kill him if he ever touched Etta.

Almost everything was getting better. They had helped Mother pull down the old dusty drapes. They went into the garage in boxes for Goodwill. Mother said the neighbors were far enough away from the trees lining their property, so they could just let the sun shine in. The shades were not a problem, so at night they could pull them down in the bedrooms when the lights were on inside.

The thing that wore everybody out was Mother's merry-go-round game. Etta had named the silliness. The three of them pulled and tugged the furniture around the rooms to see what looked best where. Nik helped to lug chairs and tables upstairs and then down again. Usually Mary Alice would start laughing after a couch or chair had been replaced in the same spot three times.

But Mother didn't frown. She just laughed with them about not making up her mind. Sometimes the solution was when Nik hauled an offending object out into the garage, which was filling up fast. Grandma did own too much furniture. There hadn't been enough room to roll a ball to Ben or layout puzzles on the floor.

Mother did a great job. She let Mary Alice and Etta and even Bob go through Grandma's books in what had been Dad's room for a week. Everyone moved their choice of books from the shelves into their own bedrooms. Nik was allowed to take his pick too. Mother said she owed him for all his help with cooking the meals. Then she asked Nik to move one bookcase into each of Bob's, Mary Alice's, Etta's and her own bedrooms. She left the bed in the little room but closed the door to it.

Dad had moved his clothes, his record player, and records over to Mr. Wilcox's. Mother said the books were hers now, and she wanted us to make the most of them.

Bob and Dick spent lots of time in the basement together playing with their father's train set. Ben was crawling, and they had gates everywhere so he wouldn't fall down stairs, or go in the sunroom or kitchen by himself. He didn't cry as much and had two teeth to show for all the fussing he had done in the trailer. Mary Alice thought he just felt better now that everyone was happier and no mean people lived in the house ... like Jean. Etta said they could keep Jean's room fixed up for overnight guests. So far neither of them had been brave enough to ask anyone over, because of what Jean had done.

Mary Alice's friend Bernie and the detective often visited before taking Nik home to Jackson, but sometimes he would stay with his own grandmother. He just needed to walk to Burns Park from their home, maybe six blocks.

Mother had taken down their grandma's picture in Dad's study. She renamed the room their exit-scheduling room. Over the fireplace, a corkboard held pages for each day of the month. Saturdays were headlined with the words, "Visit Jean." If they wanted to go, Mother said they could sign their names on the sheet. Bob was the first to print his name with his red crayon.

Mary Alice took Bernie in to show her what Mother had done. "I'm not ready to see the place where they keep Jean."

Bernie put her arm around Mary Alice's shoulder. "They're taking good care of Jean."

"I hope she can't just walk back home," Mary Alice said.

Bernie sat down on the couch. "If you go, you'll see that the doors are all locked." She stood and took Mary Alice's hand. "Show me your mother's paintings. I hear she's very good."

Mary Alice delayed, trying to keep Bernie all to herself in the study. "How far away is Livonia?"

"By car, Jean would take at least forty-five minutes to get here." Bernie also said, "I will be told if Jean finds a way to get out."

"You would come right here to protect us, wouldn't you?" Mary Alice knew that was true but didn't mind being told again.

Bernie sat back down on the couch. "First of all, I don't think Jean will ever harm another person. The mistake was big, but she was just a little girl trying to solve your family's problems. If you can think of her as having one dark spot on a handkerchief but the rest of the cloth is clean, you might be able to forgive her sooner."

Mary Alice nodded but couldn't help thinking about the little things Jean always found easy to do, like stealing Betsey's sweater and stealing Grandma's pills, and the other mean things she said and did, and all the things she didn't do. Look how Etta helped around the house, hugging Mary Alice, taking care of Ben when Mother had been ill, and cooking still.

"You don't know Jean like I do," Mary Alice said, unhappy that she was not agreeing with her friend.

Bernie said, "Try to not think too much about Jean's problems. Tell me what's new in the house."

"The house is now Mother's." Mary Alice said.

* * *

Nik heard his father's voice when Steffen entered the Lee's home. He shut off the oven but left the roasted chicken in to brown a little more. He joined the others in the living room. Dad would be pleased at the transformation in Ricky Lee.

Dad smiled at him before sitting down on the couch. "Did Mr. Wilcox have the house changed to your name?"

They all had heard Mary Alice brag about her mother's sole ownership. "Mary Alice," Ricky said, "your father suggested I be given a quit-claim deed for the house. There's no mortgage on the house."

Mary Alice nodded, but her hands were on her hips and the message was clearly telegraphed: the small soul knew some things would never be fixed. "And all the money."

"Yes," Ricky blushed. She explained to Bernie. "Jimmy's living in Chelsea with Mr. Wilcox for the time being. A divorce is not a necessity right now."

"I'm so proud of you," Bernie said. "The children need your good sense."

Ricky took Mary Alice's hand and pulled her close. The seven-year-old seemed surprised but pleased. "I'll have time to spend with each of my children now," Ricky said, straightening Mary Alice's bangs. Ricky still held Mary Alice's hand as she sat down next to Nik's dad. "Bernie told me about your loss."

Mary Alice escaped with Etta back to the kitchen, but not without first tapping Steffen's shoulder. "You look better without your black tie bobbing up and down when you swallow."

"Thanks." Steffen smiled at the imp.

Ricky tapped his knee. "I wanted you to know. I've been taken off all the medications and feel a hundred percent better. Bernie doesn't want you to worry anymore about me."

"Thank you," he said, acknowledging his gratitude with a nod in Bernie's direction, too.

"Supper's ready," Nik said.

Nik wondered if his dad noticed his apron matched Etta's. Dad did scratch his head, which might mean he was wondering if he needed to talk about not encouraging a young girl's devotion. Nik hoped he had everything under control, but he was glad his father noticed there might be a future problem.

* * *

Burns Park, Two-Story House
Friday, March 12

Nik had phoned Sam with the news. Dad was introducing Bernie to Grandma. When Nik arrived at the familiar brick house, Sam was already setting the table. "Glad you called me."

"I thought you'd be interested." Nik hugged his small grandmother. "Bernie is about your size."

"Isn't this exciting?" Grandma fussed with the lilies-of-the-valley centerpiece on the dining room table. "No one for ten years, yet here we go!"

"We like her," Sam said.

"Your opinions are as important to me as my own son's." Grandma straightened one of the napkin rings. "How long have they known each other?"

"Aunt Juno introduced them on Valentine's Day," Nik said. "She's known Bernie Johnston for years at the hospital, but she thought Bernie was too young for Dad."

"How old is she?" Grandma asked.

"Aunt Juno says she's thirty but not to worry," Sam said. "Bernie doesn't want more children."

"Well that's sad," Grandma said. "I do love grandchildren."

"Aren't we enough for you?" Nik teased.

Sam said, "Dad hasn't quoted Lincoln lately."

Their grandmother dropped a crystal goblet onto the carpet. It didn't break. "I'm so glad. Perhaps he has had enough time to let go of his …"

"Guilt about Mother's suicide?" Sam replaced the unbroken glass onto the tablecloth.

"You boys," Grandma said, correcting with a catch in her voice. "You young men are very wise. I'm not sure you haven't raised my son instead of the other way around."

Standing behind her, Nik wrapped his arms around his grandmother's shoulders. "You were always there for us too."

"And the Lord," Grandma said.

When she spied her son's Honda drive up, Grandma opened the front door even before Steffen could knock.

She tapped his chest and then hugged Bernie. The women were the same height. They smiled at each other and began to chatter as if the men had suddenly disappeared.

"How is the family you were working with?" Grandma asked Dad, almost as an aside.

"Fine," Dad said, winking at Nik.

They all knew full well Grandma had little or no interest in their activities at present. All she wanted to do was devour Dad's girlfriend and find out everything she needed to know to approve of his choice. Nik chided himself. Grandma was not a judgmental person. More an anarchist like Aunt Juno, who promptly thumped his back.

"Who's in charge of supper?"

"Grandma," Nik said. "Can't you smell the pork roast?" Then he whispered to his aunt, "Bernie's visit is too important for me to screw up."

"Better not use that term in front of Grandma," Aunt Juno said.

* * *

Helen, Steffen's mother, embraced Bernie as soon as she stepped over the threshold.

Disregarding the boys, Steffen, and Juno completely, Bernie tried answering all Helen's questions as succinctly as she could.

"Juno introduced us on Valentine's Day." Helen's home was immaculate. The dining room table was gracefully set with sparkling glassware and rose-patterned bone china on a light green lace cloth.

"Boys, bring in the serving dishes." Helen sat at the head of the table. "Pass your plates to Steffen. He'll serve—won't you, dear?"

At the foot of the table, Steffen smiled sheepishly at Bernie as he did as he was told.

"We haven't really dated, but I've met Sam and Nik." Bernie wondered if the boys had their own bedrooms here, as well as in Jackson.

And here was a fresh perspective on this lanky man: submissive instead of the take-charge bungling man she'd grown inordinately fond of. Steffen was sweet and refined in front of his mother.

"Steffen's helping me obtain a detective license," Bernie said. The pork roast was succulent, the gravy tasty, but Bernie's stomach threatened to rebel. "I quit social work, because I was getting an ulcer."

The latticed windows sparkled from the chandelier's light, while Bernie came to understand Steffen's need to quote Lincoln. Her nerves wouldn't let her shut up for long. "You're right; we haven't known each other long. Less than a month." The out-of-season lilies-of-the-valley filled the room with their fragrance. "But he's promised to stop quoting Lincoln."

Helen turned to Juno. "Did you hear?"

"The case they worked on included a very disturbed mother," Juno said. "Mother, take a break from the inquisition."

Bernie smiled at Helen. "I want to know everything about Steffen."

"Grandma's the boss in her own home," Sam said, in defense of his dad's behavior.

Juno laughed. "A man always lives in his wife's house. Remember that, boys."

Nik asked, "Bernie, couldn't you talk Dad into moving to Ann Arbor?"

"I thought you liked your high school in Jackson?" Steffen said.

Sam responded. "We'd be closer to Grandma too."

Steffen stared at Bernie as if waiting for her to encourage him. She moved the asparagus heads around on her plate. Steffen's silence suggested a word from her would start him house hunting. She tried to be noncommittal. "I'd like to visit your library more often," she said.

"We can move it here," Nik said, smiling from ear to ear.

"That would be a step in the right direction, Steffen." Helen matched both boys' grins.

Imitating John Wayne's slow monotone, Steffen said, "We'll have to see about that."

Bernie couldn't help laughing. There was no mistaking this family's intention of including her as Steffen's most significant other.

* * *

Zingerman's Road House
Saturday, March 13

Steffen was disappointed when the hostess did not take them to the booth where he had first met Bernie. "Shall I complain?" he asked.

"About what?" Bernie looked confused.

Her appeal had grown since the first day they met, a month earlier. Deciding she might become a permanent person in his life may have added to her attractiveness. After hanging her short black coat with the soft white collar next to his suede jacket, he grinned. "We're not sitting in the booth where we met."

"Does it matter that much?"

Steffen couldn't understand how she didn't realize that of course it mattered. She was supposed to be the romantic one, not him.

"I guess you can still order oysters here?" Bernie asked, actually licking her pretty lips in anticipation.

Steffen wished he'd met her in a different restaurant, one that didn't specialize in raw, slimy seafood. But here they were. The lump, consisting of a wrapped ring box, dug into his thigh. Should he wait until after the main course, or venture his future before they ate?

After ordering, Bernie smiled and moved closer to him in the booth. "I certainly like your mother."

"That's good," Steffen said. He sucked in her delicious perfume to encourage his resolve. "I should properly wait until I meet your parents."

"They're in Florida now," Bernie said, then caught on. "Wait for what?"

Steffen broke off a piece of bread from the basket and offered it to her. "To share bread with, to share my children, my life, my bed."

Bernie patted his arm. "Steffen."

"That didn't come out right." He reached for his bow tie to steady himself, but that ornery Lee kid had talked him into giving it away.

"I think you said what we are to each other, beautifully." Bernie chewed her bite of bread, securing his future with her eyes.

"Then you'll marry me?" He clutched his thumping heart with one hand and her hand with the other.

"Maybe," Bernie said, and she had the gall to wink.

Steffen couldn't eat.

Bernie kept talking light-heartedly, but he found her words didn't make much sense. Was she playing with him? Maybe? What kind of an answer was that? He searched his mind for Lincoln's saving words but found nothing.

After their dinner, Steffen drove Bernie to her condo, noticing her one-sided conversation was coming to an end. He went around and opened the passenger door of the Honda.

Bernie stood on her tiptoes to kiss him.

Steffen couldn't help himself. He lifted Bernie off her feet, kissing her warmly, thinking it might be for the last time. Finally, he sat her back down and apologized. "I hope I wasn't too rough."

Bernie stood there, watching him walk around the car.

Before he got in, Steffen looked at her long and hard. "Goodbye," he said, hoping she hadn't heard his sob.

CHAPTER 12

Dead End Street in Jackson
Sunday, March 14

"What's wrong with Dad?" Nik asked Sam.

"Wrong?" Sam continued to sort the clothes in the laundry room off the kitchen. "Is he sick?"

"He's been in his study since five o'clock this morning."

"Boy, you were up early."

"I need to finish a paper due Monday." Nik made another pot of coffee. "Cooking for the Lee's used up more time than I planned." Then Nik decided to admit, "Etta is only twelve but she's a good listener."

"Cooking took your time, or talking?"

"Both," Nik said. "Go ask Dad what's bothering him."

"Not me, little brother," Sam pushed in the washer's button. "You ask him."

"I could call Aunt Juno."

"Nik." Sam knuckled his arm. "Would you appreciate it if I knew you were having girl problems and I asked Aunt Juno to get involved?"

"Yes, but Aunt Juno knows Bernie."

"Leave it alone, Nik." Sam laughed. "Listen to your big brother for once. If he wants to talk about Bernie, he will."

"Okay," Nik said. "Do you think we'll move to Ann Arbor soon?"

"Dad's not keen about having you change high schools, is he?"

"I wouldn't mind." Nik poured himself a cup of coffee. "I like the Lees."

"One particular Lee."

"Honestly, I like all the kids," Nik said. "I can't imagine how one of them could be raised in that family and end up killing her own grandmother."

"Go work on your paper, Nik." Sam pushed him. "Trust Dad to know what's best."

"I think sometimes Dad doesn't know any better than we do about what's best. He remembers Mom too much in this house, don't you think?"

Sam got very quiet—too quiet. "You may be right, Nik. He would be closer to his girlfriend if we moved to Ann Arbor. You could certainly bring up the subject."

* * *

Steffen sat at his desk, which faced the windows overlooking the barren fruit trees Bernie had commented on. *Maybe?* Was that her promise to consider his proposal or a gentle way to dismantle their relationship? A month hadn't been enough time for her to read his genuine intentions. She needed time. Bernie hadn't asked for time. Maybe?

He turned his back on the unpromising sun. His volumes of Lincoln's sayings called to him, but he resisted their pull. No sense falling back into his system of denying pain. Nevertheless, *Gladstone's Commentaries* caught his attention. A bridge to making sense of things, the majestic volumes of law drew him.

Under, 'Self-Love, History, and God's Design,' Steffen sought comfort. "Careful study of the rules of English law would show how they were answers to man's needs, how they had served as the means of attacking obstacles to man's happiness."

Then he remembered Lincoln often quoted the Bible. Surely Bernie wouldn't fault him for turning to the source of God's law. He'd removed the Bible from the study earlier and placed it next to his bed, when he'd made a yet-unfulfilled resolution to read all of Jesus's words, printed in red in his edition of the King James.

As he passed Nik's room, Nik called out to him. "What's the matter, Dad? Your forehead is bent too far forward."

Steffen straightened, placing his hands on the small of his back. "I should tell you," he said. "Where's Sam?"

"I'm here," Sam said, coming up behind him in the hall with a load of laundry. "What's up?"

Steffen leaned against the door to Nik's room. "Bernie turned me down last night."

"No, she didn't." Nik said.

"What exactly did she say?" Sam asked.

"She said, 'maybe.'" Steffen found his throat had relaxed for the first time. He breathed in deeply as if expecting to remember Bernie's rose perfume, but the softener in the laundry Sam was holding was his only reward.

"When are you going to see her again?" Nik asked.

"I think I'll wait for her to call?" Steffen rubbed his scalp.

Sam asked, "Do you think that's a way to win her?"

"What is?" Steffen asked, honestly lost.

"Ask the Lord," Nik said.

"As if that will help." Sam gave voice to his doubts.

"Funny," Steffen said, not feeling amused. "I was headed for the King James when you stopped me, Nik."

"Sorry," Nik said.

Sam adjourned to the bathroom to replenish the linen closet. When he came back into the hall, Steffen was still standing there at a complete loss.

"Call Grandma," Sam said. "I thought Bernie got along with her. Maybe she has some insights."

"I'm not up to that," Steffen said. "But I'm glad I told you guys."

"Yeah," Sam said, "we were a big help."

"Never mind," Steffen said. "At least I know you're rooting for me."

"We are that," Nik called.

"I'll call Grandma," Sam said.

"I'll pray for you, Dad," Nik said.

Steffen closed the door to his bedroom. There was the King James, sitting unopened next to his radio alarm. He leaned against the window and flipped through the Bible's pages. Before he found any of Jesus's words, his hand found Proverbs, chapter 5: "My son, attend unto my wisdom, and bow thine ear to my understanding: That thou mayest regard discretion, and that thy lips may keep knowledge. For the lips of a strange woman drop as an honeycomb, and her mouth is smoother than oil: But her end is bitter as wormwood, sharp as a two-edged sword."

He stopped reading but didn't let go of the book. Instead he stretched out on his bed and turned to John 3:21. "But he that doeth truth cometh to the light, that his deeds may be made manifest, that they are wrought in God."

Somewhat encouraged to seek further, he read from the start of the chapter and stopped at verse six, "That which is born of the flesh is flesh; and that which is born of the Spirit is spirit." He skimmed the chapter, rereading the famous verse 3:16: "For God so loved the world, that he gave his only begotten Son, that whosoever believeth in him should not perish, but have everlasting life." Steffen knew he should stop and make a profession of belief, instead he read verse 17, "For God sent not his Son into the world to condemn the world; but that the world through him might be saved."

But what must I do, Lord? Steffen was surprised at the level of his despair.

He flipped through the pages again and found Mark 9:23: "If thou canst believe, all things are possible to him that believeth."

Steffen felt a tear slip down the side of his face. He swiped at it before it could invade his ear. Why couldn't he believe the way Nik did? What obstacle did his brain present to stop his acceptance of the Savior to solve his problems? Pride? Too much knowledge, no trust because of Pauline's death, stubbornness, intelligence, evil designs he'd witnessed in people who called themselves believers—what held him back? Steffen couldn't name the cause, but the stumbling block to belief existed. The pain of Bernie's rejection swerved his soul away from compliance with an easy religious answer to his suffering.

Sam knocked on his door.

Steffen closed the Bible and tucked it under his pillow, ashamed to let his nonbelieving son find he was mistrusting his doubts.

"Grandma says to call Bernie, right away." Sam said.

"Why?" Steffen asked.

"I agree," Sam said. "She won't turn you down. Women want to be friends with men they think love them. Think about it. Would you *not* want to be around someone who says they love you?"

Steffen weighed his hurt against the possibility of spending more time with Bernie. "I'll do it," he said.

"Hurray!" Nik called from his room.

* * *

Zingerman's Road House
Monday, March 15

Bernie arrived early in order to secure the booth where she had first met Steffen Blaine. The poor guy didn't understand her indecision. He hadn't listened to one word of her explanation. As soon as she said, "Maybe," she could tell his big ears clogged up. Not one word entered his brain.

After a good night's sleep, which she hadn't had, maybe he would be able to listen. Her reasons for putting him off dissolved after Steffen's heated embrace as they said good-bye. If he had proposed again after the kiss, she probably would have set a wedding date, but he coldly said a final-sounding good-bye and drove off.

Bernie prayed a lot for the situations surrounding the child abuse cases and found the Lord wanting as far as the results she'd hoped for. Nevertheless, the night before, Bernie had prayed earnestly for the Lord to come to her aid. And he did!

Steffen called early, apologizing for not making another date Saturday night. She had to interrupt his flow of words to say, "Yes." In fact she repeated it giddily at least three times.

She checked her watch. Six o'clock. Did he have car trouble on the road from Jackson? She wondered if he'd consider moving to Ann

Arbor before they married, just to date more conveniently. Surely Helen would appreciate his being more readily available. She knew Juno often suggested he leave Jackson as well.

Bernie wondered what her own mother and her stepdad would think of the tall, not very handsome detective she'd fallen in love with. They were accustomed to her derision of most men. Of course in her last job men rarely came out smelling like a rose. But Steffen was a real man with integrity and feelings.

She never should have said maybe. Why hadn't she just said, "As soon as I finish my training?" But that sounded so trite, so unimportant to a marriage decision. Nevertheless, taking on a new family with two teenage boys would make schooling a distant goal instead of the immediate need that she felt becoming an inspector was.

The Lord knew she was burnt out trying to seek justice for the innocents she had come in contact with. Male-dominated society and its rules of ownership regarding children disallowed ready relief for their distress. And the system of foster parenting held chasms of further harm to the souls of the children.

Becoming a police investigator promised a cleaner avenue to justice, she hoped.

From the first time she saw Steffen, she realized he was one man in a million. His traumatic defenses to deny the pain of his wife's suicide proved he was no ordinary man. Who would have thought of Lincoln as a self-help guru? No one. But Steffen had delved into Lincoln's history, finding comfort when the modern world provided none.

Of course Bernie wanted to marry him. She couldn't imagine anyone else in her life. Nevertheless she knew her motivation to start a new profession was strong.

Please Lord, she prayed, *Help me trust you more.*

* * *

Zingerman's smelled of oysters and fresh bread. Steffen found Bernie in their booth and took off his suede coat. "Will winter ever end?"

"In six weeks," Bernie promised, with her usual smile and friendly blue eyes.

He felt giddy, to the point of being silly. "You'll marry me in six weeks?"

Bernie took his hand, weighed his huge paw with her china-doll fingers. "Is six weeks long enough for you to teach me everything you know about becoming a professional investigator, a detective?"

"Oh," Steffen laughed outright. "So that's the plan. Suck me dry of information and throw me to the wolves."

Bernie stretched up and kissed the side of his face. "I think women are thrown to the wolves. Men end up with sirens."

Steffen's mood changed. "Why did you say maybe?"

"I didn't say no."

"Or yes." Steffen moved away from her side as the waitress asked for their drink order.

Bernie answered for him. "Coffee and water, for now."

After the waitress left, Steffen coughed to clear his emotions. "I'm hungry."

"Me too," Bernie said. "I'd like to see your library again. Do you lend out private books?"

"Never." Steffen moved closer to her. "I make people read them to me, if they want to see what's inside."

"I want to know every word you've read." Bernie didn't move away. "I want to know every button on your clothes, every thought in your universe."

The waitress came back with their liquid refreshments. "Are you ready to order?" she asked.

Steffen smiled, "I want to marry this woman."

The waitress flinched. "I'll be back." She turned around and left.

Bernie held her finger to her lips. "Don't laugh. She'll think you're laughing at her."

"Will you—eventually —marry me?" Steffen put both his huge hands on the small bones of her shoulders.

"Unhand me," Bernie whispered. "Or I'll promise you anything."

"Good," Steffen said, not letting go.

"I will marry you, some day," Bernie said.

Steffen leaned in for a kiss, and Bernie complied.

The waitress returned. "Now?"

"Now," Steffen said.

"We'll order now," Bernie said. "I'm going to marry the man but not now."

* * *

1830 Washtenaw Avenue
Sunday,

Mary Alice spied her father coming up the walk. He'd gotten out of Mr. Wilcox's car. Grandma's big car and their old van were both in the garage.

Etta opened the door. "Does Mother know you're coming?"

"Yes," Dad said. "I'll wait here until you call her."

"That's all right," Bob said. "Come in, Dad. I broke the engine of the train. Can you fix it?"

"Probably." Dad didn't budge.

Etta moved slowly through the living room, taking a backward glance before she entered the dining room to make sure he hadn't stirred.

Mary Alice watched as Ricky nearly ran to him. "Jimmy. Come in, come in. You needn't wait at the door. Etta should have taken your coat."

Their father shrugged away from her outstretched arms. "I did talk to Mrs. Staples," he said. "That was a good idea."

Mother nodded. "Mary Alice, Dad has something for you."

Mary Alice didn't move.

Her father came directly to her and squatted down on one knee before he spoke. "Pepper is okay. Mrs. Staples liked the canary I bought for her."

"Why did you buy her a canary?" Mary Alice was glad Etta stayed in the room. She held out an arm for her, needing her support.

127

"I traded her for Pepper." Her father opened his coat and out jumped Pepper.

"Oh, Dad!" Mary Alice put her nose into Pepper's fur. It smelled like shampoo. "Is he really ours? Did Mother agree?"

Mother nodded her head. Etta was smiling too.

Mary Alice let go of Pepper and succumbed to her father's tearful embrace. "We're going to be a family again," he promised.

Her mother nodded again.

Mary Alice thought she might grow four inches from all the happiness.

PART II

Nine Years Later

CHAPTER 13

Valentine's Day, Thursday, Nine Years Later
St. Joseph Hospital, Ann Arbor

Bernie checked her fly-away bangs' reflection in the protective glass over the cafeteria's luncheon offerings. No gray yet. Her friend, Juno, tilted her chin, probably to better survey the food choices through her bifocals. The fluorescent lights sparkled in strands of Juno's stylish white hair. Bernie wished for white too, not gray. Of course, Juno's snowy nurse uniform accentuated all that whiteness. Bernie tugged at the ends of her long apricot scarf to make sure both reached the edge of her matching long sweater.

Juno turned to her before they left the cashier's counter. "You're going to Jean Lee's parole hearing?"

Bernie followed her to their table in the far corner. "I'm worried what her sisters, Mary Alice and Etta, will think." Bernie poked at the innocuous food choices she'd made. "Fish looks good. Are you able to schedule time to come with me and testify?"

Juno pointed to her mouth, in which she had placed a large portion of a lookalike McDonald's hamburger. Bernie could smell the onions from across the table.

Nine years. Jean had spent nine years in juvenile detention, our of her fifteen-year sentence. *Please, Lord,* she prayed. *Help me follow your guidance.*

"Jean must be eighteen?" Juno had stopped chewing. "My brother says he's planning something special for Valentine's Day."

"Steffen's been awfully quiet lately."

"Aren't you ready to set a wedding date yet?"

Bernie waved her hand as if the natty problem of marriage should be dismissed. "Mary Alice is sixteen, a sophomore at Pioneer. So yes, Jean is eighteen and considered an adult. Will you come to the hearing?"

"Maybe I should blackmail you into marrying my brother."

"Oh, that'll work." Bernie laughed, surmising her faithful friend would accompany her to the hearing. Nine years was a long engagement, but life as a certified police investigator—already a partner to the man she loved—kept her busier and much happier than she'd been as a practicing social worker. She no longer needed to solve the problems of still-suffering souls. Now she made sure someone knew all the details of their out-of-control mistakes. She recognized her strong suit was not the hope of retribution. Real joy came from uncovering the truth of a situation, which was always waiting beneath the surface and demanding to be revealed. Steffen said she was a natural detective. What was he up to now?

"Which church will your wedding be held in?" Juno smiled.

"If it's still standing, I suspect Nik will want us to marry in his church, St. Andrew's."

"Nik tells me you and Steffen attended the holiday services with Etta."

"Sam won't go; but Steffen doesn't seem to mind. I love the liturgy. The shorter eight o'clock service reminds me of when I was a girl, kneeling next to my grandma for seven o'clock mass."

"And you don't need to argue with the Pope."

"Just Steffen. He believes in a Creator, but not anyone with personal interest in his life. I think that's sad."

Juno nodded. "I feel I'm on my own too. Did you ever see the flowchart for choosing your religion?"

"Are you serious?"

"I won't remember it all. It's a joke. The first question is: 'How many gods do you want to worship? If you answer a ton of them, the next question is: 'Do you want to be reincarnated?' If you answer no gods, the next question is: 'Are you rich or insane?' The first question if you answer is only one god is 'How do you feel about bacon?'"

Bernie fiddled with her scarf. "I don't know who said it, but I read there is a scientist who believes there is a consciousness between atoms. That's a marvelous thought for me. Maybe I believe in everything. But then, I do pray to the Lord … a lot."

* * *

Lorraine Street, Ann Arbor, Michigan

Steffen opened the box of matching woven gold wedding rings for the fifteenth time in the last hour. He breathed in the smell of the blue velvet lining the box. It reminded him of coffin odor. They had gone to Florida to bury Bernie's mother last year.

Snapping the box shut, he returned to constructing cardboard packing boxes for his twenty-six year old son. Sam's teaching salary at Mitchell Middle School had allowed for this move to Sam's first home, a condo across the road from their home. As Steffen cut off the sealing tape on the bottom of the box, his fear of living alone reared. Why was he determined to force Bernie to name their wedding day? He had gone directly from being a pampered son in his mother's house in Burns Park to a harried husband in his own in Jackson.

"Frowning," Sam said. "Does this mean you're going to miss me?"

"Afraid I'll rattle around in this house and lose what's left of my wits."

"Nik will pray for you." Sam laughed. "I don't mind being prayed for, do you?"

"Kind of like an insurance policy for atheists?"

"Besides, you'll have Nik and Etta's children running around here shortly."

"I was hoping to chase Bernie through these rooms for a few years. I thought Bernie and I would marry before Nik and Etta, or at least directly after—not nearly a decade after we moved here."

"Marriage then?"

Thinking he'd been encouraged, Steffen reached in his pocket and produced the box, popping it open for Sam's approval. "Tonight I'm hoping for a wedding date."

Sam examined the rings. "So the frown was worry about Bernie's reaction?"

Steffen nodded. "She doesn't seem in any hurry to assume marital bliss."

"Laundry and all that?"

"She's a top-notch investigator."

"What makes her think you want her to quit?"

Steffen pocketed his hopes with the box and shook his head. "Certainly not me. I know your Aunt Juno is all for our marriage."

"Well there you are, Dad. Aunt Juno will oil the wheels down the aisle."

"You think so?" Steffen could feel his spirits rise as he stuck out his chest. "Juno does love Bernie." Steffen's long habit of quoting Lincoln when he was stressed kicked in. "'...for unless popular opinion makes itself very strongly felt, and a change is made in our present course ... [32]'"

"Dad, you know Bernie hates for you to quote Lincoln. Besides that particular quote ends with, ' ... blood will flow and brothers' hands will be raised against brother.'"

"Right," Steffen said. "No more Lincoln for tonight."

* * *

Zingerman's Road House, Ann Arbor

Bernie was wearing his favorite color: peach. Coral? Or was it apricot? Her sweater and scarf actually threw a halo around her blonde bob. Steffen reached out to touch her soft fragrant hair. "Happy Valentine's Day. How's your day been?"

She smiled up at him. "Sit down, giant. Lovely. Happy Valentine's Day to you too. Your sister's agreed to come with me for Jean's hearing."

---

[32] P. 248, Speech delivered before the First Republican State Convention, Blooming, Illinois, May 29, 1856.

Steffen scooted into the booth, happy to bump into her hip with the ring box in his jeans. "Did I hurt you?" He fished in his pocket and produced his future. "When will we be able to put these on?"

Bernie fingered the velvet box as if it might fly open and bite her. "After I get Jean settled?"

"Well that's open-ended. Are you still upset because we couldn't get away to meet your mother in Florida?" Steffen reached for the box, but Bernie stopped him.

"Let me see the rings. Don't we need to find a home together before we marry?" She opened the box.

"Do you want out of the engagement because I'm too old now?"

Bernie put one hand on the back of his neck, pulling him down for a sweet kiss. "Is April 1 too late?"

Steffen clutched his heart as a stabbing pain disguised itself as happiness. "April 1 is All Fools' Day, and I think it's a Monday."

Bernie pulled out a pocket-size calendar from her purse. "Let's plan on Saturday, May 4."

Steffen motioned for the waitress to take their order. "She'll have the raw oysters, and I'd like your meatloaf special."

The waitress turned away, not writing down their order.

Bernie pulled on his sleeve. "Could you find a realtor for us? Jean Lee's hearing is only six days away."

Steffen nodded. "Sam is moving on Saturday. I might as well keep packing. I can arrange for your condo and my house to be put on the market, but will you have time to look for a new place?"

"After the parole hearing, there will be plenty of time. Well not really, if we're going to marry May 4. Could Juno help arrange the wedding for us?"

"She'd like nothing better." Steffen put his arm around his woman. "Thanks for getting our booth."

The waitress interrupted their kiss with the dinners they'd ordered. "Sorry," she said and scooted off.

"Tell me what you want in a house." Steffen asked as his appetite kicked in.

Bernie bowed her head and Steffen mimicked her actions. Then she slid a slimy oyster into her mouth, seemed to relish the texture, and swallowed before saying, "Let's buy a bigger condo. One with room for a housekeeper-cook to stay with us."

"How about Nik and Etta moving in with us, if we can find a big enough place?"

Bernie seemed to need time to digest the idea, or else the oysters she had finished off. "I'd like that. We could be in-house grandparents. How many rooms would we need?"

"They'd need their own floor, maybe. We could take a top floor for the master bedroom and two studies, two bathrooms on our floor. Probably 800 thousand?"

"Maybe an old fraternity house would work?" Bernie said. "Near Burns Park?'

"Wouldn't that be great? Chocolate pecan pie?"

"Absolutely! Now all I need do is figure out how to free Jean Lee."

* * *

Bernie's Condo

Bernie headed for the phone when she got home to call her mother, but Mother had died. There was no one to call except Juno, and it was way too late to call a working nurse. Her cat Buttons succumbed to old age the same year her mother died. Bernie experienced what adult orphans all over the world fear: being next in line. But no children would follow Bernie.

She busied herself feeding smelly tuna dinners to her three Siamese kittens: Zipper, Hook, and Tie. Button's replacements didn't quite measure up to her first cat's level of devotion, probably because they had each other.

How would she be able to present any new evidence in six days? Where would Jean live, if she were paroled? Would Mary Alice want to live with a convicted murderer she had helped send to prison? Who would? Was there money for Jean to go to college? What school would accept her? Where would she work?

What would Juno need to plan the wedding? Would Steffen agree to St. Andrew's for the wedding? When would she have time to have a wedding dress fitted? Would enough yellow roses be found for the bouquets and to decorate St. Andrew's aisles? Would the Lee girls want to be bridesmaids? Jean, too? Bernie readied herself for bed and her brain switched off from the overload. Sleep blessed her.

However, in Bernie's harried dream an old woman—dressed in black and wearing a multiple-strand pearl necklace which swung past her knees—chased Bernie through courtrooms jammed with bruised children. The shadow called for her to wait. Doors opened and closed rapidly, but the specter continued to pursue. Bernie spied an escape into open elevator doors only to fall down its exposed shaft. The spirit fell too.

As they floated down at an *Alice-in-Wonderland* pace, the old woman spoke. "You're dreaming, but you need to know: Jean only thinks she killed me. She's innocent."

"Who did it?" Bernie shouted waking herself and startling the three cats nestled at the foot of her bed.

Four o'clock in the morning. A fine time to pursue a case! *Please, Lord, give me the strength and wisdom I need to do your will.*

CHAPTER 14

Lorraine Street
Saturday, February 16

Steffen found a realtor, Dorothy Kerner, who *was* organized. Her red curls matched her briefcase, which produced two selling agreements for Steffen's house and Bernie's condo. "What a pleasure to work with people who know what they want."

Steffen signed his paperwork, before noticing Bernie was still reading the fine print on her documents.

Dorothy's chipper voice drew Bernie's attention. "I have a sorority house for you to look at today."

Bernie finally signed her contract and Dorothy nodded thanks, whisking the paperwork into her red briefcase. Dorothy touched Bernie's shoulder. "I'd like to show your condo on Monday. The parents of a grad student want to buy a condo close to the university."

"Do I need to take my cats to a kennel?"

Dorothy laughed. "Absolutely not. Cats never attack."

Stephen compared the two young women. Dorothy could be five to seven years younger than Bernie, but Bernie's face was smooth while Dorothy's wrinkles testified to a smoking habit or just bad genes.

Dorothy opened Stephen's front door and ushered them out. To provide enough room for his long legs, Steffen had to sit in the front passenger seat of Dorothy's yellow Mustang convertible.

When Dorothy mentioned the address of the sorority house, Bernie squashed the idea. "That's the ugly modern white monstrosity across from the Lee house, Steffen."

Steffen climbed back out of the new-smelling car, helping Bernie out of the cramped backseat.

Dorothy rolled down her window as they said their goodbyes. "One down." Her professional cheerfulness was unstoppable.

Bernie tilted her head. "Are you confident you'll find a buyer for Steffen's house?"

"I am," Dorothy said. "I do love my job. I think I was born to sell houses."

* * *

Bernie's Condo
Monday, February 18

Juno and Steffen brought over bagels, cream cheese, smoked salmon, and glazed doughnuts. Juno's yellow plastic clipboard held a range of venues, church affiliations, guest lists, floral arrangements, wedding dress shops to visit, and tuxedo rental shops.

Bernie placed the lists next to her on the couch. The dining room table and the kitchen counters were full of half-packed boxes.

"Use my red pen to mark your choices," Juno said, using a fork to take her share of the salmon breakfast feast laid out on the magazine table in front of the couch.

"Steffen," Bernie handed him the clipboard. "Which church? Don't ask my opinion, just choose."

"St. Andrew's. Hands down. Stained-glass windows always get my vote."

"Good choice," Juno threw a bagel at her brother. "They feed the hungry, and I think their political justice ideals are on the right side."

Bernie sighed, then breathed deeply, hoping the coffee fumes would stimulate her brain. She was actually doing this, getting married at thirty-nine to a man twenty years older. "Yellow roses, church basement for the reception. Give the Lee girls my charge card and tell them the more greenery and flowers, the better. Tell them to buy matching yellow gowns or reusable dresses; whatever they want. Zingerman's food is great: whatever you chose. I want my cake to be white with yellow roses for icing trim, and I want it sweet. No one reaches for cake thinking of healthy food. Zingermans will provide the cake too, three tiers with a peace dove for the top. Steffen, I'm afraid the police and social workers I know—besides your sons' friends—will be our guest list."

"And the Lees." Steffen said.

"Sounds like one hundred and fifty," Juno said. "You two are ambitious. Do you think you'll sell your homes and find a new one in time for the wedding?"

"With the Lord's help," Bernie said.

Steffen started picking up the empty wrappers and paper plates.

"What about chores?" Juno asked, helping Steffen add to the garbage bag. "Bernie hates to cook."

"And do dishes," Bernie said.

The phone rang and Steffen picked up the receiver. "Johnston soon to be Blaine residence." He winked at Bernie. "Oh, sorry. Hi, Beth Ann. Sure." Turning two shades of dark red, Steffen handed the phone to Bernie.

"You're invited to our May 4 wedding," Bernie said. "What's new?"

"I'm calling about Jean Lee's hearing. Are you planning to attend?'

"I am," Bernie said, waving her hand palm up to indicate she didn't yet know what the head of the Sheriff's Investigation Squad wanted.

"You have an established rapport with the Lee family. Could you visit them and sort of get the lay of the land?"

"In case Jean wants to go home?"

"I'm not sure about my motivation. I've been having nightmares." Beth Ann's voice sounded strangely confused.

"Me too!" Bernie said. "Does your visitor wear pearls?"

"Visitor?' Beth Ann's voice regained its dignity. "I'm wondering how a nine-year-old could have dreamt up the murder in the first place."

"What are your nightmares like? In mine, Jimmy's mother says Jean only thinks she killed her. She's innocent."

"Not relevant."

"I thought you said …"

"I'm tired," Beth Ann said. "Call me after you visit the Lees. Try to take Steffen and Juno with you as witnesses."

"To what?" Bernie persisted.

"I don't know, Bernie. Can you please just go?"

"I'm sorry, sure. We'll all go." When she hung up the phone, Bernie asked Steffen. "Is your old boss a psychic? We're both having nightmares, and mine say Jean is even innocent."

"We sent an innocent child to prison?" Steffen stopped fussing with the garbage. He put his hand on his chest as if his last bite of cream cheese might have gotten caught. Then he poured himself more coffee. "What does Beth Ann want you to do?"

"Visit the Lees. Will you two go with me? I don't even know what I'm looking for, but the judge might ask me if they want her back home."

Juno opened a small stationary box and spread the contents out on the cleaned magazine table. "I'll help if you two address these envelopes. I'll stamp them and put them in the mail tonight. People have less than two months to get ready for your wedding. Are you going to be listed in any of the department stores?"

"Of course not," Bernie said. "Are you able to slip in a note that we will only accept cards of congratulations or donations to the Ronald McDonald house?"

"I know it's extra work, Juno," Steffen patted his sister's arm. "I could go to the printer tomorrow morning and bring over the additional cards as soon as they're done." Steffen picked up one of the invitations and read out loud, "Steffen Blaine and Bernie Johnston invite family and friends to celebrate their wedding vows on May 4 at 10:00 am, St. Andrew's Episcopal Church. Reception to follow in the Parish Hall." Stephen handed the card to Bernie. "Juno, how did you manage to have these printed so soon?"

"I printed them nine years ago, when Bernie agreed to marry you. Notice the date is cleverly added in with my beautiful, matching calligraphy."

"The church is printed," Bernie said.

"I knew Steffen would choose St. Andrew's." Juno laughed. "Obviously I'm not psychic. You two took your sweet time deciding on a date."

"You're as efficient as Steffen's realtor." Bernie smiled.

Steffen turned to Bernie. "What time should we show up at the Lees?"

"Probably after lunch, don't you think? You two are making my head swim. Juno, when should I try on wedding dresses? You'll be my maid-of-honor. Steffen, which of your sons will be your best man?"

"May I have two?"

"Why not!" Juno and Bernie laughed together until their sides hurt.

After they promised to address all the envelopes before the next morning, Juno agreed to accompany them to the Lee's. Bernie prayed as they climbed into Steffen's Honda. Was she on the right track, marrying Steffen, trying to free Jean? Was the Lord leading her, or was she satisfying her own egotistical needs?

Dorothy Kerner stepped out of her yellow Mustang as Steffen started to pull away from the curb. He stopped his car halfway into the road.

Dorothy came over. "You forgot me, didn't you."

Bernie pushed the button to open the passenger side window. "The house is a mess. I'm packing."

"Never mind," Dorothy said. "The buyer doesn't have much time in town. I'll make sure they see your home's best points. It works out better if the owner is absent."

"Watch that my three cats don't get out. They don't have claws." Bernie turned to Steffen. "Changes are happening faster than I can think about them."

Steffen patted her knee. "Lincoln said, 'If you don't come down, I'll cut the tree from under you.'[33] Vicissitudes come if we instigate them or not."

Bernie realized the stress of change was causing Lincoln to emerge as Steffen's anchor again. Lincoln was all well and good, but the Lord was the surer source of strength. "The Psalms say, 'Let all those that put their trust in Thee rejoice.' I find the Bible's words more comforting."

Steffen nodded.

---

[33] Lincoln's Last Warning, cartoon title in Harper's Weekly, October 11, 1862, p.355 Abe Lincoln's Yarns and Stories, Henry Niel, 1908.

* * *

1830 Washtenaw Avenue

Ricky Lee answered the door as if she expected their visit. "This is about Jean getting freed?"

Bernie touched Ricky's arm. "We're planning to attend the hearing. You and Jimmy will be there, won't you? I don't really know what might happen."

"I'm hoping for the best," Ricky said. "But Jimmy will not be able to come. He's quite ill. Would you like coffee?"

"We've just finished breakfast," Juno said. "Are the children all in school?"

"They are," Ricky said.

"Could we visit with Jean's father?" Steffen asked.

Ricky hesitated, pulling at the knotted fringe of a brilliant aqua wool scarf. "Of course. Let me go up for a minute to tell him you're here. Before you come upstairs take a look around. The parole board will want to know about the condition of the house. I think I've made some improvements."

* * *

Steffen headed for the basement, while Bernie and Juno stayed upstairs. Disappointment knocked on his chest when he saw most of the elaborate train set had been boxed up. Some of the individual train cars were displayed on shelves around the top of the finished basement. The room was invaded by a large-screen television and five computer stations with all their screen savers blinking at him. How old were the Lee boys now? Bob must be a teenager, but Dick and Ben were surely still in grade school. Electronics had wiped out a world of creative play.

He swiped at the tears running down his giant nose. Cry baby at nearly sixty years of age. He didn't care. Whoever relinquished the pleasure of childhood toys needn't speak to him. The best part of having children was being able to play with their toys.

When he returned upstairs, Bernie and Juno had already ascended to the second floor to question Jimmy Lee. Steffen stood at the bedroom door, unwilling to interrupt Bernie's questions.

* * *

On the hospital bed near the bay window, the bald, cadaverous person bore no resemblance to the strutting dandy who had been Jean's father nine years earlier. "Jimmy," Bernie said. "Is there anything we can tell the parole board about bringing Jean home?"

The disappearing man turned a slightly darker shade of green. "Don't." He waved at Ricky in her position near the door. "No" was all he was able to moan. His eyes shifted upward; his forehead and upper lip broke out in sweat.

Ricky stepped forward and ushered them into the hall. "His pain medications for bone cancer don't relieve the pain enough. I don't know how much longer he'll last. Hospice volunteers come in the evening so I can get some rest."

Juno spoke first. "He doesn't want Jean to come home?"

"Not his decision anymore," Ricky said.

Juno led the way down to the first floor.

As Ricky handed them their coats, she turned to Steffen. "Etta tells me Nik is quite impressed with your legal aplomb—expertise—and your spiritual progress."

Bernie turned Ricky in her direction so she wouldn't see Steffen's discomfort. "Nice to hear they are expecting."

Juno took the hint and pushed Steffen out the opened door.

Bernie fiddled with her coat buttons. "I wish Steffen's beliefs were closer to Nik's."

Ricky nodded. "I talked to Steffen at Etta's wedding. He's a very staid man."

"Steffen thinks the world rests on his shoulders."

Ricky said, "Thank the Lord we're able to believe in His power and glory."

144

CHAPTER 15

Trailer at Packard and Eisenhower
Tuesday, February 19

Etta stirred the yellow paint again. Nik and Mary Alice wouldn't let her use the roller or climb the ladder, so she was relegated to making sure the paint color remained constant. Nik suggested the brightest shade to enlarge the small room. "Not enough windows." Etta sighed.

Mary Alice, still the eternal optimist and a curvaceous sixteen, swung her loaded roller toward the wall opposite the trailer's undersized window, sprinkling the drop cloth with yellow drips. "If you hang a big mirror on that wall, you'll have twice the light."

As if to approve the suggestion, Etta's child leapt in her womb, making her laugh. "The baby agrees with you."

"Has to be a girl," Mary Alice said. "Nik's aunt will be here shortly. Should I keep painting or clean up?"

"How fast can you roll that thing?" Etta laughed, pouring more paint into the tilted flat container. "How are we going to find matching dresses for the wedding?" Etta patted her stomach. "Does the paint smell yellow, or just smell?"

"It is stinky. I figure the salesladies at Jacobson's will earn their commission. Besides, this won't be the first time a pregnant mother was chosen as a bridesmaid. Nik and Sam will look handsome in tuxedoes."

Etta giggled. "You don't suppose Bernie will make them wear yellow?"

"Maybe a yellow rose as a boutonniere." Mary Alice busily rolled the paint in widening swaths. "Were you surprised at the church they chose?"

"Bernie's a believer like you and Nik, but Steffen and Sam don't take their beliefs very seriously. Besides, Episcopalians are Christian."

"Nik told Sam to start writing down five things he's thankful for every day so he can be given the gift of faith too."

"Is that how Nik converted you?" Mary Alice stopped working. "I thought you had to confess your sins and be baptized."

"True. But not until a person realizes how much the Lord loves them will they feel stricken with humility at His generosity. Hey, keep rolling the paint. Nik told me to ask the Lord for saving peace, when I was so homesick a month after our wedding. I finally gave up, or gave my will over to the Lord's care. I do feel His daily, loving presence. 'His rod and His staff, they comfort me.'"

"I think I was born believing. Except for you, I didn't have anyone I could count on but the Lord. Do you think Steffen and Sam are too prideful to be saved?"

"I do not! Jesus didn't come to call the righteous, and their souls are really none of my business."

"Sure, sure." Mary Alice laughed. "But my big sister is glad the godmother of her baby is a believer."

"I am, and you know Nik is too." Etta heard someone knock. "Keep painting. Aunt Juno's early."

"If Bernie is with her, send her in."

Nik let the threesome in. "I'm making macaroni and cheese with tomatoes and chips of sautéed green peppers. You're invited."

Without asking, Steffen seated himself on the loveseat. "Sounds good to me. I miss your cooking. Bernie and I have a proposition for you and Etta."

Nik had insisted Etta's parents' old recliners prevented him from touching her enough. The Salvation Army hauled the chairs and the two sets of bunk beds out of the trailer to make room for their new furniture.

"Meat sickens me," Etta said. "I guess the baby will be a vegetarian." As she offered to take their coats, she noticed Bernie never seemed to age, but Aunt Juno said her knees were giving her fits from the cold, damp weather.

Bernie, always ready to make everyone comfortable, said, "We visited your mother yesterday."

"Dad doesn't want Jean home," Etta said.

"Where's Mary Alice?" Bernie asked.

"In the boys' old room. It's going to be the nursery. She wants to finish painting. I mean I want her to complete the job before we go shopping for our bridesmaid dresses."

When Bernie left to talk to Mary Alice, Etta eased herself down into one of the matching wingback chairs.

Juno sat down in the other, facing her. "Is your father afraid of Jean?"

Steffen cleared his throat. "Bernie and Beth Ann think Jean might have been innocent. They both had dreams. Beth Ann won't tell us what she dreamt but Bernie's was of your grandmother insisting Jean only thinks she's a murderer."

"Fine time to be deciding that. Why did they think she was guilty nine years ago?" Etta's baby kicked at her cantankerous mood.

"She confessed," Steffen reminded her. "Jean must have thought she killed your grandmother; but someone else must have instigated the crime. She was only nine."

"My father? I think Dad doesn't want Jean to see him now because he's so ill. She thought the world of him. You think Dad talked Jean into the crime."

Bernie and Mary Alice joined them. Mary Alice's habitual frown always appeared when the subject of Jean was discussed. "I'm not going home, if Jean starts living there."

Etta pushed herself up from the chair and went over to embrace her younger sister. "You'll stay with us. You can have our old room all to yourself."

Bernie said. "I dreamt about your grandmother."

Mary Alice accepted a Kleenex from Bernie. "What did she say?"

"That Jean only thinks she killed your grandmother."

"You never lived with Jean," Mary Alice said. "She's as mean as her name."

"Nine-year-olds don't have the brain power to premeditate murder," Steffen said.

"She wanted the house," Etta said.

"Your grandmother seems to think Jean's innocent," Bernie said.

Mary Alice shook her head. "The trouble with believers is that we often give credence to outlandish superstitions. Why didn't you ask her who did kill her?"

Bernie patted the paint-splattered knee of Mary Alice's jeans. "Never mind, let's go shopping for your bridesmaids dresses."

"Shouldn't I change?"

Bernie hugged her. "You don't know how beautiful you are, do you?" Then, Bernie scooted Steffen over so she could sit next to him on the love seat. "Nik's dad has a great idea." She elbowed Steffen

"When we find a house to buy that's big enough, we would like you all to move in with us. You, too, Mary Alice."

"How long will it take to find a house?" Mary Alice stood behind the chair Etta had occupied.

Juno answered. "They'll surely find one before the wedding."

"Nik, can you slow down supper, so we can take the girls shopping?" Steffen stood but realized the headroom in the trailer required he sit back down.

Nik asked Etta, "Will you be able to wait for dinner?" Turning to the older adults he said, "She's always hungry now."

"A good sign for a pregnant mother," Aunt Juno said. "Let's eat before we shop."

* * *

1830 Washtenaw
Wednesday, February 20

Bob was engrossed watching an old second-generation Star Trek video while finishing his math homework, when Mary Alice found him in the basement. "'Lo," he said, not raising his head.

"How do you know it's me?"

"You're the only female left in the house."

"What about Mother?"

"Heavier footfall on the stairs."

"I don't want Jean to come home."

Bob turned toward her but the backlighting from the flickering television screen kept his face in the dark. "You're frightened because you testified against Jean."

Mary Alice moved to a seat next to him to watch his expression. She could smell the orange he'd just eaten. "Not in open court."

"Doesn't matter. Jean knows you did."

"What do you talk about when you visit her?"

"Mom and I usually pray with her. At first she just sneered at us. For years really." Bob cocked his head as if wanting to listen to his own words. "Then about five years ago, she started listening to the prayers. Asking us questions."

"Which prayers did you say?"

"You know, St. Francis' prayer for peace."

"The 'comfort, love and understand' one?"

"That's it. Jean slowly opened up. She realized we were not there to punish her. We just wanted to spend time with her. She did well in school."

"I never said Jean was stupid. I worry she used you and Mom, learned how to put up a false front to convince you she was becoming less of a psychopath."

"Psychopaths are unredeemable. I admit Jean makes money into an idol, but neurotics can be cured. Dad doesn't want Jean home because the neighbors will start treating us like lepers again."

"Leopards?"

149

Bob pushed Mary Alice's wheeled desk chair away from him.

They laughed together, before Mary Alice heard her mother's heavy shoes come down the basement stairs.

"The bottom line is Jean is coming home," Mother said. "Your dad will need to reconcile himself with her before he meets his maker. Mary Alice, the same goes for you. Jean has paid the heavy price of losing her whole childhood for a nine-year-old's mistake. I am not going to let anyone ruin the rest of her life."

Mary Alice couldn't think of an appropriate reply. She didn't have the courage to explain it didn't matter because she was moving out to live with Etta and Nik and his Dad, and—thank the Lord—Bernie.

After Mother went back upstairs, she said to Bob, "Maybe they won't parole Jean."

* * *

Washtenaw County Court House
Thursday, February 21

The parole board—two women and three men—sat in the jury box. The judge's desk was empty. A large webcam screen was set up to broadcast Jean's testimony from her prison in Waterloo. Ricky and her three sons sat together. Etta, Nik, and Mary Alice were in the row behind them. Bernie, Steffen, Juno, and Beth Ann Zhang were seated behind the prosecutor and defense attorney desks to answer questions from the board. Only Jimmy Lee was absent.

Bernie watched Mary Alice cross her arms as the grainy, flickering picture of eighteen-year-old Jean appeared on the screen. Neither Etta nor Mary Alice had visited their sister while she was incarcerated.

The oldest male member of the release board asked Jean, "What do you have to say for yourself, young woman?"

"I admit to a nine-year-old's heinous crime of poisoning my grandmother with her own pills. I ask my family to forgive me, and I ask the state for a chance to prove my worthiness as a productive citizen.

I plan to study law to ameliorate the plight of abused and neglected children."

The members of the board spoke together for a few minutes. Then the same man said, "Your perfect scores on your SATs and good conduct record leave me only one choice. Parole granted for Friday, March 15."

Mary Alice shook her head, and then waved at Bernie.

"Do you have any objection?" the parole officer asked.

"You all better pray hard that none of us falls into her plans again— or rather, disrupts her plans."

The screen was shut off and the members of the panel marched out of the jury box.

Ricky walked over to Mary Alice. Mary Alice raised her chin. Bernie put her arm around Mary Alice's shoulder. "Ricky, I've invited Mary Alice to make her home with us."

"I think that would be best," Ricky said. "I love you all, Mary Alice, but Jean needs a place to live."

Mary Alice turned away, and Bernie followed her out of the courthouse.

* * *

Bernie's Condo

Mary Alice fell asleep in the guest room as soon as they got home. Her emotions left her wrung out, devoid of reaction or energy. Bernie lured the curious cats out of the room with a can of fresh tuna and shut the door.

Juno would understand, wouldn't she? Bernie rang her cell. "I want to reopen Jean's case. The family is not going to be whole until I can prove Jean's innocent."

Right to the point, Juno said, "Steffen will accuse you of stalling the wedding plans."

"May 4 is not going to disappear." Bernie took a deep breath. "And I intend to show up, don't you?"

CHAPTER 16

Washtenaw County Court House
Friday, February 22

Steffen pulled open the heavy glass door of Beth Ann's second-floor office. He didn't remember the door being a problem before. Bernie didn't notice his difficulty. Even though the wedding plans were still on track, her awareness of him dimmed as she focused on Jean's future.

His heart seemed to take a hit each time she smiled or didn't smile at him. Bernie was even lovelier than when he first met her as a social worker. She was right to become an investigator. The hunt seemed to thrill her, making her eyes sharper, twinkling with curiosity. The line of her chin was up, and her shoulders drew back ready for the fight for truth. His Joan-of-Arc. Now if he could just bring her home as his wife. "The ides of March usually bring ill winds." He was trying to cheer Bernie up, or at least get her attention.

Bernie ignored his negative reference to Jean's release date. "We'll be married shortly after, what can happen?"

"Are you still fighting, this close to your wedding?" Beth Ann seemed cheerful enough, but nine years of investigating criminals had hardened her complexion and dulled the scope of her intelligence, as if she'd been beaten down by witnessing the results of human cruelty. "Sit down," she said. "Let's reason together. The department doesn't have money to throw around."

"On a dream vision's hint?" Bernie asked.

"I'm sorry I mentioned my nightmare to you," Beth Ann grumbled. She swiped at her bangs, which were as black as the day they first met. "What do you hope to find?"

"You did agree a nine year old can't carry out a premeditated murder by poison without help." Bernie moved to the edge of her chair.

Beth Ann ran her hand over her lips. How many years had it been since she applied lipstick? "Well, you're still friends with Mary Alice." She met Steffen's stare. "I don't need to find a search warrant for you to investigate Jean's dead grandmother's insight."

Old. He felt older than he should. These women sucked all the energy right out of him. Or maybe he was just beginning to notice how much fortitude and stamina were required to chase down truth in its hidden lairs.

* * *

St. Joseph Hospital
Saturday, February 23

Bernie pulled at Steffen's hand. "Jimmy Lee's hospitalization puts a time limit on how quickly we need to find out the truth."

"Denial, the Nile, is not just a river in Egypt." Steffen's chest ached. He couldn't count any other cold symptoms. "You're trying to terminate our wedding plans."

"I'm not." Bernie stamped her small foot.

"I love you," he said, as his chest pain let up.

"Me too, you. Do you want to ask the questions? He's chauvinistic enough to answer you."

Steffen put his hand in his pocket to keep from clutching at his chest. "I think I'll sit this one out. If you forget something, I'll remind you."

Bernie brightened immediately. She opened Jimmy Lee's door, walking with purpose to the side of his bed. "Jimmy, what can you remember about the week before your mother's death?"

"Jean's in the back bedroom with Ricky." Jimmy pushed a button. A nurse rushed in.

"Please," he said, pointing to his IV.

The nurse nodded, and they waited as Jimmy relaxed under the additional narcotic.

Steffen sat down in the visitor's chair, wondering if he could borrow the IV. He planned to make a doctor's appointment for an antibiotic prescription for what must be a serious bronchial infection as soon as he got home. Funny he didn't feel like coughing.

Bernie resumed her quest. "When did you first hear there were rats in the neighborhood?"

Jimmy's eyes glazed over, and he almost smiled. "Jean said Mr. Prettinhoffer told her."

Steffen shivered at the skeleton of a man's crooked grimace.

Bernie was relentless, "Describe Ricky's relationship with your mother."

Steffen wondered how she could shut off her reactions to the horror of death happening before her.

Jimmy blinked once at the door, checking to see if Ricky was in the room. "I know they hated each other." He rubbed his hands together. "The medication reaches the bones in my fingers last."

Nevertheless, to Steffen the gesture still resembled a greedy man's glee at the prospect of more money.

"Where did Ricky buy the rat poison?" Bernie asked, moving to Steffen's side of the bed so they could both judge Jimmy's truthfulness.

Jimmy rolled his head from side to side, as if listening to an unwelcome and unseen guest. "Jean borrowed some from Mrs. Staples."

"I've been dreaming about your mother," Bernie said. "She says Jean only thinks she killed her grandmother."

Joe Wilcox barged into the room. "Why are you questioning my client? I'll have to ask you to leave."

* * *

Lorraine Street Home
Sunday, February 24

Bernie brought McDonald's breakfast sandwiches to Stephen's house. St. Andrew's mass was nearly empty, and the lines for communion had been short. Usually she kept the handout and readings, but with everything packed for the move to a new home they hadn't yet found, one additional piece of paper to file was too much to ask. "The straw that broke the camel's back," she said, as Steffen opened the door.

He hugged her while shutting the door behind her. "Because I didn't go with you?"

"Talking to myself." Bernie stayed in the hug long enough to shake off the winter chill. "Have you eaten?"

"I can smell bacon." He'd set the table with linens and dishes.

"I'll love you forever if the coffee is fresh."

After Bernie said a prayer to bless her breakfast, Steffen told her the good news. "Dorothy's on her way. She's found two fraternities."

* * *

When they drove past the fraternity house on Hill Street, Steffen turned Dorothy's first prospect down. "Look at the view we would have."

Across the street from the attractive brick fraternity, the stark orange-and-metal siding of the admittedly innovative architectural creation for the Business School's new addition stared back at them.

"It wouldn't be that bad, if the garbage bins were not situated directly opposite our front door," Bernie said.

Dorothy said, "I'd like to show your house, Steffen, on Monday to a couple new to Ann Arbor. They want to place their children in the grade school across the road."

"Mitchell School," Steffen said. "My son, Sam, teaches at Mitchell."

"Okay," Dorothy said, a little less enthusiastically, "Your final fraternity house choice is in Burns Park."

* * *

Burns Park Home

Steffen liked the brick Tudor house immediately. The three-story house had a lavish mahogany entryway, with a large front room stretching the entire length of the house back to French doors leading to a small but cultured garden. Flower beds could be seen outlined under the snow. Plastic cones hid roses from the worst of winter.

The dining room to the left was bright and charming without being massively furnished. The kitchen's cabinets, appliances, breakfast nook, and attached media room with a fireplace were perfect for the combined family home.

Steffen and Bernie followed Dorothy up to the second floor, where one huge master bedroom with a screened-in balcony overlooking the garden flaunted two bathrooms and walk-in closets on opposite sides of the room. Across the hall enormous studies shared a sitting area near the steps.

"We couldn't have designed a better plan," Bernie said.

"Now the linchpin." Steffen said.

Dorothy's didn't seem to understand the reference, but the third floor was a complete four-bedroom apartment with a fully-equipped kitchen and two bathrooms.

"Sold," Bernie and Steffen said together, laughing at their luck and agreement.

"You're good," Bernie said, shaking Dorothy's hand. "I was really worried when you showed us the first two choices."

"I love my job." Dorothy flipped out the necessary paperwork from her case. "Closing—once you are approved—will be scheduled for Friday, March 1. I told the sellers you wanted to move in before your wedding on May 4."

Steffen shook her hand. "Are you sure they will accept our offer?"

"Absolutely," Dorothy said. "Or I would not have showed you the property. Eight hundred thousand and they pay all the closing costs."

* * *

Trailer at Packard and Eisenhower
Monday, February 25

Mary Alice climbed into the back of Steffen's Honda hybrid. Juno sat next to her brother. Bernie needed to show Nik and Etta the location of the house they'd bought, so they drove together in the Lees' old Blazer, which Etta had claimed when she was sixteen and able to drive.

Mary Alice had no desire to drive a car. People were so crazy, passing each other just to be first in line at the next stop signal. Besides, she didn't have a job, and Mom said she needed to pay for her own car insurance. The bus was fine for when everyone was too busy to chauffeur her around.

What would Mom think if she went to live with Bernie's family? She might have her feelings hurt. The house on Washtenaw never felt like home. Maybe because she was so guilty about living there after Grandma died. Dad had been ill from the first night he reconciled with Mom. Probably knew he was sick. No one wants to die alone, but everyone does.

They pulled up to a mammoth house on a tree-lined street. Steffen unlocked the door, but Bernie came over and took Mary Alice's hand. "Stick with me, kid," she said. "I think you'll like your room."

"Could I call you Aunt Bernie?"

Bernie pulled her closer. They were the same height now. "I'd like that," she said.

The home's first-floor ceilings were a story-and-a-half high. The formal front room and the garden through the French doors were as elegant as the dining room. The kitchen opened out into a big family room, where bookshelves on the walls promised room for all the books she could ever read.

Bernie showed her the master bedroom and the enormous closets on the second floor. They followed Etta and Nik up to the third floor. Mary Alice heard Etta squeal with pleasure. Even there, windows vied for every available space. Besides the master bedroom with its own bathrooms, three other bedrooms were available with a full bathroom between two of them.

"Pick one," Etta and Bernie said as they stood in the hall with her.

"I love the sun," Mary Alice said. "I guess I'll pick the one facing the front. Are we really going to live here?" She embraced Etta.

"We really are," Etta said. "And Mother is only three blocks away."

"Bernie." Mary Alice rubbed her forehead. "Nik and Etta might have twins. We don't have room for Jean, do we?"

Bernie shook her head. "No. The people I love need a safe place to lay their heads."

Mary Alice sat on the steps and broke down. "Give me a minute. I'll get out of your way."

"They took the back steps down to the kitchen," Bernie said. "You cry as long as you want. I'm glad we get to live together too."

* * *

Burns Park House
Friday, March 1

Steffen was thankful that Dorothy Kerner's expertise allowed the closing of Bernie's condo, his house on Lorraine, and their new home in Burns Park to last for less than two morning hours in the Maple Street Chase Bank.

The movers cleaned out his Lorraine house with Sam's help, and Juno supervised the loading of Bernie's belongings onto the moving truck. Nik and Etta's, along with Mary Alice's, additions to the truck were unloaded first and hauled up to the third floor of the Burns Park house before Bernie and he arrived.

Mary Alice met them at the front door, stepping quickly to the side as the movers brought in Bernie's couch for the family room.

For the first time Steffen could remember, Mary Alice took his arm and guided him to a stool next to the kitchen counter. Without his asking, she poured him a glass of ice water.

Then she brought Bernie to his side. "Is he feeling well?" she asked Bernie instead of him.

Bernie laughed, and then sobered when she took a good look at him. "Steffen, you are as white as a sheet. Are you well?"

"I was going to call the doctor," he said, lightly pounding his chest with his fist. "I think I'm a little clogged up … with a cold."

"Run. Go get Juno," Bernie said.

Juno appeared before he finished his glass of water. The cold must have made him thirsty.

Mary Alice was busy listing all the people who had died since her grandmother was poisoned. "Pepper, Mr. Prettinhoffer, Mrs. Spradlin, Mrs. Staples, Dad is dying and now …"

Bernie hushed her. "Old people like us get a little winded with excitement. I'm sure Steffen will live to see the wedding. She clapped him on the back, which seemed to relieve what ever was knotted in his chest.

Juno took his pulse, pulled his eyelids down and pronounced him fit for supervisory work with the movers. "Steffen, no lifting."

Bernie patted his cheek, but Mary Alice didn't leave his side. "I worry," she said, not moving more than three feet from him for the rest of the day.

CHAPTER 17

Friday, March 15
Jean's Release from Waterloo

Driving Steffen's Honda through the winding roads to Ann Arbor from Waterloo, Bernie tried not to worry about her new husband. Antibiotics had not broken up the phlegm in his bronchial tubes as quickly as Juno had predicted. Nik was at home with him, serving chicken soup to the invalid while he pursued his sudden addiction to Star Trek reruns.

Bernie stopped at the Mud Lake picnic area to brag about her knowledge of sand hill crane habits. "They usually make a nest in those marshes each year."

Jean touched her shoulder. "They don't want me home, do they?

"Your mother did tell you about your father's hospitalization?"

"Because I'm coming home." Jean leaned against the car door. "He's afraid of me."

"Actually, Jean, he does seem afraid of the truth being discovered."

"The truth? Didn't Pilate ask Jesus, 'What is truth?'"

"He did!" They held a respectful silence. Then Bernie dove into the heart of the discussion. "Nine-year-olds cannot conjure up complicated murder scenarios. Someone in your family tutored you to think in terms of gratification-motivation, methods of execution, and the deadly means, without providing an adequate scenario for you to avoid punishment."

Jean opened the passenger door and got in. "Does Mother agree that because Dad is avoiding me, he must be the culprit?"

"He does act guilty, but he's so ill the District Attorney may not prosecute."

* * *

1830 Washtenaw Avenue

Ricky was waiting at the front door. "Jean, you cut your hair."

Jean and her mother embraced for a long time.

"I miss my mother," Bernie said, embarrassed to interrupt them to explain her tears.

Ricky recovered her good manners. "Come in, come in. I've boiled the tea water twice already. Mary Alice is helping set up Etta's nursery but Bob, Dick, and Benjamin are looking forward to eating cake."

Bernie followed Ricky and Jean into the sun room. "Have you stopped painting?"

Ricky poured tea at a round table where Bob, Dick, and Benjamin accepted kisses on the cheek from their returned sister. "No, no. I moved my paints to Jean's old room." Ricky chatted away. "I felt I was keeping in touch with Jean by sharing her space."

Jean accepted a petti-four from Bob. "I was looking forward to getting my old room back."

Ricky passed a crystal plate of cucumber sandwiches to Bernie. "I made up Etta's old bed for you to share a bedroom with Mary Alice."

Jean made a face at Benjamin, who turned to Bob for help in dealing with this new-to-him grown sister. "You were just a baby, Ben, when I went away. Do you remember me at all?"

With his mouth happily crammed with cake, Ben shook his head.

Bob intervened, "You were too young, Ben, to visit Jean while she was away."

Dick patted Ben's arm. "I was too young too."

"Where were you?" Ben asked Jean.

"In Waterloo, where they help young women grow up," Ricky said cheerfully.

"Do I get to stay home to grow up?" The poor boy seemed honestly concerned.

Bernie tried to think of some way to reassure the youngster.

"You always get to stay home if you want to badly enough," Jean said, which eased Ben's mind enough to take another small bite of cake. "What does Mary Alice think of sharing a room with me?" Jean asked her mother.

Ricky rescued the plate of cakes and passed it to Jean, who offered the first choice to Bernie. "Mary Alice is staying with Etta until after the baby comes," Ricky said. "The baby is due in a week. Bernie and Steffen gave an apartment in their house to Etta and Nik. Nik is a great cook."

"I hate to cook." Bernie found it necessary to mount a defense for herself. Should she tell Jean that Etta and Nik had invited Mary Alice to stay with them, or let Ricky tell her? Before she could decide, Jean changed the subject.

Jean said, "I'd like to see the old trailer."

Bob said to his mother, "Me too. Can we go see the old trailer, Mom?"

"We can as soon as tea is over. I hear no one has rented it since we moved out."

Bernie prepared to leave. "Jean, you're settling in just fine. Ricky, may I invite myself to tea next week?"

Jean—ever the scamp—asked, "To check on me?"

Ricky interjected. "Please do, and bring Mary Alice along."

* * *

Washtenaw County Court House
Monday, March 18

Bernie marched into Beth Ann's office before noticing Steffen lagged a few steps behind her. She reached back and held the door for him. "Terrible cold," she explained to Beth Ann. "Can't seem to find his old get-up-and-go."

"Won't married life be too strenuous for you, Steffen?" Beth Ann enjoyed her own joke.

Steffen didn't smile as he sat down with a heavy sigh. "Careful. I might decide to share my deadly virus."

"Sorry," Beth Ann said. "Are you on antibiotics?"

"That I am." Steffen managed a short-lived grin.

"They make him nauseous." Bernie explained, before getting to the reason for their visit. "Ricky was definitely not involved in the death of her mother-in-law."

Steffen straightened in his chair: "Is Jimmy too ill to prosecute?"

"Bring me the evidence," Beth Ann said, "and I'll have him moved to the prison hospital."

Steffen asked, "Could you have him transported to the prison for questioning?"

Bernie understood the implications. "His family should be present to hear his confession. They need to move on in life as a unit without unresolved issues."

Steffen grabbed his shoulder. "Bernie," he whispered, before falling out of his chair onto Beth Ann's carpeted floor.

"Call 9-1-1," Bernie yelled, as she pounded on his chest.

* * *

University Hospital

Sitting in the hall, while the nurses attended to some routine, Bernie worried about Steffen's future with her. Bypass surgery was a positive thing, according to Steffen's doctors.

Nik, Etta, and Sam had urged her to return to Burns Park, but she didn't have the courage to leave. Instead she gave them directions to feed her three Siamese cats. If she lost Steffen, no one on earth would be able to step into his shoes. *Please, Lord, I need this good man in my life. Forgive me for not marrying him sooner. Please give me a second chance.*

The nurses allowed her back into the room, and she leaned her head against the wall in the uncomfortable visitor's chair. She closed her eyes to rest them from all the blinking lights on the equipment surrounding Steffen's bed.

"Who did it?" Bernie shouted, waking up in the hospital chair looking into Steffen's frightened eyes. "You're okay," she said, rising to take his hand and kiss his cheek. "You had bypass surgery."

Steffen motioned for the water glass, and Bernie held it while he drained the contents using the bent straw. Finally his tongue was wetted enough to speak. "Who did what?"

"Jean's grandmother is still chasing me around in my nightmares, claiming Jean is innocent."

"But she didn't answer your question?"

* * *

Steffen watched the fluorescent lights dance in Bernie's golden hair as she shook her head. His angel had saved him and promised to marry him. He pushed himself up to a seated position. Bernie must have rung the buzzer, because a nurse and a nurse's aide rushed through the door.

"You need to lie back down." The head nurse monitored the machines, while the aid took his pulse.

He complied but asked, "How about if you tilt my head up?"

The nurse nodded to the aide, who barely slanted the head of the bed. "You require rest. Try not to talk very long. You should leave, Miss. He does need to sleep."

"A kiss will relax me." Steffen winked at the nurse.

Bernie immediately touched his shoulder and kissed him gently on the lips.

Her scent occupied his senses. He wanted to hold her, be rid of all these dinging monitors and invading antiseptic smells, and rush down the aisle with her. However lethargy—possibly drug induced—overcame his senses. "I can't believe it. The nurse must have increased the pain medication. I'm getting sleepier, but I love you. Go home and rest. I'll have the nurse call you when I'm more awake. We'll figure out who else could have killed Mrs. Lee."

* * *

Bernie stayed at his side, ignoring the nurse and Steffen's dictates. She needed time to pray before leaving the room. *Lord, thank you for restoring Steffen to me. Please help me clear Jean's name and find the real murderer. Help me to find the strength to carry my burdens and bring justice to the innocent.*

Reluctantly Bernie stepped out into the hall, but not before she looked once more at the man she was going to marry. Just fifty-nine, Steffen's long, white, blanket-covered limbs appeared older than she imagined an ideal bridegroom's body should be. His nose and Adam's apple accentuated his lean face, and his shock of thick white hair needed smoothing. Instead of being the helpmate she had delayed marrying for nine years, she understood he might now be someone who only needed caretaking.

Maybe Juno could move into the Burns Park house too.

Contrary to the realities she faced, she felt joy push up from the pit of her stomach, making her soul sing with happiness and thankfulness for her Maker's intrusion into her selfish plans. Steffen needed her, and she wanted nothing more than to love this good man.

CHAPTER 18

Margaret Mitchell School
Monday, April 15

Nik drove Etta's old Blazer around the jam of school buses and mothers picking up their children in status cars. He spied his older brother, Sam, walking half way down the long drive. Nik beeped his horn, but Sam continued to trudge along toward his condo without raising his head. Finally Nik lowered both windows and yelled. "Hey, Sam!"

Sam's quick smile answered. When he climbed into the car, he said, "You'll have to go all the way through. They'll never let you turn around."

"Wave to all your students," Nik said. "You really love this job, don't you?"

"About as much as you love showing old duffers how to better their golf game."

"Loving a job sure helps in the morning." Nik shoved his brother's shoulder. "Dad's doing great. He and Bernie take walks every morning."

"So we'll need to get this bachelor party planned, I guess." Sam waved back at a tall, buxom girl. "Can you believe she's fifteen?"

"I can see why teachers get in trouble."

"You wouldn't believe how aggressive they are—sexually I mean. How's Bernie progressing with Jean's case, speaking of aggressive teenagers?"

Nik laughed. "Well Jean's legal as far as age goes, but I wouldn't recommend any attachment to her."

Sam shook his head. "I'm more worried about Mary Alice. She's such a sweet kid. Loves her family, dedicated to Etta … and you."

"Sweet on her?"

"Hey, I'm way too old."

"Dad's got twice the years over Bernie that you have on Mary Alice. Does she even know you're alive?"

Sam laughed. "Absolutely not. She thinks I'm an old man teaching at the school she attended last year. Never thought I'd feel old at 26."

As they passed their former home on Lorraine, Sam said, "Remember when there was an oak tree across the street next to the school?"

Nik nodded as he braked when a crossing guard asked him to wait for a line of children. "They chopped it down."

"I killed it."

"What?"

"It's your fault too. Always telling me to pray for something. So one day I challenged God. I told Him, 'Let me see your power. Make blue roses grow on that oak tree.' I think the process killed the tree."

Nik digested the story. "Have you thought of seeing a psychologist?"

"No, but Mary Alice's beliefs are getting to me, more than yours ever did."

"She's a sweeter pill to swallow."

"I guess. Anyway, I've been writing down five things I'm thankful for—most especially Dad's recovery—and I can tell you that I'm thankful to somebody."

"Praise the Lord," Nik said, swiping at the wetness clouding his vision.

* * *

Burns Park Home

Etta met her husband and brother-in-law at the front door. "Nik, Dad said to bring your oven trays down to the main kitchen."

"Fine with me." After kissing her, Nik clapped Sam on the back. "I'll go check on them. We're celebrating Sam's conversion."

Etta grabbed Sam's arm. "Really?"

"Probably as close as I'm going to get," he said.

In the front room, Mary Alice closed her school book with a bang. "Etta, the Thanksgiving list worked! Right, Sam?"

"It did, it did." Sam put his hands behind his back. His ears turned a slight tinge of pink, and Etta recognized religion was not the only draw on Sam's attention.

Mary Alice thumped Sam on his chest. "About time you got educated, professor."

He grinned, then stuck his hands in his blond hair; a gesture similar to Nik's when he was ruffled. "Teacher—I'm just an old teacher."

Mary Alice left the room with a wink for him. "Not that old."

Etta shook her head. She hadn't let go of Sam. "She probably doesn't even know she's flirting, Sam."

Sam patted her hand. "Etta, you know I would never touch a child."

Etta trusted him. Nevertheless when she was helping Mary Alice set the table for seven in the main dining room, she cautioned her little sister. "Don't tease men. The Lord has made you beautiful for a reason."

Mary Alice held a butter knife in midair. "Sam's like an uncle to me."

"There are fewer years between you two than between Steffen and Bernie."

Mary Alice skipped to the next place setting. "You think he'll wait for me to get through college?"

"I didn't mean to encourage you."

"Hey, sister, what's good enough for you might do well by me too."

"Oh stop!" Etta held her hand over the place where she was receiving a serious kicking bout from her expectant child. "My baby's kicking me around the table."

Mary Alice leaned over her bump to embrace her. "The Lord works his wonders."

Etta joined the rest of the crew in the family room, finding the most comfortable chair had been reserved for her use.

Bernie was filling out some legal paperwork. "Your father's interrogation will be held at the Milan prison hospital this Friday. Etta, do you think you would want to come?"

"I'll be there, unless my baby has other ideas."

Mary Alice sat on the arm of Bernie's chair. "Is Mother very angry about Dad being taken to the prison?"

"I did talk to her." Bernie patted Mary Alice's knee. "She's not sure your father knows where he is from all the pain medications. She would like you and Etta to visit more often. The boys miss you both."

Etta knew who else Mary Alice wanted to hear about. "Jean?"

Bernie nodded. "She's renting your old trailer, by herself. She told your mother she's been living in a sea of humanity for nine years and would like to find out who she is by living alone for a time.

"My idea of nothing to do," Steffen said. He no longer seemed so pale. Another healthy sign was that Mary Alice had stopped following him around as if he might fall over any minute. "Nik, what's for supper?"

"Stuffed shells with three cheeses and spinach." Nik's tone got silly with pomposity, "As well as a bean dish of corn and garlic."

Juno applauded. "Girls, what about a shower for Bernie?"

Bernie shook her head. "At my age, that's ridiculous."

"See, boys," Steffen said. "I told you I was too old."

"For the wedding? You want to call it off?" Bernie stood, forcing Mary Alice to stand too.

Steffen held out his arm to have her sit back down on the love seat. "No, no. The stupid bachelor party. If you're not going to have a shower, I ... I ..."

Mary Alice jumped to his side. "Is it your heart?"

Steffen laughed, and they all relaxed. "I was trying to find a Lincoln quote, and my head is emptied of all his words."

* * *

Milan Prison
Friday, April 19

Please, Lord, Bernie prayed earnestly, *Allow this family peace and understanding of each other, if it be Your will.'*

Fourteen-year-old Bob had stayed home with his brothers, Dick and Ben. In the jammed room, behind privacy glass, Jean was seated in the front row next to her mother. Bernie was in the front row too, holding tightly to Mary Alice's left hand. Etta held her right hand. In the stadium-like viewing room, Juno, Steffen, Beth Ann Zhang, and Judge Wilson sat on a higher level directly behind them. Nik and Sam—along with several reporters and television cameras—were crowded into the back row of seats.

The male prison nurse attendants wheeled in the cart with Jimmy Lee propped up nearly in a seated position. Joe Wilcox, his lawyer-friend throughout the years, seemed harried and exhausted.

Bernie spoke into the microphone first, "Mr. Wilcox, does your client wish to make a statement?"

Jimmy looked into the mirror, which he probably knew shielded his family from his view. He passed a hand over what was left of his hair. Bernie thought she heard Jean gasp. Mary Alice clung to Bernie's hand, pulling her closer to her side. Etta patted her other hand.

"I believe my Maker requires me to confess." Jimmy's voice was nearly a whisper, but they could hear him clearly enough. "First I told you all the lie that I could have moved into Mother's house on Washtenaw as soon as Father died. It wasn't true. He despised me and was sure I would not be able to pay even the taxes on the house. I always hated Mother for not taking us in and wanting more and more grandchildren."

Bernie saw Ricky stiffen.

Jimmy continued. "Mary Alice and Etta were leery of me from birth, but Jean loved me, I think." Jimmy started to cough, and one of the male nurses helped him take a sip of water. Jimmy argued with him about letting more morphine into his intravenous drip.

Juno said, "He'll pass out if they give him too much."

"So," Jimmy waved at the mirror as if to wash away his deeds. "I told Jean all the stories I could about my mother's lavish expenditures, while we had barely enough to feed everyone. Of course I explained the house would be ours if anything sinister happened to Mother. I frightened all the neighbors and Ricky about rats infecting the trailer park. Jean did borrow rat poison from Mrs. Staples—or was it Mrs. Spradlin? I don't remember which now. I even suggested that Mother took so many pills she might overdose herself someday, and we would have enough room for everyone. I didn't see Jean change the powder in Mother's pills, but I made sure Etta was the daughter to find Mother dead that Sunday. I even told Jean to clean up the table so people wouldn't think Mother kept a dirty house. I was hoping Jean would get community service; she was so young to commit a murder. I am sorry she had to spend nine years in prison, but I didn't really want her home. I was afraid I had created a psychopath who might turn on me."

Jean broke down, and Ricky ushered her out of the viewing room. Jimmy was wheeled out. Mr. Wilcox followed him, looking even older than a few minutes before.

Bernie turned to Mary Alice. "Are you able to forgive your sister now?"

Mary Alice stood up and faced the small gathering, as if ready to make a statement to the press. "My Savior requires us to forgive those who sin against us. My grandmother was taken away from us by her own son, who used my sister's weaknesses. I do forgive them, but I'm not stupid enough to overlook Jean's ability to kill a person I loved. Don't anyone forget that Grandmother favored Jean above the rest of us. Jean killed a person she knew loved her. I don't want to be called the sister of anyone who could manage that, even if she had been five years old. I was six and knew better."

One of the reporters stepped forward as if to ask a question.

Bernie said, "That's all for now. The Lee family has suffered enough. The truth has finally been told. We'll all try to move on."

* * *

St. Andrew's Episcopal Church
Saturday, May 4

Halfway down the aisle, Bernie noticed Steffen was swaying slightly. His son, Sam, nudged his shoulder, and Steffen perked up, holding out his hand as Bernie climbed the tiled steps to greet him. Mary Alice and Etta wore long shimmering yellow gowns. Juno—her maid-of-honor in a lime green dress to complement her red hair—lifted Bernie's veil and removed the bouquet of yellow roses she'd been gripping as if they were a life-line to get her down the aisle.

Reverend Nieman's words were repeated by both of them, and then they stood for the photographer's dictates before adjourning through a line of well-wishers to the parish hall in the basement of the church. It was when she was cutting the cake that Bernie noticed Steffen's ears were bright red.

"Are we embarrassing you?" she asked.

"I'm overwhelmed with happiness," he said, poking at his chest in what was becoming a sweet habit.

Bernie took Steffen away from the crowd as soon as she could, whispering to Juno, "We're going home to rest up for our honeymoon."

"I thought you were staying home," Juno whispered back.

Bernie winked. "We are."

PART III

Three Years Later

CHAPTER 19

Burns Park Home
Three Year Anniversary

"Wake up, sleepy head." Bernie stretched her arms over her head, kicked off the covers, and straightened her legs, toes wiggling and reaching for the ceiling. She'd had a great anniversary party in bed with Steffen last night. He seemed so driven to please her, so she had teased him. "Hey, we can do this again tomorrow."

A sudden chill made her pull the covers back up to her neck.

"Steffen?" He was really sound asleep.

The birds were greeting the full-blown day.

She craned her neck to check the digital clock. 7:52.

"It's almost eight. We need to get moving, Steffen. Steffen?"

Well if he was going to be lazy, so was she. She rolled over and cuddled into her pillows, but the smell of coffee tempted her. She slipped out of bed. When she returned from her shower, he still hadn't budged from his side of the bed.

She pulled her terrycloth robe tighter and slipped on a pair of socks for the hike downstairs to the kitchen. Thankfully, Steffen had rigged the coffee pot up with a timer to make sure they would be greeted each morning with a full pot.

Finches were attacking the bird feeder hanging off the patio in force, while a female cardinal ate what they dropped as her mate stood watch.

Feeling guilty for finishing her cup without him, Bernie trudged back upstairs with two full mugs. She sat the blue cups down on his bedside table. "Coffee, big guy. Are you ever going to wake up?"

She nudged his shoulder, brushed his unruly hair away from his face, and saw his eyes were open. Fixed. His smile lingered on her favorite face.

But he was gone!

"Steffen, oh Steffen, not yet. Don't leave me alone."

Collapsing on the floor next to him, she held his cold hand, pressed it to her face, and smelled a trace of Old Spice.

She heard a keening far away, growing louder and louder, but she couldn't stop it. Salty tears ran into her mouth. She choked, but the sound kept increasing as if she could rouse him back from the other side.

Mary Alice was pulling her to her feet, but Bernie couldn't hear what she was asking because of the loud shouts coming from her own throat. She put a hand over her mouth so she could listen to her young friend.

"He's with the Lord, Bernie. You'll be all right."

"No," Bernie said. "No." But at least she'd stopped yelling.

"Come downstairs," Mary Alice said. "Etta is calling Nik. He is teaching an early golf lesson. We'll wait in the living ... " She coughed. "Downstairs. Wait with me." She continued talking as Bernie let herself be led out of the bedroom, down the circular stairs, and into the front room. "We could hear you on the third floor. Susan started whimpering from the noise, so Etta said they'd stay upstairs. Can I bring you coffee?"

Seated on the comfortable loveseat, Bernie pulled her robe closer to her. "I should dress."

A detached calm descended. "I left Steffen's coffee on his bedside table. Mine's up there too. You could nuke them if they're cold. Steffen didn't touch his."

Mary Alice's face was very wet when she placed Bernie's hand on her cheek. "The Lord will ease your pain. We'll get through this together." She restored Bernie's hand to her lap. "Let me call Juno."

"I don't think Juno can help Steffen now," Bernie said. "He must have passed in his sleep. Did you see the smile on his face?" A blackness filled her mind, and she could feel the comfort of fainting. *At least I'm sitting down,* she told herself, and she let her head fall back against the couch.

Juno was shaking her shoulders, but Bernie fought to stay in the dark, peaceful place where her brain felt no pain. Juno wouldn't give up, so Bernie reached for Steffen's comforting words: "'I felt, that for (us) now to meet face to face and converse together was the best way to efface any remnant of unpleasant feeling, if any such existed.[34]'"

"She's quoting Lincoln," Mary Alice said.

"He comforted my brother when he was grieving." Juno scooted next to Bernie. "Bernie will stop when she's able to."

"The Lord wants me to live alone?"

* * *

Mary Alice climbed the back stairs to Etta's third-floor apartment in Bernie's house. Her three-year-old niece, Susan, was happily playing with a miniature wooden train set Steffen had insisted she needed.

Etta, still a head taller than Mary Alice, wrapped her arms around her younger sister. "How are we going to survive without Nik's Dad?"

Mary Alice fought for composure. "Could you wait downstairs with Aunt Juno for Sam and Nik to get home?" She sat on the floor and put the toy train back on its wooden tracks.

Susan came over and hugged her. "Do you have a booboo?"

Mary Alice inhaled the shampoo scent in the baby's black hair. "Aunty will be better soon with all these hugs." She stood up to talk to Etta. "I need to help Bernie get dressed in my room."

"Let me take Susan down to Aunt Juno, then I'll come with you to get clothes for Bernie out of their bedroom. We're going to need gallons of coffee. Can you start the thirty-cup pot that's under the corner cupboard?"

Mary Alice was grateful for a sister who understood the situation better than she did. Seeing Steffen's body by herself might be too much

---

[34] See note 4. IBID

for her. He'd been her friend—more than a friend. Steffen was the father she never really had. He valued her and accepted her foibles. No one on earth knew her as well as Steffen Blaine. Now this loving man of integrity was gone.

She dragged out the large coffee pot, clanked it into the stainless-steel sink, and filled it with water. It was heavier than she'd thought when she tried to lift it onto the counter.

Sam, Steffen's oldest, touched her elbow. "Let me help."

She turned and threw her arms around his neck. "Oh, Sam."

He stroked her hair until she realized he was sobbing too.

She pulled away slightly and wiped his face with a dish towel. "This pot is too heavy for me to lift."

He pulled her close again, and she could smell his father's favorite Old Spice cologne. Then he stepped to the side and looked at the coffee pot. "We might as well empty it. We'll need the coffee downstairs, right?"

"Okay." She watched him empty the fool thing. "Can you come with me. Your dad is still on the bed, and I need to find clothes for Bernie to wear."

Nik and Etta came up the back stairs. Nik knelt down next to the kitchen table; he held out his hand to Mary Alice. "Could we pray for Bernie's strength?"

Mary Alice knelt next to one of the red-bottomed metal chairs.

Etta placed her Bible on the matching chair. "Lord, we come to You in this time of need. Bring us through this trial praising Your holy name."

Sam picked up the Bible and randomly chose a page to read. "Isaiah 10:3, 'And what will ye do in the day of visitation, and in the desolation which shall come from far? To whom will ye flee for help? And where will ye leave your glory? His hand is stretched out still.'"

Nik and Sam embraced. Sam was a taller than Nik, just like Etta was taller than Mary Alice. Aunt Juno watched Susan on the first floor while the four of them entered the second floor's master bedroom.

Etta opened the windows, although Mary Alice couldn't smell anything untoward.

After Nik changed out of his golf-pro outfit, the boys dressed their dad for the undertaker while Etta and Mary Alice picked out several outfits for Bernie to wear.

After Mary Alice straightened the covers in her bedroom across the hall at the front of the house, Etta arranged Bernie's clothes on the spread. "Should I disturb the boys to get a suitcase so Bernie can stay with Juno for a few days?"

"Use my suitcase," Mary Alice said. "We should probably not interrupt them right now."

After they packed Bernie's belongings, Jean followed Mary Alice down the back stairwell.

Facing the family room's blank television, Nik said, "Aunt Juno cautioned us not to bother Bernie with too many questions right now."

Etta was pouring the coffee Sam had started. She extended a fragrant cup to Mary Alice.

"We're waiting for the funeral director," Sam said, pulling Mary Alice to his side on the couch. "There are no good options."

Aunt Juno came into the kitchen, holding Susan on her hip. "The hospital says since we can't determine the time of death, his organs can't be donated."

"I think Steffen should be cremated," Mary Alice said. "Should we ask Bernie?"

"Tomorrow will show up soon enough for that decision," Sam said.

Mary Alice leaned her head on Sam's shoulder. He placed his hand on her cheek, then brushed her hair behind her ear. If she hadn't met Bernie—because she hated having her hair cut—Mary Alice would never have met Sam. Steffen was the investigator of her grandmother's death, so maybe they would have seen each other then. But if Bernie hadn't taken her in when she couldn't return to her mother's house, they might have only passed by each other—never felt the love they shared.

"I've always relied on Bernie's good sense," Mary Alice said.

Aunt Juno set Susan on Nik's lap. "You might need to trust your own resources while Bernie comes to grips with losing my brother." As she walked back into the front room to check on Bernie, Juno's shoulders shook with sobs.

Mary Alice started to get up, but Sam drew her next to him. "I need you too."

* * *

First Presbyterian Montieth Hall
May 15, Steffen Blaine's Memorial Service

A flock of twenty birds flew past the upper section of the window behind the altar. Mary Alice's attention was drawn back to the alabaster jar holding Steffen's ashes, placed in the middle of a delicate lace cloth which draped the communion table.

Sam and Nik were holding up better than she had expected. Their newly-purchased black suits complemented their broad shoulders. They sat on either side of Bernie, who looked presentable dressed in the requisite black dress. Her hair was perfect and her make-up sparse, but the shock seemed to baffle her.

Sam rose and told the gathered crowd, "I didn't know my father was at risk. We will take his love to our own graves."

Nik's turn was performed by Etta, who said, "This gentle man filled our lives with his love and integrity. The Lord has called him home, and we dreadfully miss his comfort."

Bernie rose as if to speak, but did not turn to the audience. Instead, facing Steffen's remains, she quoted Lincoln, "What was their process of reasoning, I can only judge from what no single one of them told me. But I believe they all could have said, 'We are not to do evil that good may come.[35]'"

For her own grief, Mary Alice turned her confusion toward the Lord. Of course death was not an unusual occurrence, but she poignantly remembered each time Steffen had looked ill, or touched his chest when his emotions ran high. He no longer quoted Lincoln when he was troubled, but his sentiments cost him more energy than was normal. His heart wasn't made of cold substance, and he perished too soon.

---

[35] See Note 1.

Sheriff Beth Ann Zhang walked briskly to the front. She stared at Steffen's remains for a few minutes, which seemed to stretch out to a half hour. Then she moved in front of Bernie. A deep red line between her thick eyebrows telegraphed an outburst was forthcoming.

Mary Alice rose to her feet and attempted to move between the two women.

"Why didn't you let me see him for one last time?" The sheriff slapped Bernie before Mary Alice realized her intent. "You knew I loved him too."

Nik and Sam seized the unstable, grieving woman's arms and walked her toward the exit. That's when Mary Alice noticed her mother and brothers had attended. She looked briefly for Jean, but rather hoped she wouldn't need to speak to her.

Juno Blaine stood and addressed the mourners. "We all grieve in different ways with various stages of denial, anger, acceptance and sadness. My brother's affections were experienced personally by many of you. Thank you for coming."

Mary Alice put her arm around Bernie's waist. "We'll go home now."

Bernie breathed deeply before saying, "We shall have no split or trouble about the matter; all will be harmony.[36]"

Mary Alice could taste blood from biting her lips. Patience had never been a quality she possessed. She shook her head at Sam when he returned after depositing the sheriff—in a garbage can she hoped!

"Nik says to ask the Lord to forgive people when you are not able to understand them."

He gripped her hand and helped her lead a distracted Bernie to Steffen's Honda.

---

[36] See Note 3.

CHAPTER 20

Washtenaw County Sheriff's Office
May 16

She could have faced Sherriff Zhang's wrath by herself, but Bernie appreciated Mary Alice's support—even if her young friend disagreed about this trip to apologize. "There is no dispute as to the facts. The dispute is confined altogether to the inferences to be drawn from these facts. It is a difference not about the facts, but about the conclusions.[37]"

Mary Alice shook her head as she locked the Honda's doors.

Bernie tried to sound lighthearted. "I know, I know. I gave Steffen such a rough time when he quoted poor old Lincoln to help him get a grip. Why do you think quoting the lines I memorized helps me?"

"Your mind demands you switch your attention away from emotional turmoil." Mary Alice held the heavy door of the building open. "I'm sure praying or reading the Bible allows the same remedy but taps into the source of all life too."

Bernie hugged Mary Alice's shoulders. "Thanks for coming. This may not be pleasant. I do need to make amends to the poor woman. Beth Ann misses Steffen too."

Walking down the long hall to the sheriff's office, Mary Alice slackened her pace. She was hanging her head the way she did when she was six. Her long bangs and soft hair nearly hid her saddened face. "We will never stop missing him."

---

[37] See Note 7.

Bernie's stomach pain prompted her to send a plea. *Lord, give us strength for the day, mercy to our friends, and peace that surpasses understanding.*

Sheriff Beth Ann Zhang had her back to the wall of windows which faced the inner hall. When Bernie tapped lightly on the open door, the sheriff's shoulders slumped. She raised one hand to touch her greying short hair before turning toward them.

"Beth Ann," Bernie gulped at the tragic sight before her. "I came to apologize. Is there anything I can do?"

Mary Alice sat down in one of the chairs facing Beth Ann's metal desk.

The upholstery had been changed from purple to a soft-textured bright blue. The mirrors with the Van Gogh irises were gone. Now the walls were painted a cheery shade of yellow.

Beth Ann pulled out her desk chair and sat down. "I need to apologize too. I am sorry I made a spectacle of myself at Steffen's ..."

"Memorial service," Mary Alice provided.

"I knew you loved him too." Bernie took it upon herself to fix them all a cup of tea at Beth Ann's credenza. "Lincoln would have told you, 'If (I) have been out of order in what I (did) or said, I take it all back so far as I can. I have no desire, I assure you all, ever to be out of order – though I never could keep long in order.[38]'"

Bernie removed the tea bags, serving Mary Alice and the sheriff, before she gripped her own cup and sat down to listen. The fragrance of the tea calmed her a bit.

"She's taken to quoting Lincoln?" Beth Ann asked Mary Alice, as if Bernie had suddenly disappeared from the room.

"You're both grieving," Mary Alice said. "Anger." She actually pointed at the sheriff, then she flipped the back of her hand toward Bernie. "And denial."

"I know he's gone," Bernie said. "The waves of panic are filled with Lincoln's words. I hear them in Steffen's voice."

---

[38] See Note 5.

A beat of silence invaded the room. There were no words to fill the void Steffen left, no explanations, no prayers to bring him back, no answers. Except for one. Bernie knew with her entire being that the Lord knew what she was feeling and had not left her side. "I'm not alone."

"You mean Steffen's spirit is with you?" Mary Alice asked in a tone of rising alarm.

"No." Bernie patted her arm. "I mean the Lord has not abandoned me."

"I'd been calling Steffen," Beth Ann said. "In the last two weeks. We were both concerned ..."

"About his health?" Mary Alice half rose from her chair, but Bernie reached over to calm her back down.

Beth Ann shook her head. "There has been an unusual death at St. Joseph's continued care facility."

"How unusual?" Mary Alice asked.

"Your sister, Jean." Beth Ann pushed a case file toward Bernie. "She applied for a job at St. Joe's, but was turned down."

Mary Alice scooted back into her chair. "How is it possible children of the same parentage turn out so differently?"

"Jean's father took special care to turn Jean away from loving others," Sheriff Beth Ann said. "I remember his confession."

"Did Steffen start an investigation?" Bernie asked. "He never mentioned anything."

"I'm not sure he took my calls seriously." Beth Ann swiped at her bangs. "I asked him if he was happy in his marriage."

"You came on to him?" Mary Alice stormed out of her chair, banging her untouched tea onto Beth Ann's desk and splashing its contents onto several files.

Bernie calmly went back to the sideboard for some much-needed paper towels to wipe up the mess.

Beth Ann helped her find a fresh roll of towels behind the credenza's lower sliding door. She blocked Bernie's return to her desk. "Steffen said he hadn't thought the Lord loved him enough to reward him with all the happiness his marriage to you had brought him."

"Thank you, Beth Ann." Bernie reached for the sheriff's shoulder, but she stepped away from the offered comfort.

Mary Alice helped clean up the spilled tea. "Do you want us to go out to the hospital for you?"

Bernie said, "I believe it was Shakespeare who said, 'Where the offense lies, there let the axe fall.[39]'"

Beth Ann and Mary Alice only stared in her direction.

"I could take her with me," Mary Alice said. "She does have the detective's license."

"Steffen always said you were a natural, Mary Alice," Beth Ann said. "With better instincts than himself."

"I'm right here," Bernie said. "Why are you mentioning me in the third person?"

"Because," Mary Alice said, leading her outside to Steffen's Honda. "You have decided to withdraw into Lincoln's black world."

* * *

Burns Park Home

After Bernie agreed she needed a nap before lunch, Mary Alice called Sam to see if he could join them for tomato soup and grilled cheese sandwiches. "Sheriff Zhang gave Bernie and me a suspicious-death case to work on. Jean might be involved."

Sam was there in a heartbeat. "No school today. Have you told Etta or your mother?"

Mary Alice shook her head. "Need to find out more before I do." She poured their soup, adding the mugs to the luncheon arrangement at the kitchen counter, then came around to where he was sitting on one of the stools.

Steffen held out his arms, and she stepped into his embrace. He rubbed her shoulder with one hand and tipped her head up. "Am I too old for you, do you think?"

---

[39] See Note 19.

Mary Alice put her arms around his neck. "Only if you think I'm too ugly for you."

"You?" He laughed and kissed her mouth. "You sweeten my dreams." He kissed her left eyelid. "You let me hold onto hope." He kissed her right eyelid. "You make me thank the Lord for being near you every day."

Mary Alice kissed his cheek. "We'll be all right then." Then she claimed his mouth.

Bernie coughed at the entrance of the kitchen. "Kissing in the kitchen is allowed."

"I thought you were napping?" Mary Alice scurried to add another placemat and food to the counter.

"Tell me about Zhang's new case." Sam helped Bernie pull up her heavy wooden stool.

Mary Alice bowed her head. "Bless us our Lord, and these Thy gifts which we are about to receive."

"I read the file. Seems a woman at St. Joe's was about to be sent home," Bernie tasted her soup. "But she died during the night."

Sam looked at Mary Alice as he chewed his first bite of grilled cheese. "Tomato in the sandwich, too. How is Jean involved?"

"Zhang said she applied for a job at St. Joe's as a nurse's aide but they turned her down because of her record." Mary Alice wasn't as hungry as she thought she was. "How do you recognize evil and faked redemption?"

"Only the Lord really knows," Sam said.

Bernie was stirring her soup. She hadn't touched her sandwich. "If (she) can not or will not (confess), if on any pretense or no pretense (she) shall refuse or omit it, then you should be fully convinced of what I more than suspect already—that (she) is deeply conscious of being in the wrong and that (she) feels the blood of (her grandmother) like the blood of Abel, crying to heaven against (her).[40]"

Sam tipped his head at Bernie. "Would Dad approve of you using Lincoln now?"

---

[40] See Note 2.

Mary Alice chose to ignore Bernie's affliction. "Psychopaths can decide to mimic socially acceptable behaviors. And, Bernie, you need to eat something before we go."

Bernie stuck her tongue out. Mary Alice and Sam couldn't help but laugh.

* * *

St. Joseph's Assisted Living Facility

Bernie showed her detective's license to the receptionist just inside the front door. "These are my assistants. My stepson, Sam Blaine, and Mary Alice Lee. We'd like to speak to the manager."

The blonde focused her attention on Sam. "What shall I say is the nature of your visit?"

"The investigation into the latest death to occur here." Bernie raised her voice and purposefully nodded to several of the residents and their family members in the posh lobby.

They were quickly ushered down the hall to a spacious office with floor-to-ceiling windows facing a well-kept courtyard garden. The receptionist left them without taking time to make the necessary introductions.

A kindly-looking beauty with masses of brownish-auburn hair stood as the skittish receptionist exited.

"We are looking for the manager." Bernie checked to see if Sam realized the attractiveness of the woman before them.

"I am Sister Mary-Louise Strafford." She motioned toward the small, tan couches arranged in a half circle in front of her undersized desk. The scent of lemon oil testified to the cause of its gleaming dust-free surface. "How may I help you?"

"Give her your card," Mary Alice said.

After handing over her identification, Bernie regained her voice and professionalism and pointed to the couple on the couch. "My assistants, Sam Blaine and Mary Alice Lee."

"You are here because I called Beth Ann when Mrs. Kerner passed," Sister Strafford said. "I expected Steffen Blaine. Your father, Sam? I did read his obituary. So sorry for your bereavement and for all of our loss of a good man."

Bernie could feel the wave of hurt swelling in her breast. "No (woman) can be silent if (she) would. You are compelled to speak; and your only alternative is to tell the truth or lie. I cannot doubt which you would do.[41]"

Sister Strafford kept her seat behind her desk.

Sam tried to explain Bernie's strange outburst. "Bernie is Steffen's widow. My father quoted Lincoln whenever his emotions threatened to overtake his reason. My stepmother has assumed his bad habit."

"It is," Bernie admitted.

Mary Alice returned to their task. "Was Mrs. Kerner scheduled to go home? Did she live by herself?"

"She did," Sister Strafford said. "We had her interview several of the volunteers from hospice to help her at home, but after the last one talked to her, she insisted she didn't need anyone."

Mary Alice hung her head, as if anticipating the answer to the next obvious question.

So Sam asked it: "What was the name of the last hospice applicant?"

"Jean Lee," Sister Strafford said. "Did you say your name was Lee?"

"I did," Mary Alice said. "Do you know what the conversation between the two covered?"

Sister Strafford nodded. "When I left them together, Mrs. Kerner was describing the abundant number of medications she needed to keep track of."

"Sheriff Zhang said Jean Lee applied as a nurses' aide in your facility." Bernie twisted her watchband so she could read the time.

"I'm not aware of her application, but I do remember Marie Lee's death and her granddaughter's false imprisonment. However St. Joseph's does not hire felons, even if they have been paroled."

"Hospice does?" Sam asked.

---

[41] See Note 15.

"I don't know their policy," Sister Stafford said. "I will say when I recognized Jean, I didn't prevent her from interviewing for the job of taking care of Mrs. Kerner. So there would not have been continued rancor on Jean's part, if that's what you are implying."

"My sister keeps long grudges," Mary Alice said.

Bernie asked, "May we see Mrs. Kerner's old room? Did she leave any belongings behind?"

"I'm afraid her room is already occupied. Mrs. Kerner was buried in our cemetery two—no, three weeks ago." Sister Strafford undid a barrette holding her hair to the side. She shook it forward and then replaced the clip. "We do have a file system set up to keep belongings, other than clothing and medications, for the relatives. After a year, if no one claims them, we donate everything to charity. Let me have someone take you to the storage area."

A less attractive, portly woman escorted them to a basement area lined with steel shelves holding dozens labeled boxes. "They are all in alphabetical order," the sister said. "Mrs. Kerner's box will be in aisle eleven."

Sam pulled the box off the third shelf in the long passageway. "Antoinette Kerner?"

"We only had one Mrs. Kerner," Sister said. "There's a table near the door. Call me when you are finished." She smiled a once-winsome smile at Sam. "You can help me lift it back in place."

Sam cut the tape on the box, opening it before stepping away for Mary Alice and Bernie to go through the items.

Bernie handed the daily devotional books to Mary Alice. Four albums of family pictures, a harmonica, two empty ring boxes, a small glass globe with a white daisy inside, and a diary comprised Antoinette's relics.

Bernie flipped to the last entry in Mrs. Kerner's diary. It read, "When I used the bathroom, that stinker stole all four of my rings. No one is going to believe me. I don't care. At least I get to go home tomorrow. Thank you, Lord, for restoring me to good health."

Bernie handed the journal to Sam, who read it quickly and gave it to Mary Alice. "I'll have Beth Ann issue a warrant for the diary. We probably need to have Antoinette's body exhumed too."

As they passed Sister Stafford's office, Mary Alice's voice broke as she said, "We'll be back."

* * *

Sam's Lorraine Street Condo

'Bernie knocked hard on Sam's door. It was after ten o'clock at night but she couldn't sleep. The picture of Mary Alice kissing Sam kept reappearing as soon as she shut her eyes.

"Bernie," Sam buttoned the top of his jeans. "Is Mary Alice okay? Come in, come in."

"Coffee?" Bernie wrapped and unwrapped the apricot scarf matching her sweater. "I needed to come."

Sam hit a button on his coffee pot and dug two cups out of the cupboard. "The living room is more comfortable," he said, as Bernie started to pull out a kitchen chair in the dinette.

"Fine," Bernie couldn't think of what was so urgent. Why had she needed to drive over from Burns Park? "I parked out front. Is that okay?"

"Of course, Bernie." He handed her a cup of coffee and watched as she sipped it, slowly trying to assemble words in her scrambled brain.

"I miss your father."

"I know." Sam sat quietly.

Did he realize how soothing his silent presence was? "I want to talk about your kissing Mary Alice."

"I understand," he said. "I am much older."

"Your father was twenty years older than me. I wish someone had had the sense to tell me to hurry up and marry him. I wasted ten years worrying about my career goals." Bernie purposefully went to the place in her brain where Lincoln held sway. "…besides this open attempt to prove by telling the truth what (I) could not prove by telling the whole truth. So that I cannot be silent if I would.[42]"

"And what are you trying to tell me?"

"He died." Lincoln was of no help now.

Sam merely nodded.

"I could have been with him … longer." Sam didn't respond to the significant statement. "Marry her before you squander one more moment."

Sam took her cup from her, pulled her to her feet and hugged her. "I thought you were here to tell me to stop seeing Mary Alice. You want me to marry her! I'll do it tomorrow." He swung her around the room, the way Steffen had twirled her behind old Mr. Prettenhoffer's trailer.

Bernie was sobbing uncontrollably when he set her down.

"Oh, Bernie. I'm sorry. Did I hurt you?"

"I miss him," she managed. "Maybe you should drive me home and propose to Mary Alice."

"I can do that." He looked at his jeans. "I wanted to be more romantic."

Bernie grasped his meaning. "But you won't wait six months."

"I promise," he said.

Appeased by his response, Bernie drove home. She'd done her best to move the couple toward marriage. Why hadn't Juno pushed a little harder? Then Bernie remembered Juno had their invitations printed before Bernie had set her wedding date. "My fault," she told the Lord. "I wanted to prove myself to Steffen. Love has nothing to do with competition."

---

[42] See Note 6.

CHAPTER 21

Washtenaw Sheriff's Office
June 15

Mary Alice assumed Beth Ann had called them in to review the evidence of Mrs. Kerner's death. Sweet old Sam had to work or he would have come with them. He wanted to marry her as soon as she would set the date. Bernie was pushing too. Of course Mary Alice understood. Steffen's loss made all of life's passages urgent.

Bernie had been a widow for only six weeks, but she seemed happier. She still wept at the drop of a hat, or fork for that matter. At least she was taking more care with her clothes, worrying about a slight weight gain, and fussing with her beautiful hair. Perfection didn't erase her sorrow.

Sheriff Beth Ann met them at her office door. "Two more."

Mary Alice and Bernie looked at each other before following her into her office.

"Two more seniors died?" Bernie asked.

"A couple, married forty-five years, in their home. Various hospice personnel are being investigated, including Jean Lee. We need to know their whereabouts the night of the murders."

"You're sure they were murdered?" Mary Alice asked. "How old were they?"

"Mrs. Kerner's autopsy said arsenic," Beth Ann plopped into her chair.

Mary Alice pulled out her iPad. "Four of Mrs. Kerner's rings were stolen. Have you searched Jean's trailer. What could have been the motive for the couple?"

"Sorry, what were the victims' names?" Bernie asked. "Could I ask for a cup of Earl Grey?"

"Losing my manners as well as my mind," Sheriff Beth Ann said. "Carl and Martha Brandt." The sheriff read the file's label before opening it and pushing it toward Bernie." She stood and busied herself with the tea as they scanned the details.

"Any children?" Mary Alice asked.

"Nine," Bernie read from the file. "Could we ask a member of the family to accompany us to their home, to see if anything is missing?"

"The oldest, Johnny, compiled a list." Beth Ann pulled a yellow legal sheet out of the file. "The thief was thorough. No heavy items. Most of the jewelry and cash would fit in a small bag or purse."

"Hospice workers carry a first-aid kit, don't they?" Mary Alice surveyed the list.

"You have a warrant for me?" Bernie closed the file before sipping her tea. "Beth Ann, could you visit the hospice office and ask them to put Jean on leave until we solve who is targeting older people?"

"Why not arrest her now?" Mary Alice insisted. "Before she hurts anyone else."

"We haven't linked her conclusively to any of the deaths. The prosecutor would laugh me out of the office."

* * *

Brandt Residence
Scio Church Road

Bernie loved the place as soon as Mary Alice turned into the tree-lined drive. Not much grass existed between the evergreens littering the front lawn. "They lived in a forest."

Built of rectangular tan stones, the house could have been situated in any European city. When they opened the front oak door, the stained-glass windows shone glory on the well-oiled wooden floors.

"Wow," Mary Alice said. "I thought your house was beautiful."

"Our house. After all these years, don't you feel at home there?"

"Sam's condo will be all right."

Bernie wanted to nail her down on a wedding date but knew her young friend too well. Pushing would achieve no result.

"What are we looking for?" Mary Alice headed for the dining room, which functioned as a library since every available wall space held bookshelves crammed to overflowing. "Look! The books are double shelved. Each shelf has two rows of books."

"Good people," Bernie said. "Books sell freedom, and freedom begets affection."

"That wasn't a Lincoln quote."

"Nope, just my own ramblings." Bernie held her stomach. "I wonder if all widows get nauseated as easily as I do."

Mary Alice pulled down a book by James Joyce. "Only if they are pregnant."

Bernie gasped.

Mary Alice turned around just as Bernie headed for the nearest chair.

She put her head down between her knees. "I'm too old."

"Forty-three is too old to get pregnant?" Mary Alice knelt down next to her. "I'll buy one of those test packages, if you're too embarrassed."

"On the way home," Bernie said. "Let's tend to business. So you are pretty sure the thief doesn't read."

"Not one empty space." Mary Alice surveyed the room. "Do you think each of the nine children has their own libraries?"

"If they were brought up right." Bernie pointed to a dark doorway at the far end of the dining room. "Let's have a look at the kitchen."

Straight out of the eighteenth century, the black stove, red pump on the skirted sink, and benched table could have been the complete set of an Amish movie.

"Someone loved antiques to a fault," Mary Alice said.

The bedrooms upstairs sported homemade quilts, a spinning wheel for show, and lace-covered dressers. Chairs were hung on the wall, in the Amish fashion. The bathroom was jarringly modern with a washer and dryer in the attached closet.

"I smell kitty litter," Bernie said. "Wonder where the cat is."

"Would a thief steal a cat?"

"Maybe a lonely one," Bernie said, thinking of Jean alone in the Lee's old trailer.

* * *

Sam's Lorraine Street Condo

Mary Alice ran her fingers through Sam's blond hair. "I need to concentrate on nailing Jean to the inside of some prison."

Sam shoulders slumped. "Bernie claimed her career goals helped her procrastinate too."

"You are not sixty-three years old."

"Dad was fifty when they met. Bernie told me she made a mistake in not marrying Dad sooner. She intends for us to marry quickly."

Mary Alice tried a new tactic. "Maybe our grief makes us think we're in love."

"What! Don't be ridiculous. You love me, you idiot." Sam stormed around the room, kicking a hassock and fluffing a pillow with entirely too much vigor. "Don't you want to start a family?"

"I want to marry you." Her words sounded lame.

"But not now." Sam stood stock still. "By Christmas?"

"We'll probably start the new year together."

"Probably?" Sam sank onto the couch. "I can't take it, Mary Alice. I'm not made of stone."

She went to him to embrace him, but he pushed her away. Why was he being so pig-headed? "I'll call you later."

"Don't bother." He said the two words too softly.

She didn't want to believe him. "Don't bother?"

"Call me when you've decided on a date."

"That's ridiculous.'

"So sue me." His eyes flashed.

Mary Alice moved to the door, wanting him to stop her. "We need each other."

"I don't want to be your lap dog," Sam said. "I want to marry you."

So she left, slamming the door to make her point. What, that she was gone? She loved him. She stood on the stoop for a minute then turned to Bernie's Honda.

It was all Bernie's fault. If she hadn't interfered and insisted they marry immediately, Sam would have let their relationship take a more natural course before a wedding was even mentioned.

Why was she so adamant about putting her sister behind bars?

And then she knew—if she were married, her happiness would wipe out some of her resentments toward her sister for dragging the Lee name through the mud again. *What shall I do Lord? I love him, but Jean has to be stopped.*

* * *

Burns Park House

Bernie heard Mary Alice stomp up the stairs. Sam must have pushed her to set a wedding date. She should have told him to be subtle. Mary Alice would not pick up a spoon to eat her own soup if you made a point of demanding she do it.

Maybe she could wait until morning to find out what happened, but Bernie had never been called a coward. *Lord, be a guide to my tongue. Help me find words of understanding.*

Bernie stepped into the hall. Mary Alice's door was open—maybe an invitation to talk?

"Did you bring me the pregnancy test?" Bernie asked, sticking her head around the door.

Mary Alice pointed to a pharmacy bag lying next to her on the bed.

"I'll be right back," Bernie said, mainly to avoid talking about Sam.

Back in her own bathroom Bernie waited for the truth to be revealed. She wondered if Sam and Mary Alice would move into the Burns Park house after they were married. Sam wouldn't be able to walk to work at Mitchell School anymore, but they would both be more comfortable. Steffen's bathroom wasn't being used on the other side of the bedroom. And Bernie could be just as happy in the front bedroom, the one Mary Alice was mucking up with her self-pity right now.

Bernie looked again at the plastic strip and found out Steffen and she were going to be the parents of a child who would never know his or her father. But a joy crept through the haze of grief. A baby. *Thank you, Lord.*

Apparently Mary Alice's curiosity got the best of her because she knocked on Bernie's bathroom door.

Bernie burst out into the bedroom. She hugged Mary Alice, feeling like jumping up and down. "A baby," she said and then repeated in case she hadn't been heard. "A baby."

Mary Alice smiled. "Oh, Bernie. Let's go wake up Etta."

"We can wait until morning. What a blessing. 'Intoxicated with unbroken success, we have become too self-sufficient to feel the necessity of redeeming and preserving grace, too proud to pray to the God that made us: It behooves us, then, to humble ourselves before the offended Power, to confess our (national) sins, and to pray for clemency and forgiveness on a day of humiliation, fasting, and prayer.[43]'"

"Steffen repeated the quote on Thanksgiving Day." Mary Alice moved toward the door.

"No, don't go. I promise to leave Lincoln alone. I'm just so happy, so exalted."

"The Lord has surely given you a great gift." Mary Alice shuffled her feet. "But I'm still mad at you."

"You're right to be angry. I never should have talked to Sam."

"I want to deal with Jean before I jump into anything."

---

[43] See Note 27.

"Mary Alice, you know my brain has been coasting around, and sometimes '(she) knows not where (she) is. (She) is bewildered, confounded and miserably perplexed.[44]'"

"And you were going to avoid Lincoln, remember?"

"But I'm apologizing."

Mary Alice shook her head. "Two can play this game you know. I've heard enough of Lincoln around this house, too. 'No one is good enough to govern another without the other's consent.[45]'"

"What if I never bring up the subject of your marrying Sam again?

"Better," Mary Alice smiled. "That would be a whole lot better." She hugged Bernie. "And a new baby in the house. Wow."

* * *

University of Michigan Hospital
July 15

On the way to the hospital, Mary Alice explained to Bernie why she had rushed her out of the house. "Hospice called Sister Stafford who relayed the message to Sheriff Zhang. Jean Lee used them as a reference when she applied to the University for a nurses' aide job."

"Jean probably thought no one would question a hospice volunteer's credentials." Bernie tugged at the buttons on her tightening blouse.

"Well Jean was wrong about their checking, but they gave her a uniform after her initial interview. She's scheduled for duty at the 7:00 pm shift, because the hospital realized the problem too late."

It was only six o'clock, and Mary Alice could have called Sam to help. But after a month Sam was still sulking, not calling her, and not even visiting Nik, Etta, and Susan on the third floor of the Burns Park house.

Sheriff Zhang met them at the emergency room entrance.

---

[44] See Note 8.

[45] See Note 28.

The three women were directed to the Cancer Center's fourth floor. Beth Ann showed her badge at the nurses' station. A burly security guard opened a side gate for the sheriff to enter.

"Wait here," the sheriff said. "I'll find out where we should set up watch."

Four elderly women walked their way. One was in street clothes. The other three were dressed in various assemblies of pajamas, robes, and hospital gowns. Two were entirely bald. Two—one leaving and one staying—wore wigs of questionable worth.

Bernie nodded in their direction.

Mary Alice approached the group. "I bet I can guess who gets to go home tonight."

The four laughed with her.

"I'm Mrs. Laura Plagga," the winner said. "But I won't be checked out until seven. A hospice volunteer is driving me home."

The exercise group proceeded down the hall, and Bernie joined Mary Alice. "Let's just ask the floor nurse which room is Mrs. Plagga's."

"Leave a note for Beth Ann," Mary Alice said.

They moved extra chairs into room 66.

Predictable as the morning, Jean Lee crept in Mrs. Plagga's hospital room backward and shut the door.

* * *

Bernie yelled, "Stay right there, Jean. I'm making a citizen's arrest."

Mary Alice had jumped toward the door as if to restrain Jean, but Jean pulled out a short revolver, then pulled Mary Alice's arm behind her back. "You don't want your precious Mary Alice hurt, do you?"

Jean dragged Mary Alice out of the room.

Bernie bolted toward the door still yelling as loud as she could. "She's got a gun. Everybody down!"

CHAPTER 22

University Hospital

Cool as a cucumber, Jean pushed Mary Alice into a janitors' closet. "Now we can have a little chat, until those idiots decide to stop looking for us."

"Why are you killing old people?" Mary Alice rubbed her wrenched shoulder as she backed up into a wall of hung brooms and mops. The smells of bleach and disinfectants made her eyes tear.

"Hey, I already paid the price." Her sister grinned. "Nine years, six more to go."

They could hear feet pounding down the hall past the closet.

Mary Alice thought she heard a bomb ticking, but it was probably the pulse in her ears. The yellow windows close to the ceiling were webbed with chicken wire. The room was hot. Could she smell the light bulbs? Probably fear smelled like ozone.

"Turn around," Jean whispered.

Mary Alice hadn't anticipated the blow to the head. She blacked out before the floor crashed up at her, and she tasted her own bloodied lip.

* * *

Sam Blaine was kissing the side of Mary Alice's face. She couldn't turn her head because the pain was so great she thought her head might fall off her neck. "Did I die?" she asked. "Is that why you came?" She could smell the Old Spice cologne he'd copied from his father.

Sam moved his frowning face closer. "You're still an idiot."

"Nurse!" Bernie called out into the hall. "Would you check her morphine drip?"

"Did they catch Jean?" Mary Alice asked softly. "Bernie, don't yell. Just whisper."

"She slipped away." Bernie's face was blurring, but Mary Alice could still hear her say to a growling Sam, "Well, she was wearing that nurses' aide uniform."

"She admitted to murdering three," Mary Alice thought she better get the truth out there before she died. The pain was not subsiding. "She said she has six more to go."

"Please, Lord," Bernie said, taking Mary Alice's left hand. "One for each year she served?"

A nurse arrived and Mary Alice slipped into Elysian, morphine-fed fields where white horses romped among sunflowers. She could feel Sam still holding her right hand. That was good. She gave his hand a squeeze before running after one of the slower horses.

* * *

Washtenaw Sherriff's Office
July 16

After Jean had been taken into custody, Bernie no longer felt up to the task of questioning her. True Jean hadn't killed Mary Alice, but harm was harm. The doctors expected Mary Alice's full recovery. The effects of the concussion were supposedly temporary.

Etta left her baby with Aunt Juno and drove Bernie to the sheriff's office. "They're both my sisters," Etta said. "Maybe I can help the sheriff too."

Mary Alice wasn't Bernie's child, but she might as well have been. Seeing her poor swollen face and her head wrapped in bandages did not allow Bernie to rise above her anguish to professionally question Jean.

Beth Ann Zhang entered the viewing room with three steaming cups of tea.

"It's up to you and Etta," Bernie placed her hand on her stomach. "I have good news. Do you want to hear it now or after you question Jean?"

Beth Ann guessed because of her gesture. "How old are you?"

"Forty-three, you?"

"Never mind. How lucky you are. Steffen's child. More than Nik or Sam."

"As much," Bernie said. "I'll love the new one as much. I am blessed."

Etta squeezed Bernie's arm after accepting her cup of hot tea from the sheriff. "Could I help with Jean?"

Jean had her back to the two-way mirror.

Looking into her Earl Grey cup, Bernie shook her head. "I know there is a God, and that he hates injustice ... truth is everything. A house divided against itself cannot stand. God cares, and humanity cares, and I care.[46]"

"Jean has destroyed our family with her evil intentions." Etta said. "I've never been afraid of her."

"You can tell her arsenic was found in all three victims." Beth Ann turned to Bernie. "We searched the trailer and didn't find the cat or any of the stolen jewelry."

"Won't her confession to Mary Alice qualify her for a trial?" Bernie wasn't sure the adult legal system had any more access to true justice than the child-protection courts.

"No linking evidence," Beth Ann said. "Mary Alice's testimony could be thrown out because there were no witnesses to it."

"If she confesses now, will it be admissible?" Etta asked.

"Not always," Beth Ann said. "But everything is being taped.

Bernie said, "Here, I haven't touched my tea. Take her my cup."

Beth Ann and Bernie watched as Officer Schultz opened the door for Etta. Without greeting her sister, Etta set the cup of tea in front of her.

"How long are they going to keep me for questioning?" Jean sipped the hot tea.

---

[46] See Note 21.

"I don't know the system very well." Etta's voice wasn't hostile, but she said it almost as a question. "You did hurt Mary Alice."

"Not intentionally." Jean finished her tea and slid the empty cup back to Etta's side of the table. "Our little sister was in the wrong place at the wrong time."

In the safety of the viewing room, Bernie's baby fluttered as if in response to the chilling comment.

Etta didn't back down. "Mary Alice was helping Bernie investigate the murders of the senior citizens. But you always have an excuse for your cruelty."

"You don't have the brains to be a psychopath, Etta." Jean laughed.

"You don't have a heart behind your ribcage. Dad ruined you with his love of money. I hope I don't have any more children. One of them might turn out to be just like you."

Beth Ann tapped the window. "This isn't getting us anywhere."

Jean heard the tap and turned in their direction.

Bernie sucked in her breath. She pointed at Jean. "Evil incarnate. The Lord will need to forgive her, because I'm incapable of understanding."

* * *

Burns Park Home

Nik Blaine's happy home had been transformed from a serene haven into a fortified battle station. On the first-floor's family room, Mary Alice was ensconced on the couch. His young daughter, Susan, refused to leave her auntie's side even for supper, so they both had television tables in front of them. Nik had used Bernie's kitchen to fix fish stew for everyone.

Sam had brought over his favorite cartoon video, *The Triplets of Bellevue.*. His brother was as afraid as Susan to let Mary Alice out of his sight.

Etta carried their emptied plates into Bernie's kitchen. "Susan, after the movie, you promise to come up to bed."

"No," the three-year-old shouted. "Why didn't you keep Auntie safe?"

Nik and Etta looked at each other.

"Yeah," Mary Alice said, "Why didn't you all keep me from getting bonked on the head?"

Sweet Bernie must have felt the blow deepest, because she went off into Lincoln's solace. "I shall try to correct errors when shown errors; and I shall adopt new views so fast as they shall appear to be true views.[47]"

Nik moved to his stepmother's side. "Bernie, she's only being flippant." He whispered, not wanting to alarm Susan, "There was no defense against Jean's gun."

Susan jumped down from the couch, knocking over the empty folding table. "No secrets, Grandma. Sorry."

Sam set the table to the side. "Yeah, Grandma, no secrets."

Bernie laughed and held out her arms for Susan. "I can tell you a big secret, or Auntie can tell everyone."

Mary Alice frowned from the pain or concentration. "Well, let's see."

Susan abandoned Bernie and ran to Mary Alice's side. "Tell me, tell me."

"It's a riddle, okay?" Susan didn't seem to be agreeing, so Mary Alice continued, "You are going to have another uncle or auntie, who will be younger than you. Just a baby!"

Sam stood in disbelief. "You don't want to marry me because you're pregnant?"

"Wait a minute," Nik said. "That would be Susan's cousin. She said aunt or uncle."

But Mary Alice was off the couch pounding on Sam's chest. "I never want to marry you. You don't love me. I'm just a convenient possession. How could you even think I would touch another man?"

Susan was crying from all the confusion and yelling.

Etta picked her up. "You big babies. Now look what you've done. Mary Alice, straighten up. Who is pregnant?"

---

[47] See Note 22.

"Me." Bernie sat down on the floor and wept.

Susan struggled to be set down. "Now Grandma is crying?" She pointed at Sam. "What did you do?"

Sam collapsed on the couch, where Mary Alice joined him. "Sorry," he said, holding out his arms in innocence. "I am an idiot, but I love you, Mary Alice. When will we have a wedding?"

Now Susan danced over to Sam. "A wedding. You and auntie will have a wedding? I want to be the flower girl."

Sam picked her up, hugged her to his chest, and wept bitterly.

Etta rescued Susan. "It's raining inside today," she told the child. "In the morning everyone will be sunny again."

"I hope so," Susan said, hiding her head in her mother's neck as they went up the back stairs.

Mary Alice leaned on Sam's shoulder. "August 17?"

Sam dried his eyes with a dish towel provided by Bernie. "I almost lost you."

Nik motioned for Bernie to follow him upstairs to his third-floor digs. "They need make-up privacy."

Bernie seemed reluctant.

Engrossed in her embrace with Sam, Mary Alice waved over his brother's shoulder.

Nik held open the entry way door at the top of stairs. "Bernie, the Lord has blessed this house, wouldn't you say?"

"I am happy." Familiar with the apartment's layout, Bernie headed for the front room. "I don't know why I broke down in tears."

"So much has been happening to the family. Your nerves must be strained to the limit."

"(Her) mind, taxed beyond its power," Bernie touched her forehead. "...is running hither and thither, like some tortured creature on a burning surface, finding no position on which it can settle down and be at ease.[48]"

Nik understood her fixation with Lincoln paralleled his own father's flight from his emotions. He hoped the new baby would ease Bernie

---

[48] See Note. 11.

onto more stable ground. His King James Bible was open on the coffee table. He'd been reading the Psalms. He closed the Bible and opened it at random, asking the Lord to guide him to words of peace for Bernie and the whole family.

He read out loud to her, "'Jesus said, "Whosoever shall receive this child in my name receiveth me: and whosoever shall receive me receiveth him that sent me: for he that is least among you all, the same shall be great."'"

Bernie smiled. "Do you want me to wait for Etta to put Susan to sleep?"

"I know you're tired."

"Read Etta the passage you just found. Then she'll know I'm at peace." Bernie headed for the front steps to the master bedroom on the second floor. "Do you think Sam and Mary Alice will live with us, after they marry? Your dad's bathroom is just sitting there."

Nik laughed. "We'll see, Bernie. They're both kind of independent."

"I noticed that."

CHAPTER 23

Washtenaw County Court House.
July 17

Bernie's best friend and sister-in-law, Juno, drove her to the arraignment of Jean Lee. "Steffen and I made a mistake in helping Jean get paroled. '(We should) have gone farther with (our) proof if it had not been for the small matter that the truth would not permit (us). A further deception was that it would let in evidence which a true issue would (have) exclude(d).[49]'"

Juno didn't seem inclined to fault her brother for Bernie's Lincoln habit. "I was at Jean's father's confession. Remember? He admitted encouraging his daughter to murder his own mother."

Bernie changed the subject, falling back into her role of child-protector. "Do you think Ricky will be at the trial?"

"It's not a trial." Juno brushed her white hair away from her eyes.

"The arraignment. Will Ricky bring her three sons?"

"I would not bring my children to witness the crimes of their own sister." Juno stared at Bernie as they waited for the light to change at Main.

"Etta told Jean she hopes she doesn't have any more children, because she's afraid they'll turn out like Jean."

"Not something I would mention to a murderer, even if she was my sister."

---

[49] See Note 9.

Bernie pulled at her seat belt. The safety apparatus was apparently not designed for expectant women. Dire things happened in courtrooms. "I have sometimes seen a good lawyer struggling for his client's neck in a desperate case, employing every artifice to work round, befog, and cover up with many words some point arising in the case which he dared not admit and yet could not deny.[50]"

After Juno locked the car doors, she ignored Bernie's concerned reference and complimented her. "You are looking grand this morning."

Wearing black slacks with a long blue jacket to mask her silhouette, Bernie had hoped her pregnancy bump wouldn't be telegraphed to the world. But she stopped Juno as they exited the parking structure elevator. "I'm worried."

Juno encouraged her with Lincoln's words, "(We) can not fail in any laudable object unless (we) allow (our) minds to be improperly directed.[51]"

Bernie sought the source of her strength. *Lord, prepare your way for justice, protect us from evil hearts, and help us trust you more.*

The small, paneled courtroom lacked a jury section. The two rows of long pews behind the prosecutor and defender tables were nearly filled with family and a few spectators Bernie didn't recognize.

Ricky, Jean's mother, had dragged her children along to hear the charges read against their sister. The family sat behind the defendant's table. Bob, the oldest boy, wore a dark blue tie with his school uniform. As always his face was somber, but he did lift a hand to salute Bernie. Dick, the fourteen-year-old, had his shirt collar unbuttoned, but Bernie suspected his tie was carefully folded in his jacket pocket. Ricky's loving upbringing was reflected in all three youngsters. Ben, two years younger, respectfully held his baseball cap in his hand.

If only the children hadn't been born so close together, maybe Jean would have received more of Ricky's positive influence. Instead Ricky's postpartum depression arrived at a time when her greedy husband used

---

[50] See Note 13.
[51] See Note 18.

the frustrations of his nine-year-old daughter, Jean, to teach her how to murder innocent seniors.

When Jean was brought in, wearing an orange jumpsuit, Ricky leaned forward to consult with Joe Wilcox and the young defender.

Sam and a still-bandaged Mary Alice were seated behind the empty prosecutor's table. Bernie and Juno joined their side of the camp.

Etta and Nik arrived, with Susan walking between them.

Susan dropped their hands and ran toward Bernie. "Grandma. We're all here." She stood on the seat next to Bernie, surveying the people across the aisle.

Just then the court clerk entered. "All stand. Judge Silas Chapski presiding. Court is in order."

Judge Chapski marched up the steps to his podium duly robed in black.

"There's my other grandma. Grandma, do you like my red dress?" Susan pointed at Ricky.

Ricky crossed the aisle to hug the child. "Etta, isn't she too young to hear all this?"

Judge Chapski banged his gavel. "Order, order in the court room. Will the spectators please take their seats?"

Etta said loudly enough for her retreating mother and the entire audience to hear, "We're all too young, Mother."

"Silence, silence in the court room." Another pounding of the gavel. "Or I'll have you removed."

Etta gathered up Susan and sat her on her lap.

Susan wasn't frightened. "Is the man-witch mad at us, Mommy?"

The court-room erupted in laughter, but Judge Chapski moved on. "Where's the prosecutor?"

"Here, your honor." Officer Schultz opened a side door, and Sheriff Beth Ann Zhang and a slim reed of a man entered.

"Charges?" the judge asked.

"Aggravated assault," the underfed prosecutor said.

"How do you plead?"

Jean stood, "Not guilty, your honor—honest."

The sheriff pulled on the prosecutor's coattails. He brushed her off. "We'd like the defendant to be remanded without bail."

"Nonsense," Judge Chapski said. "Obviously this is a family dispute."

Sheriff Zhang leapt to her feet. "She is under investigation for a string of murders, your honor. She's already been convicted of killing her own grandmother."

Ricky stood without speaking.

The judge noticed. "Who are you, may I ask?"

"Her mother, Judge Chapski. My daughter was wrongly convicted of the murder and my husband admitted to coercing Jean into the crime. She was nine at the time."

"You have a penchant for rhyming evidence." Judge Chapski smiled. "Are you willing to provide a surety bond for the upcoming trial?"

"Gladly," Ricky said. "My daughter is welcome to stay in my home."

"So ordered." Judge Chapski rose and left the bench.

"You're kidding," Sam said.

Jean sneered at them. "You haven't had the benefits of a loving mother, have you?"

Ricky spoke to Bob and then followed Jean out of the courtroom.

As Bernie's stunned family got up to leave, she noticed Sister Mary-Louise Stafford from St. Joe's was sitting in the back row. She reached for Mary Alice's hand.

"Wait for us in the hall." Bernie stopped next to the sister's pew.

"The trial will see that justice is done," Sister Stafford said.

"Not sure," Bernie said. "I've been around the justice system for many years."

Sheriff Zhang caught up with them. "I need to warn you, if Jean ..."

"Warn us?" Mary Alice hung her head. "You should arm us with machine guns. That fool is going to do serious harm to more people."

In the hall Nik, Etta, and Susan were surrounded by a group of people Bernie couldn't identify. "Bernie, Sam, Mary Alice: these are Carl and Martha Brandt's nine children: John, Michael, Rose Marie, Dorothy, Anita, Angela, Timothy, and Jeffery. And Mrs. Laura Plagga's family: Gary Pierce and his wife and sisters. Would you join us in prayer?"

Juno and Sam linked hands with the crowd of victims' families.

They bowed their heads to Nik's prayer. "Our Father who art in heaven, hallowed be thy name. Thy kingdom come, thy will be done on earth as it is in heaven. Give us this day our daily bread, and forgive us our debts as we forgive our debtors, and lead us not into temptation but deliver us from evil. For thine is the kingdom and the power and the glory, forever. Amen."

* * *

Dexter Assisted Living Home
August 15

Mary Alice pulled down the Honda's visor mirror for the third time since they had left Ann Arbor.

"You're beautiful enough," Bernie said. "I'm the one who is beginning to *not* look like a serious detective." She patted her stomach. The growing baby apparently liked the ride out to Dexter. "Have you been reading more of Steffen's library?"

"Don't expect me to start quoting Lincoln."

"Once infected with Lincoln's words, it is hard to cure." Bernie hit the side window's button, inviting in the countryside's dusty smell of ripening cornstalks.

"I think I'll be ready for the licensing exams before Christmas."

"Did the sheriff give you any more details?"

Mary Alice parked under the columned verandah. "Two senior deaths last night. Hopefully there is nothing suspicious."

Inside they were directed past a courtyard filled with bright yellow marigolds banked against contrasting rows of purple and white chrysanthemums. On their right they passed a library with a grand piano, a small ice-cream stall, and a large dining room where white table cloths and blue napkins awaited the lunch crowd.

Next to a bank of elevators, they found the director's office. "Greg Olsen." The fit young man introduced himself after Bernie produced her credentials. "Sheriff Zhang asked me to delay calling the family or the undertaker until you arrived. She's already upstairs. Fourth floor, Room 420."

When they entered the apartment's bedroom, Beth Ann covered the face of a slight form on the bed. "Lydia Pinkerton has strangulation marks on her neck."

"Jean poisons her victims." Mary Alice needed to see the red and purple marks for herself. "Did you close her eyes?"

"I did." Beth Ann said. "Bernie, should you be sitting down?"

"Serial killers change their methods when they've been successful, right?" Bernie did sit down in the victim's recliner.

"When they don't get caught, you mean. Or a stupid judge lets them out on the street again."

Beth Ann shook her head. "Anger is going to overwhelm your ability to find evidence."

"She's right, Mary Alice. 'Neither let us be slandered from our duty by false accusations against us. Let us have faith that right makes might and that in that faith, let us, to the end, dare to do our duty as we understand it.[52]'"

"How long did Steffen take to stop quoting Lincoln?" Beth Ann went through the mahogany dresser drawers of Miss Pinkerton.

The pink wallpapered room smelled of lavender. A flowered coverlet matched the small couch and the recliner's upholstery. Dark undersized furniture lent an elegant style to the dead woman's abode. Framed family pictures covered the walls and every available surface.

"He didn't stop until Bernie threatened to end their relationship."

Bernie promised. "As soon as we find enough evidence to put Jean Lee away for good, I'll rebury Lincoln."

"Weren't there two deaths?" Mary Alice asked.

"Next door," Beth Ann said. "Bernie, do you need help getting up?"

Bernie struggled to her feet. "In six months I'll look like a monster."

Mary Alice muffled a laugh. "No you won't. You'll look like you're ready to give birth."

---

[52] See Note 23.

In the adjacent room, Beverly Petersen's body lay on the bathroom floor. Someone had covered her with two large, dark blue towels. Mary Alice pulled the towel covering her face down just enough to notice the marks on her neck matched those on Miss Pinkerton's neck. She waited for Beth Ann to see them before covering the body again.

"Why is Jean continuing to kill innocent women?" Beth Ann seemed to be sweeping away troubling thoughts by brushing aside her thin, grey bangs.

"She told me she'd served nine years." Mary Alice touched the back of her bruised and tender head. "So she plans to kill a total of nine old women."

Beth Ann accompanied them down to the first floor. She stopped in the director's office for a moment. "I told him the bodies were cleared for removal."

Bernie asked. "He'll notify the families."

Mary Alice hadn't moved. "How do we connect this to Jean?"

"She might have worn gloves to strangle them," Beth Ann said. "Otherwise there will be fingerprints on the skin."

"She worked as a nurse's aide," Bernie said. "She would have worn surgical gloves."

Mary Alice moved down the hall but sat down in the dining room. "We need to pass around a picture of Jean to see if any of the patients—sorry, residents—have seen her."

"The director won't like that," Bernie said. "I'm just going down the hall for a chocolate shake. You don't need anything, do you?"

"Coffee," Mary Alice said.

"Tea for me. Might save their lives," Beth Ann said. "I'm going to use the director's computer to print off copies of a police picture we have on file."

"Make about fifty," Mary Alice said, estimating the number of places set for lunch. She pulled out her iPad to review the notes she'd already made.

The first death by poisoning was Mrs. Kerner at St. Joseph's Assisted Living Facility in Ann Arbor. Four rings were missing. Mrs. Kerner's diary implicated a hospice worker.

Then Carl and Martha Brandt were poisoned in their home, where cash and jewelry were stolen as well as a cat.

Next was the attempted murder of Mrs. Laura Plagga at the University of Michigan's hospital. Jean had been turned down for a position with St. Joe's. She had presented hospice references—which were checked out too late—and was given a uniform. She was asked to report for duty at 7:00. The stake out for Jean resulted in Mary Alice being clubbed over the head with Jean's gun.

Jean was released into her mother's care after the arraignment for the assault.

Now Lydia Pinkerton was killed by strangulation in Dexter. And Beverly Peterson also lost her life by strangulation in Dexter.

"Four more to go," Mary Alice told Beth Ann when she returned with the fliers. "How are we going to catch her before it's too late to save four people?"

They placed a flyer with Jean's smiling face, wearing a nurse's aide uniform, under each plate. Beth Ann's phone number was printed in bold type with the warning, "Dangerous and armed. Do not approach!"

* * *

Before Bernie and Mary Alice closed the doors of their Honda, Beth Ann ran toward them.

"Thank goodness," Bernie said. "Someone has recognized her?"

"No," Beth Ann said. "We need to go back to Greenwood Hills in Ann Arbor."

"How many?" Mary Alice asked.

"Three." Beth Ann hurried back to her police car. Sirens blared and the flashing lights cleared a path down Dexter Road for Mary Alice to follow.

"They're already dead," Bernie said.

So Mary Alice slowed the car to a safe speed when they reached Miller Road. "She's too smart to stay on the scene."

They lost the sheriff but continued down Huron to Division, on to Fuller past the Gandy Dancer Restaurant and the back of the University of Michigan, out to Gallup Park where the road changed its name to Geddes. "Which road is Greenhills on?" Mary Alice asked Bernie. "Is it past route 23 on Dixboro?"

"Maybe there will be a sign at the roundabout." Bernie called the facility on her cell phone when they reached Dixboro Road.

The receptionist had them turn around to go west to Earhart Road. "Then take the first right north by the old barn across from Concordia University."

When they arrived at the sprawling V-shaped brick building, Beth Ann's sheriff car was parked under an outlandish white-peaked façade tacked onto the front of the four-story sprawling facility.

"Was this a factory?" Mary Alice asked.

"No it's built to look like a hospital," Bernie said. "I wonder how old it is. I thought there were independent living apartments and separate cottages."

Mary Alice noticed a woman seated on a bench near the side of the main door. Dressed in light blue scrubs with a large purse beside her, she appeared to be waiting for a bus. A horn beeped in the parking lot, and she rushed to catch her ride.

Once inside a woman about Mary Alice's age outfitted in a maroon business suit, fashioned for success, led them to the library. As if conducting a tour for new residents, she explained the layout. "The Lodge is for assisted-living guests, and the Mews are the apartments for more independent residents."

A garish, bright green carpet with geometric purple trim steered them down three halls to a bank of elevators.

"Aren't there cottages available too?" Bernie asked.

"The Chalets."

The windowless library was the size of a small living room. Two comfortable-looking arm chairs, about five straight-backed chairs, and two writing tables filled the small room. One antique writing desk stood unused in the corner nearest the open entry way. The top two shelves of all the bookcases held no books.

The tour guide explained the scarcity of books. "The Ann Arbor library brings requested books out every week."

"I think we can find our way now. Thank you for your help." After the young woman scurried away, Bernie called from the archway. "Beth Ann?"

"Back here," she called.

Mary Alice led the way past the only free-standing, wooden shelf, which seemed to be holding up the ceiling.

At the far end of the room as they turned around the back corner of the bookcase, a crumpled woman was propped up in the corner. Her feet were splayed out, drawing attention to grey socks slipping over her orthopedic shoes. The book *Forever Amber* was still clutched to her breast. Her wig had been pushed down to her nose.

"How was she killed?" Bernie asked.

"I think she was smothered," Beth Ann said. "The coroner is on the way."

"There's no door to the place," Mary Alice said.

"The body is well hidden," Bernie said. "Are there more victims?"

Officer Schultz appeared with the busy tour guide. "Sorry I'm late. Couldn't find Earhart Road."

"Stay here until the coroner comes." Beth Ann motioned for Mary Alice and Bernie to follow her down long hallways, through several doorways and right turns.

"We'll need bread crumbs to find our way back," Bernie said.

The carpeting had changed to a less austere floral pattern. Some of the doors listed the apartment occupants' names. At the very end of the hall, a police officer seated on a hall bench stood when he recognized the sheriff.

"I haven't let anyone in since I called you," he said, nearly using a military salute.

Rhoda and Edward Power's names were listed under the brass knocker.

"What was the lady's name in the library?" Bernie asked.

"Jennifer Gordan," the officer said. "We found her first. The Powers' evening tag was still on their door at two this afternoon. So the staff called me to investigate. He's in the bedroom, and she's in the kitchen."

Inside, the entryway's bright red carpeting showed signs of fading at the far end of the dining room, where the sun danced through floor-to-ceiling windows. Just to the right of the entry door, above a spotless stainless-steel sink, a serving shelf for the dining room let sunlight gleam onto the red-tiled kitchen floor.

Rhoda's body lay face down next to the open refrigerator.

Edward looked asleep in the master bedroom, except for the bloodied pillow next to his bruised face.

"She's killed eight now," Mary Alice said. "Is there any chance we can save her final victim?"

CHAPTER 24

Washtenaw Sheriff's Office

Sam met them at the entrance of the building. Mary Alice wondered if he was ever going to end their embrace. She wasn't in any hurry either. He shut out the evil world. She could feel his good heart beating against her. Old Spice never smelled so good. She whispered in his ear, "Marry me tomorrow."

He pushed her away. "Are you teasing me?"

She clung to his shirt front. "No. Please. I don't want to be alone anymore." Her tears shocked her.

"I believe you," Sam said, kissing her wet cheeks. "I believe you."

She could taste her salty tears on his lips.

Bernie touched Mary Alice's shoulder. "Beth Ann is waiting. Sam, we might have caught Jean on security tapes at Greenhills. The cameras were well-hidden. We don't think she noticed them. Come in, and keep your fingers crossed. Will Reverend Nieman let you have a church wedding on such short notice?"

"We'll ask." Mary Alice hadn't let go of Sam's hand. "Midnight would be fine."

"You don't have a dress." Bernie fussed.

Sam's grin didn't let up. "She wants to marry me now. That's all that matters. Let me make a few phone calls out here. I'll be right in."

* * *

Beth Ann motioned for them to hurry up. She was standing at the door of the tape viewing room.

Mary Alice ran down the hall and hugged the sheriff.

Bernie thought Beth Ann's knees buckled from the impact. "We're not sure," she said, staggering back.

"I am." Mary Alice steadied the older woman. "I'm marrying Sam Blaine tomorrow. You're invited."

Bernie nodded to the truth of the statement.

Beth Ann shook Mary Alice's hand, but she was drawn into another exuberant hug.

Bernie intervened. "The tapes," she reminded Mary Alice.

"There are five." Beth Ann opened the door.

Judge Chapski, the prosecutor, and Ricky Lee, Jean's mother, were already assembled.

Beth Ann barred the door. "None of you are leaving this room until I have an arrest warrant for Jean Lee on eight charges of premeditated murder and one charge of attempted murder. She's armed and obviously dangerous. She intends to add another victim to wipe out her nine years of incarceration for murdering her grandmother."

"I'll need all the names," Judge Chapski said in a subdued manner.

Mary Alice pulled out her iPad. "I have them all." She handed the screen to the judge.

Ricky held out her hand, and the judge gave her the list. Ricky read the names out loud. Her voice was out of control, rising and falling with each name, finally sobbing out the final three names. "April 15, Mrs. Antoinette Kerner, St. Joseph's Assisted Living Facility, poisoned and robbed; June 15, Carl and Martha Brandt in their home, poisoned and robbed; July 15, Laura Plagga, University of Michigan Nursing Home, attempted murder, and Mary Alice Lee, aggravated assault; August 15, Lydia Pinkerton, Dexter's Nursing Home, strangled; Beverly Peterson, Dexter's Nursing Home, strangled; Jennifer Gordan, Greenhills Assisted-Living Facility, smothered, and Rhoda and Edward Power, smothered."

Bernie stepped across the hall from the silenced room to call Juno. "Ricky's probably going to need some medication. Could you join us at the Sheriff's office?"

"I'll arrange for someone to greet the children when they come home." She paused. "Do you think Nik would mind?"

"I'm sure he will take care of them," Bernie said. "The Lord couldn't ask for a better servant."

* * *

The tapes for Greenhills were in vivid color. Mary Alice watched her sister first enter a backdoor marked, 'Employees Only.' August 15 was clearly marked on the bottom tag on the screen.

Jean walked confidently down the green carpet with the geometric trim. She wore the facility's light-blue staff uniform. Near the library Jean didn't look around to see if anyone noticed her entrance.

The next tape clearly showed her face, unmoved by her recent crimes, as she opened the unlocked door of the Power's apartment.

"Justice will be done," Judge Chapski said.

"After five murders in one day that could have been prevented by listening to me!" Sheriff Zhang slammed out of the room. A window to the hall cracked with the percussive force from the door.

Mary Alice spoke to her mother. "If she comes home, remember Jean is looking for one more death to wipe out her resentment."

"I wish it was me." Ricky broke down, crying inconsolably.

The young prosecutor started speaking. "Psychopaths are brilliant. They learn how to mimic sane society in order to be accepted. None of this is anyone's fault except the murderer's."

"No," Mary Alice said. "Since I was six-years-old I've been telling people Jean was evil. No one listened."

"I don't believe in the incarnation of evil." The prosecutor shuffled papers on the table in front of him. "Saying, 'The devil made me do it' doesn't excuse the crime. Responsibility still lies firmly with the perpetrator."

"As does ignoring the truth." Mary Alice wondered if the Lord minded very much if she didn't feel inclined to forgive either Judge Chapski, the prosecutor, or her own mother. "Don't forget Jean is still out there, free to do mayhem with a gun—thanks to the three of you."

* * *

Bernie was standing in the hall and put her arm around Mary Alice. She could feel from the jut of her young friend's shoulders that anger filled her heart. "Sam's Aunt Juno taught me how to pray for people whose actions I couldn't condone."

"How?" Mary Alice's red eyes snapped.

Bernie pulled her into Beth Ann's empty office. "'Then I ask, is the precept, 'Whatsoever ye would that men should do to you, do ye even so to them; obsolete? Of no force, of no application?[53]'"

Mary Alice kicked one of the blue desk chairs, but finally sat down. "Lincoln's solace, is it?"

Bernie moved the second chair to face Mary Alice. "Listen, please. When Jesus was hanging on the cross in great agony with his tormenters at his feet, he asked his father in heaven—remember? — 'Father, forgive them for they know not what they do.' You can ask the Lord to forgive others when your heart doesn't understand their motives."

"Why doesn't the Lord stop Jean?"

"Maybe he's giving her a few more seconds on earth to repent."

"I'm going to need forgiveness if anyone else dies. I want to lay hands on her myself."

Sam joined them. His happiness enthused the room. "Midnight tonight, Mary Alice. Can you believe it? Tomorrow when you wake up, you will be Mrs. Samuel Blaine."

"Here's love." Mary Alice pointed to Sam. "The Lord has wiped evil from our view. Only happiness and trust in the Lord remains."

Bernie spoke only to the Lord, "*...as his faith is, so be it unto (her).*[54]"

---

[53] See Note 16.

[54] See Note 16.

*   *   *

1830 Washtenaw Avenue

By mistake Juno had kept her keys to Ricky Lee's home from thirteen years before when Ricky needed nursing care. She handed the key ring to Nik with a cryptic warning. "Jean has a gun, and Bernie said she's suspected of killing five older women today. I don't think she'll harm her little brothers, but she did attack Mary Alice. I'll call you after I get Ricky stabilized."

After leaving a cell phone message for Etta, Nik stayed in his van until Bob and Dick arrived from school. "We need to pick up your little brother."

"Where's Mom?" Bob asked.

"She's been detained, but you remember my aunt Juno is taking care of her."

"Mom's sick again," Dick said. "Jean gets her upset."

"You boys get in and fasten your seat belts." Nik started the car. "Should we eat out, or should I cook for you?"

"We better eat at home," Bob said.

"Yeah, in case Mom can come home." Dick lowered his head.

"We're too old to cry," Bob said.

"Not me," Nik said. "I'm a little older than you two, nearly double your age. When I'm moved by sadness or the Lord's beauty, I let the tears fall."

"Really?" Dick said. "What about men not crying?"

Nik laughed. "I think that's why women live longer. They get to release all their frustration by crying. Jesus wept in the Bible."

"He did?" the boys asked in unison.

"He got angry too." Nik told them. "He was a human being. We all cry, laugh, get angry, and forgive. It's all part of the deal."

Dick said very lowly, so that Nik had to strain to hear him, "I've never seen Jean cry."

After picking up Ben from Mitchell School, Nik knocked on Sam's condo—only a block away—but his brother wasn't home. He left a note on the door. "I'm cooking at 1830 Washtenaw, if you'd like to join the boys and me."

Bob moved to the front seat, and Ben buckled up in back with Dick.

Ben asked, "Could you make us your pizza? I remember it, don't you?"

"That's a long memory," Nik said. "We'll see what your mother has in the house, okay?"

"Can you make pizza dough with biscuit mix?" Bob asked.

"Yep."

"We have breakfast sausage," Dick said.

"And lots of cheese." Ben jumped up and down as much as his seat belt allowed.

"What about tomato sauce?" Nik asked. "Do I remember your grandmother canned tomato sauce?"

"It's too old to eat, isn't it?" Bob asked. "I know we have new tomato sauce in jars."

"That will do," Nik said as they piled out of the car at their home.

Once the two large pizzas were baking, Nik made a trip to the basement where the train set had pulled him years ago. Now computer screens entertained the boys, one for each.

When he returned upstairs to check on the pizza, he heard the doorbell. Etta and Susan were turning away. "Wait, wait," Nik said. "Sorry, I was in the basement."

"I smell pizza," Susan crowed. "Where are the boys?"

"Your cousins are probably in the basement, right?" Etta said, giving Nik his expected warm kiss.

Susan was off running for the basement without even a hello for her dad.

"Wife."

"Nik, Sam and Mary Alice are getting married tonight. Jean has been up to no good and Mary Alice finally realized what a find your brother is. Sam tried to call you at home but he got me."

Nik looked at his watch. "What time?"

"Midnight at First Presbyterian." Etta hurried into the kitchen. "Reverend Nieman said no, so Sam called his principal, and he recommended Reverend Fair. I need to shop for Susan. She's going to be their flower girl."

"I hope I'm the best man."

"You are to me, dear. Of course you are. You can wear your dark blue. My emerald green will do. I'm maid of honor."

"Who's going to give the bride away?"

"Bob," Etta called down to the basement. "You have a suit, don't you?"

"A sports jacket."

Still calling down to them, Etta said. "Mary Alice is getting married. We need you to walk down the aisle to give her away."

"Don't do it," Ben said. "I like Mary Alice. I know she's sharp sometimes, but she likes us."

"Don't talk like a baby," Dick said. "It's a wedding. She's still our sister."

"She certainly is," Etta laughed.

Nik grasped her to his chest to enjoy her excited warmth.

She pushed him aside. "We need to hurry. I'll set the table for six.f

"Seven," Jean said, popping her head into the kitchen.

CHAPTER 25

First Presbyterian Church
Montieth Chapel

Bernie wished she'd had more time to prepare for Mary Alice's wedding. Her baby squirmed to remind her life was still happening quickly enough. She'd found a blue lace top she could wear unbuttoned over a darker blue dress, which was really too tight.

Mary Alice burst into the Chapel. "How do I look?"

"Great, but let's hide down the hall in the toddlers' room until everyone arrives." Bernie laughed. "You are to walk down the aisle, not jump into the room."

"Sam won't find me to give me my bouquet. What time is it?"

"I'll watch for him. You are beautiful. It is exactly a quarter to twelve. Is that Etta's dress?"

"She said I could wear it. I didn't like the veil. It needed to be ironed."

"It's just that I don't remember it being quite so low cut."

Mary Alice tugged at the lace top. "I think I'm fuller than she is."

The dress dragged on the floor.

"You're shorter than Etta, too."

"I'll just hold it up when I walk." Mary Alice pranced around the room. "I can grab it with the same hand that holds the flowers, if Sam ever gets here."

"Oh, he'll be here." Bernie laughed again. "Here, I brought you something borrowed, but they are yours to keep."

Mary Alice opened the jewelry box holding the pearls Bernie had worn at her wedding.

"They were my mother's." Bernie held the pearls up. "She passed away before I had enough sense to marry Steffen."

"They're beautiful." Mary Alice turned around to let Bernie fasten the double strand of pearls under her shock of hair. "Etta left her blue garter on top of the dress for me."

Beth Ann Zhang knocked on the room's door. "Sam brought these."

They opened a large box of yellow roses, one large bouquet, a crown of roses for Mary Alice's hair, a flower girl's basket filled to the brim with rose petals, a corsage for Bernie, and a smaller bouquet for Etta.

"Where is my bridesmaid—and flower girl? And Bob?" Mary Alice started to open the door, but Bernie shooed her away.

"Sam will see you. I'll go ask." Bernie tugged at her jacket.

Beth Ann laughed. "I'll do it. I'll do it. You're both too nervous. The church isn't going anywhere."

"Oh, Beth Ann," Bernie said. "I meant to tell you, your dress is beautiful. Where did you find it?"

"From China. My mother sends me clothes every season. Does she think I don't shop?"

"Well, it is beautiful," May Alice said. "The colors seem to shift when you move."

"Too bright for a wedding?" Beth Ann asked.

"Perfect," Mary Alice said.

"You always are elegant." Bernie hugged her friend.

Ten minutes later, Reverend Fair knocked on the door. "Sheriff Zhang wanted me to tell you not to worry. Apparently she's kept a watch, a stake out, on Jean Lee's home. They reported seeing her enter the back door."

Mary Alice sat on the floor, her dress billowing around her. "Etta and Susan went over to tell Nik and dress Bob. Etta still had to buy a dress for Susan."

Bernie tried to calm her down. "Maybe they got out of there before Jean arrived."

"No," Reverend Fairfax said. "Sheriff Zhang said to tell you it's a hostage situation. Would you like Sam to join us to pray for them?"

"He'll see her dress." Bernie sat down in one of the room's rocking chairs.

"Bad luck has already descended," Mary Alice said. "I'll call him in."

Bernie stayed seated as she held Sam and Mary Alice's hands, while Reverend Fairfax prayed. "Lord, keep our loved ones safe from the anger and insanity threatening them. Bring them home without harm, in Jesus's name we pray."

* * *

1830 Washtenaw Avenue

Etta Blaine shuddered. Of course she didn't smell burnt beans, did she? "Nik, the pizza is burning."

Jean moved out of the way of the oven door. "Where is Susan?"

"With Mary Alice," Nik said, as he pulled out the two pizzas. "She's going to be her flower girl."

Jean laughed. "Nik, you need lessons in prevarication." She moved to the basement door, and Etta tried to block her way.

Jean tossed her aside. Etta felt Nik catch her.

"Jean," Nik's voice was too calm. "You've hurt enough people, haven't you?"

"Just one more to even the score, Nik." Jean's face showed no emotion. "Did you know your wife told me she didn't want any more children with you?"

Nik was silent.

"Aren't you going to ask her why?" Jean rubbed her hand on the basement door jam. "She's afraid her future children might turn out like me. So I thought I would solve her worry by getting rid of Susan."

Bob slid under her arm, coming into the kitchen. "You better never hurt Susan."

"What are you going to do about it, shorty?" Jean pulled out her gun.

Nik grasped Bob to his chest. "Please, Jean."

"How come you never visited me in prison, Nik? Aren't Christians supposed to visit incarcerated people?"

"I'm sorry," Nik said. "Please don't hurt my daughter."

They could hear crying in the basement.

"Who's the crybaby?" Jean asked.

"It's Ben," Bob said. "Nik told him it was okay to cry."

"Well it's not," Jean said. "Nobody likes a crybaby. Smiles." Here Jean smiled a horrendously sincere smile. "Smiles are what people need to like you."

Etta tried to reach her sister. "Jean, we love you. The Lord can forgive anything. Please don't hurt our baby. I'm sorry I said something so mean. Dad is to blame for teaching you how to hate. We'll stand by you."

"Yeah, I saw a lot of you when I was in prison too. Hey, Bob, you want to make an appeal to my better side?"

"I'll pray for you, but never touch Susan. I don't think the Lord will forgive that."

Etta felt time had decided to stand still. Behind Jean's head, three spiders on the back door's window constructed silvery lines in three corners. A grating sound came from the basement as if bars were being closed.

"Susan," Jean called in a garish voice. "Come upstairs, sweetie. Let Aunty Jean see you. Aunty wants to put a nice hole in the middle of your forehead so you never turn out like her. Susan, ..." Jean descended one of the basement stairs.

Nik rushed at her, but she turned the gun on him. "Watch it big boy. There is more than one bullet in this gun. Back off."

Etta pulled Nik back.

Dick ran up the basement stairs into the kitchen. "Jean."

Jean had let him pass. "Dick, go down and bring Susan up."

"Nope." Dick held out his hand toward the gun. "Where did you get the gun?"

"Oh, I was rummaging around one of the homes where I played nurse. Why?"

"What kind is it?" Dick took a step closer to his big sister, almost touching the gun.

"Hey, Etta, get a load of this. I'm not the only gangster in the house."

"Dick," Etta whispered. "Get back. She'll hurt you."

Dick grabbed the gun barrel, just as Ben hit the back of Jean's knees with his shoulders. Jean tumbled over him and down the stairs. Ben slammed the door shut and locked it.

They could hear Jean's cries as she stumbled down the stairs. Loud cursing and swearing erupted.

"Susan's outside," Dick said. "We pushed her through the old coal vent; you know, where they dumped coal when the furnace wasn't gas?"

Etta ran to the front door, opening it to a member of the SWAT team holding her grimy daughter. "Susan, Susan." She kissed her cheek and smelled the coal dust and then motioned toward the kitchen. "Jean is in the basement. She doesn't have a gun."

"The boys were bad, Mommy."

Nik joined their embrace.

Beth Ann arrived. "We need to vacate the building. Are the boys safe?"

Bob, Dick, and Ben came to the doorway.

Ben spoke first. "A big man in black took Jean's gun."

Dick nodded. "He said to go outside."

"Through the front door." Bob touched Susan's foot. "We got you all dirty."

Outside, Nik fell to his knees. "You boys saved Susan." He stretched out his arms and the boys ran to him.

"The wedding," Beth Ann said. "They're all waiting for you. Make my apologies."

Etta couldn't let go of Susan. "Call them for us. We need to give this young girl a bath and then go shopping."

"I'm hungry," Ben said. "The policeman said to leave it when I tried to grab the pizza."

Etta sniffed. "I smell smoke."

One of the other officers must have called the fire department, because they could hear the fire engines coming. Flames were climbing out of the basement windows.

"My books." Bob moved toward the house.

"No," Nik said. "Everything can be replaced. Let's take them home, Etta. I'll make more pizza while you give Susan a bath."

"Come along, boys." Etta opened the van doors. "Your sister has decided her own fate."

CHAPTER 26

Burns Park House
Two Years Later

Bernie's two-year-old toddler, Jason, banged into the back of her knees. "Mommy, Susan says I can't go to school."

"Not today, baby." Bernie dried her hands after filling the dishwasher.

Jason put his hands on his hips. "I'm not a baby. Susan says her mommy is making two babies."

"That she is." Bernie thanked the Lord in her heart. "The twins will be two years old when you start school."

"Kindergarten." Jason followed her into the laundry room. "Will Sam be my teacher, too?"

"I'm not sure, baby."

"Please," Jason wagged his tiny finger at her. "Don't call me baby."

"Okay, big boy."

Satisfied, Jason returned to his cartoons in the family room.

Little problems were easier solved than the big problems facing her. The night before, Bernie had called the family to join her for dinner to talk about their options. Ricky Lee wanted the boys' temporary custody order rescinded. The house on Washtenaw was finally rebuilt after the fire. Ricky threatened to take legal action if the boys didn't move back with her.

Bob was not the only holdout. He insisted his brothers were safer living with Bernie and Jason than they would be at home. Last night after he'd said grace for the family, he'd stated his main reason: "She's still on those drugs."

"She is stabilized," Juno said.

"Bob, you know I love having you and Dick and Ben living here with me." Bernie had passed him the plate with the ham that Sam had sliced.

"But Mom says we cost you money to feed us." Dick's practical bent kept him worried beyond his sixteen years.

Nik intervened. "Money is not an issue, Dick. We want to know what you boys think about moving."

"Don't leave," Susan said. "Who will I play with?"

"Me." Jason had jumped down from his chair to thump her arm.

Sam picked him up and reseated the two-year-old. "Hey, no hitting, big guy. We never hit women. Even if they're twice your size." He winked at Mary Alice.

"Oh," she said. "Now I'm twice your size. Can I help it if sisters are inclined to be fertile at the same time?"

Bernie wondered if another leaf could be added to the table for family get-togethers. Three more children in the house. Nevertheless, she had no intention of encouraging Ricky's sons to leave. They loved being together in the master bedroom. Bob had commandeered Steffen's bathroom. Dick and Ben peacefully shared the other. She loved going into the busy room, which they kept in nearly perfect order.

Jason had demanded he be allowed to bunk with the boys too. But she wasn't ready to relinquish his presence in her bedroom.

Nik had been right about Mary Alice and Sam. The independent couple moved into Sam's condo as soon as their interrupted wedding resumed the busy night of Jean's fiery death.

"If I could stay here," Ben said, "couldn't Mom visit us?"

"She says she's too alone in that big house." Dick separated a stray pea from touching his mashed potatoes.

"Emotional blackmail." Bob said. "And what if she forgets to take her medicine? She's not going to let you count her pills."

Mary Alice sympathized with him. "I haven't completely forgiven Mother for championing Jean's release or the judge for believing Jean's lies." She bowed her head. "I do ask the Lord to forgive her. The only answer I've gotten is there is a difference between forgiveness and recognition of criminally insane people."

The oldest sister, Etta, made a suggestion. "Bob, why not let Dick and Ben return to Mother's house? She is not mentally ill. Her depression is understandable, and she is under a doctor's care. Aunt Juno is an expert and saw Mother when she was really very ill in the trailer. You remember when she couldn't speak."

Bob shifted in his chair.

"How about if Juno and I arrange to have tea with your mother every Friday? We can check on Dick and Ben and see if the house is being taken care of."

"She'll know you're checking on her," Dick said.

"Good," Bob said. "I hope she knows someone needs to govern her behavior. She hasn't established a good record of parenting so far."

"Problem solved," Nik said. "Thank the Lord."

Bob hadn't addressed all his concerns. "Etta, remember Jean said she wanted to hurt Susan because you told her you didn't want your children to turn out like her?"

"I'm sorry I said that," Etta said. "My anger triggered more violence."

"But what made you forget what you said?" Bob pointed to Etta's sizable waistline.

"Now, Bob," Bernie cautioned, "Don't be rude."

"He just wants an answer," Mary Alice said.

Etta rubbed her tummy. "I looked at all of creation, Bob. Each being of the Lord's is unique in spite of parentage. I've read that the birds' beaks evolve nearly every season. Life needs to go on."

Bernie ended the meal. "Time for dessert. Bob, it is always the truth that sets men free."

Notes
In Lincoln's Shadow

1. Abraham Lincoln, to Williamson Durley, Springfield, October 3, 1845, p. 10; Volumes 1 to 8; The Life of Lincoln, 1858-1865, P.F. Collier & Son, New York, 1906. "What was their process of reasoning, I can only judge from what no single one of them told me. But I believe they all could have said, 'We are not to do evil that good may come.'"

2. Abraham Lincoln, page 38, IBID. "If he can not or will not (confess), if on any pretense or no pretense he shall refuse or omit it, then you should be fully convinced of what I more than suspect already— that he is deeply conscious of being in the wrong and that he feels the blood of his mother like the blood of Abel, crying to heaven against him."

3. Abraham Lincoln, to Joshua P. Speed, Springfield, May 18, 1843, page 3, "The Writings of Abraham Lincoln," Volume Two, 1843-1858, P.F. Collier & Son, Publisher, New York, 1906. "We shall have no split or trouble about the matter; all will be harmony."

4. Abraham Lincoln, to James Herdan, Springfield, April 26, 1846, page 14, IBID. "I felt, that for (us) now to meet face to face and converse together was the best way to efface any remnant of unpleasant feeling, if any such existed."

5. Abraham Lincoln, House Remarks, January 5, 1948, page 23, IBID. "If (I) have been out of order in what I said, I take it all back so far as I can. I have no desire, I assure you all, ever to be out of order—though I never could keep long in order."

6. Abraham Lincoln, Speech to the House, January 23, 1848, page 28, IBID. '... *besides this open attempt to prove by telling the truth*

what he could not prove by telling the whole truth. So that I cannot be silent if I would.'

7. Abraham Lincoln, page 24, IBID. "There's no dispute as to the facts. The dispute is confined altogether to the inferences to be drawn from these facts. It is a difference not about the facts, but about the conclusions."

8. Abraham Lincoln, page 42. IBID. *He knows not where he is. He is bewildered, confounded and miserably perplexed.'*

9. Abraham Lincoln, page 29, IBID. *(He) would have gone farther with his poof if it had not been for the small matter that the truth would not permit him. A further deception was that it would let in evidence which a true issue would exclude.*

10. Abraham Lincoln, page 39, IBID. *'How like the half-insane mumbling of a fever dream …'*

11. Abraham Lincoln, page 41 IBID. *'His mind, taxed beyond its power, is running hither and thither, like some tortured creature on a burning surface, finding no position on which it can settle down and be at ease.'*

12. Abraham Lincoln, page 31, IBID. "I bet you're wondering, 'how any man with an honest purpose only of proving the truth, could ever have thought of introducing such a fact to prove such an issue is equally incomprehensible.'"

13. Abraham Lincoln, page 36, IBID. "I have sometimes seen a good lawyer struggling for his client's neck in a desperate case, employing every artifice to work round, befog, and cover up with many words some point arising in the case which he dared not admit and yet could not deny.'"

14. Abraham Lincoln, page 38, IBID. "Then let her answer fully, fairly, and candidly." He stood abruptly. "Let her answer with facts and not with arguments."

15. Abraham Lincoln, page 48 to William H. Herndon, Washington, 2-1-1848, IBID. "No man can be silent if he would. You are compelled to speak; and your only alternative is to tell the truth or lie. I cannot doubt which you would do."

16. Abraham Lincoln, page 101, IBID. "Then I ask, is the precept, 'Whatsoever ye would that men should do to you, do ye even so to them' obsolete? Of no force, of no application? 'as his faith is, so be it unto him.'"

17. Abraham Lincoln, page 66, to Rev. J. M. Peck, Washington 5-21-1848, IBID. 'Whatsoever ye would that men should do to you, do ye even so to them' obsolete? Of no force, of no application?"

18. Abraham Lincoln, page 90 to W. H. Herndon, Washington, 7-10-1848, IBID. "You can not fail in any laudable object unless you allow your mind to be improperly directed."

19. Abraham Lincoln, page 268, IBID. "I believe it was Shakespeare who said, 'Where the offense lies, there let the axe fall.'"

20. Abraham Lincoln, page 65, Volume Four, Lincoln Douglas Debates, II, 1858. "I would like to know how it then comes about that when each piece of a story is true the whole story turns out false."

21. Abraham Lincoln, page 209, after reading Mr. Bateman's list of Springfield clergy, who would vote against Lincoln, before November 1860. "I know there is a God, and that He hates injustice ... truth is everything. A house divided against itself cannot stand. God cares, and humanity cares, and I care."

22. Abraham Lincoln, to Hon. Horace Greeley, 8-22-1862, Vol 8, 1862-1865, G. P. Putnam's Sons, 1906. "I shall try to correct errors when shown errors; and I shall adopt new views so fast as they shall appear to be true views."

23. Abraham Lincoln, page 188, Volume 8, Chapter XIV, After a Great Struggle Speech early in 1860 in Plymouth Church where Henry Ward Beecher was Pastor. The audience was too big and the venue was changed to Cooper Union. "Neither let us be slandered from our duty by false accusations against us. Let us have faith that right makes might and that in that faith, let us, to the end, dare to do our duty as we understand it."

24. Abraham Lincoln, page 189, IBID, Chapter XV, Cooper Union speech. "You say you will destroy (their marital) union; and then you say the great crime of having destroyed it will be put upon us. That is cool. A highwayman holds a pistol to my ear and mutters through his teeth, 'Stand and deliver, or I shall kill you, and then you will be the murderer.'"

25. Abraham Lincoln, Fragment: Notes for Law Lecture, July 1, 1850, IBID. *'Discourage litigation. Persuade your neighbor to compromise whenever you can.'*

26. Abraham Lincoln, IBID. *'As a peace-maker the lawyer has a superior opportunity of being a good man.'*

27. Abraham Lincoln, page, 271, Thursday, the 30th of April, 1863; Proclamation Appointing a National Fast Day, IBID. "Intoxicated with unbroken success, we have become too self-sufficient to feel the necessity of redeeming and preserving grace, too proud to pray to the God that made us: It behooves us, then, to humble ourselves before the offended Power, to confess our (national) sins, and to pray for clemency and forgiveness on a day of humiliation, fasting, and prayer."

28. Abraham Lincoln, page 209, Speech at Peoria, Illinois in reply to Senator Douglas, October 16, 1854, IBID. "No one is good enough to govern another without the other's consent."

29. Abraham Lincoln, page 161, Eulogy for Henry Clay, State House at Springfield, July 16, 1852, IBID. "With other men to be defeated was to be forgotten; but with him defeat was but a trifling incident, neither changing him nor the world's estimate of him."

30. Abraham Lincoln, page 163, IBID. "He never spoke merely to be heard."

Printed in the United States
By Bookmasters